Daddy's Girl

Also by Beverly Lowry

COME BACK, LOLLY RAY
EMMA BLUE

Daddy's Girl

Beverly Lowry

The Viking Press New York

Copyright © 1979, 1981 by Beverly Lowry
All rights reserved
First published in 1981 by The Viking Press
625 Madison Avenue, New York, N.Y. 10022
Published simultaneously in Canada by
Penguin Books Canada Limited

Library of Congress Cataloging in Publication Data
Lowry, Beverly.
  Daddy's girl.
  I. Title.
PS3562.092D3   813'.54   81–50517
ISBN 0–670–25393–6   AACR2

A portion of this book appeared originally in *Woman's World* magazine under
the title "Post Oak Blues."

Grateful acknowledgment is made to Peer International Corporation and
Peer-Southern Organization for permission to reprint a selection from the
song "Georgia on My Mind" by Hoagy Carmichael and Stuart Gorrell. Copyright 1930 by Peer International Corporation. Copyright renewed by Peer
International Corporation. All rights reserved.

Printed in the United States of America
Set in Janson

For Colin and Peter

I.
Llavots Willy-Nilly

June Day

And-two-and hit it: the beat's hot and she's on it, marking time with her left high heel. In tight swingy dress and strappy red shoes she's a picture, hair pinned back on one side with a Brazos Belle gardenia, one ear out being her June Day style. It's the Kikker Kuntry Ballroom tonight, out the Pasadena highway east of town. Sometimes it's Broken Spoke in Jake City, or Texas Jam near Humble; anyplace country's all right, even Grits Casserole over in Clute, as long as it's outside the Loop: beyond the city limits of Post Oak Place, out from her part of Houston and home.

She's got on lipstick and lashes, a bra to lift her breasts. There's a Rita Hayworth wave that falls just so across the eye on the covered ear side: she flings it back, cups the microphone to her lips.

THANK YOU VERY MUCH LADIES AND GENTLEMEN AND ALL YOU COWBOYS. AND NOW I'D LIKE TO DO A SLOW NUMBER FOR YOU, A SONG RECORDED ON THE RCA LABEL A COUPLE OF YEARS AGO BY THE GREAT OPAL BLOOM. IT'S DEDICATED TO ALL THE DAUGHTERS IN THE AUDIENCE AND YOU KNOW WHO YOU ARE. IT'S CALLED "WHAT'LL I DO ABOUT DADDY?" AND I HOPE YOU LIKE IT.

The fiddle tunes up. It's a sad one, written by M. S. Sue.

There will not be a dry eye in the house when the song is done; June Day will drag out the daddy parts to make double certain. The trick in country singing is not to cut the treacle but extend it, to pick out the soft spots and keep pressing. She loves it. The stage, the music, the spotlight. The cornball moment. She eats the moment absolutely up.

Looking up into the lights, she flutters her lashes as the intro whines, setting the beat. There's a way to take the light; you can feel it in the heat. It's a downhill ride if you just let go.

On the edge of it now. And-two-and. Accent on one. Hit it.

What'll I Do about Daddy?

I'm a newfangled kind of girl,
Sign my checks, my Master Charge is mine.
I've read the books and know the code.
ERA, YES, I'm not afraid to fly.

Mama died when I was only two,
Leaving me here not knowing what to do.
Daddy was the one to help me out,
Backing me up, seeing I got through.

He's an old-fashioned kind of man,
Likes his jokes, football on TV.
When he sees me, he says, "Well, how's my girl?"
Like time was stopped and I was on his knee.

He wants things to be just like they were,
Remembering when he said, "Whose girl are you?"
I can't say, don't tell me what to do. . . .

Our Bodies, Ourselves, No More Masks,
But what'll I do about Daddy?

(. . . hum . . .)
Daddy's girl, I'd say, and hug him tight.

(. . . hum . . .)
When bad dreams came, he saw me through the night.

I've told him, "Move ahead, Dad, like I do."
Boys or girls, look around, they're all the same.
He can't do it, to him it's just not true. . . .

My Mother Myself, Against Our Will,
But what'll I do about Daddy?

The Feminine Mystique, whose girl are you?
What'll I do about Daddy?

Betty Friedan, Bella, and Kate,
What did you do about . . .
What'll I do about my daddy?

It's me singing. My feet in her shoes, my songs she's wailing: June Day is M. S. Sue is me. Names is all. Labels stuck on. We're the same. At night, some nights, not many, Sue Shannon Stovall Muffaletta turns into June Day singing the songs of M. S. Sue at Kikker Kuntry or Texas Jam, outside the Loop at any rate, in the redneck suburbs near the refineries where nobody calls me by my Post Oak name.

After all, I'm a Stovall and Stovalls rename everybody at least once. Mama Two I call myself as well, to distinguish myself from my own mother, Mama One, and the Mamas Zero, those dead grandmothers passed on. My own daughter, Caroline, who's fifteen, is Zero Mama, though Caroline herself will have none of this legacied labeling, not to mention motherhood itself, which she isn't planning on.

He's an old-fashioned kind of man.

This song never made it big. Not the way "Sylvia Brown" did. You never can tell. I've always thought "Daddy" was better.

Likes his jokes, football on TV.

Daddy goes by a number of names too, including Chunk, Big, Baby, and The Kid. Sometimes we forget. People come to town, call us up, ask for some old name. We have to stop and think. Is that us? Is Chunk Stovall the same as Big?

He wants things to be just like they were . . .

I have learned to whisper into the mike as if it were a secret ear, to caress the air waves with a throaty hum, to trill lightly so the sound comes out a noodling loop, never shrill or too loud. The beat of the bass matches my pulse. It's hot in the lights. There's a track of sweat forming down my spine, running the distance, another tracing the curl of my ear. By the time I finish, my feet will slide like fish in these shoes, my ears will be salty, my hair wave will droop. And well, I will love it.

Our Bodies Ourselves, No More Masks,
But what'll I do about . . .

I don't sing that well, actually.

Daddy?

But I have a certain knack with my own tunes and club-owners like to have me come by now and then for a hometown thrill. "Houston's Own," they announce me. And songs are easier to write than you might think. The beat's the key. Once you get the beat it's a matter of filling in the blanks. The thing about the words is, you just have to be shameless.

The Mrs. other rest of me lives inside Traffic Loop 610 in a respectable, up until recently all-white (read respectable) town within Houston's city limits called Post Oak Place. Or Post-oh. Or POP. As a girl I was Sue Shannon Stovall. (Double initials were big: Mama went the trend one better and made me SSS.) In POP I am Sue Stovall Muffaletta, three kids and a white Mustang, a daddy who often is in her home. (Her daddy that is. Mine. Big Stovall.)

SING THE SONG, JUNE DAY. SING ABOUT DADDY.

In Post-oh, I am such a mother. As Team Father of my boy's
Little League team, today I made calls to Yankee parents, asking
them to show up Sunday for our annual Field Day, when we
prepare the community diamond for another season of ball. I
have made my sno-cones and Frito pies, attended my PTA Talent Nights, played witch at Halloween suppers. I have marched
for school bonds and on cancer. I have gone to Astroworld and
Peppermint Park and the Fat Stock Show. I edge my yard. I
have, in other words, done my All-American Mother share of
the Aren't We Doing Right by Our Children works. In Kikker
Kuntry I put on swingy skirt and perfect Brazos Belle gardenia,
pin one side of my hair back, do it: singing my June Day song.

My Mother Myself, Against Our Will,
But what'll I do about . . .

For a while Daddy was Big Daddy. In time, however, that
name has been narrowed to plain and very apt Big. Big doesn't
live in Post-oh with us. He has an apartment nearby, in Signs
of the Zodiac, one of those huge apartment cities Houston's
known for. But he's around a lot. He's there now in fact, sleeping over with my kids.

. . . Daddy?

He'll be in Robby's bed.
Robby will have rolled out the convertible couch for himself.
Ricky will be in the twin bed next to Big. Ricky's the only one
who can sleep through Big's snores.
Caroline, our princess, will be off to herself, closed up in her
room in her pink Neiman-Marcus hotshot peignoir.
I ask you, peignoir? I ask you, pink? Oh, color. Oh, Daddy.

Whose girl are you?

Jane Bartholomew, a pal, lives in the house next door to mine.
Jane and I are located on POP's lesser edge: west of the Poor

Farm ditch near Fed Mart and the railroad tracks. Jane's house is barn red with white trim. There's a wrought-iron eagle over her front door, love seats on the porch. She's got scallops and ruffles and roosters and stencils of cute people, curtains that match the wallpaper and cut-out hearts: the, in other words, Early American works. Jane was after change when she redecorated. Anything but the Danish Modern of her long-gone marriage. The avocado green. The harvest gold. The walnut and foam.

In a fit of the same kind of fury I painted my house too. Originally it was white, but a new color was going around in the arty section of Houston, close to the museums. A rich lady over there was having her houses painted this ritzy color, something between gray and beige. Putty maybe. Maybe clay. Ritzy at any rate; anyone could tell. The rich lady had the window screens taken off, the woodwork painted flat white. Looked nice. Fancy.

Thought I'd copy. Cadge some prestige. Went to Sears, bought nine gallons. Sears Best Coverall, America's Choice.

On the card, Sears best Linen looked the same as the Putty I was hoping to copy.

Fat chance.

"Elephant," Jane declared, surveying my work. "Hide of Elephant Gray." This was after I'd set my elbow in a permanent crook painting all week.

"What's wrong with white?" Big said.

I took off the window screens, put them out with the trash. Now, on a precious dry day, we open the window and: Fly City. Mosquitoes, june bugs, roaches. Ragweed and pollen, stuff in the air to give Robby's asthma the blues. Roaches.

"What's wrong with screens?" Big said.

Anyway, my pal Jane said to me once, "Sue. Do you realize when you introduce Big to people you never tell them his name?"

I said it wasn't true and she said oh yes it was.

"You say, 'So-and-so, I'd like you to meet my daddy,' but you never tell them his name."

But I do. I say his name all the time. I sing about him in this song. His name for me has never changed, never mind all the labels he has gone by. I've tried to switch to more adult versions —Father, say, or Pop—but the switch won't take.

Daddy. His name is Daddy.

What'll I do about, what did you do about . . .
Our daddies.

Big says it's whore hair to pin a flower behind one ear and leave the other one sticking out. Probably. But that's my June Day style. You need those things to keep yourself up on who you are. At home I cover them both.

THANK YOU VERY MUCH, THANK YOU THANK YOU, *YES.*

And in the morning good news: Big will get the kids up, fix their breakfast, see them one by one off to school, Caroline, then Robby, then Ricky, the order of their birth having come to be, in some great who-knows plan in the sky, the routine sequence of their arising.

Me? Sweet City: I will lie in bed all ears, pretending to be asleep. Big will know I'm awake but Big won't say. It's one of our pacts. I'll rest, he'll make coffee; when they're gone I'll have a cup. I'll do something for him in return, maybe fix him liver for dinner tomorrow night, which he loves and I can eat but am not much on.

It works out, we do our dance. Buck and wing, dip and twirl and timestep; ball-change, ball-change.

ALL RIGHT, JUNE DAY. ALL *RIGHT*!

Big's alarm however will be noisy; it will rattle the windows and buzz the piano. The floors will shiver, my bones will object

PLUM JAM CITY! he'll shout.

DOOWAH DITTY, to rouse them.

Never mind. I get to sleep in.

Oh, Daddy.

To whom my heart, my heart. Does not belong but well there's a lot of feeling there.

OKAY FOLKS AND NOW FOR AN UPBEAT NUMBER. YOU MAY REMEM-
BER THIS ONE. IT'S A TRUE STORY, TAKEN FROM THE PAGES OF THE
Houston Post, ABOUT A LITTLE LADY WHO REFUSED TO STAY HOME. IT
WAS A BIG HIT A FEW YEARS BACK. . . .

Trash. Fringe, flash, and sequins, top-forty cornball, one-two: I love it. The beat hits. They recognize this one, here's the applause. And I love it. I am a college graduate, understand; went to the "W," majored in English, got my degree. Top per-cent of my class, all-American honor girl, best of the best down the line. Daddies in Ophelia, Mississippi, thought I was the berries. Now look. I have this fantasy: when I walk in a room, people notice. How I move, what I look like, how I flip my hair. I'm old enough to know better but hotshot notions die slow. Up here on the stage, the dream comes true. They're noticing.

And I eat it absolutely up.

I will whisk into the house when I get home tonight, race through the kitchen to my room, strip off June Day dress and shoes in the dark, go to bed salty. This will do me for a time. I won't sing again for several weeks.

In the morning I'll be me again. Sue. I'll think back over tonight and wonder, Was that me? Singing those songs? Wear-ing that dress? Skirt so swingy? Lord. I'll check myself out for traces: sniff an arm, feel behind an ear. And yes, it will be there. The scent of salt at my wrist, the leftover dead gardenia crum-pled into a brown toadstool in my hair, that rank and too-sweet smell.

Me. In my Post Oak bedroom alone. Mascara in clownish smears, licking off the taste of June Day lipstick. Shoe straps still on my arch—faint white shadows etched in Kikker Kuntry dust —toenails painted scarlet. Whore feet, Big would say.

Meantime now. The song. The nighttime, outside the Loop version of Post-oh me.

SING THE SONG, JUNE DAY. SING THE SONG.

Big in the Morning

A quarter till, Big's awake. Sue's house is dead quiet, the sound of safe sleeping, its even, even pulse. Only Big stirs; listens. His time.

From the convertible couch in the living room, Robby wheezes, his seasonal sleep, troubled by early-spring weeds and new blooms. Yesterday bees were in the ligustrum, a certain sign: Robby's starting to sneeze and whistle, he'll have to take pills. More than likely he's on his stomach, knees bent, feet up. Such a boy. Who could sleep that way? A thin, stalky arm might hang to the floor. With his dark Italian complexion and starved, skinny look, Robby might be a refugee from some war, some street child begging coins. Stovalls are never thin. Breath comes hard. Stovalls never have allergies, do they.

As always, Caroline's door is closed, her sleep her own. Princess Grace, Big calls her. Her Very High Lama-ness, Lady Queen, Miss Bud.

Sue's breath is deep and measured, a healthy good-bye, yet is it. He thinks sometimes she puts on, feigning dreams to pinch sacktime. Like her mother. His Sue, his girl, his daughter.

His Sweet Sally Jane.

SUE CITY. She's his girl. DOOWAH DITTY.

Big's eyes opened at five-thirty without an alarm. He will rest awhile before getting up. Up too early, too much time to fill. Anyway, he has his routine all timed, down to the wire. In the twin bed next to him Sue's youngest lies sprawled on his back, uncovered, head flopped against an arm. His light snore rides the morning pulse.

Big told on him once. "Snoring is in Ricky's blood," he announced. "He's a Stovall. My Daddy snored and so do I."

That night, Robby stayed up to record his brother's sleep and, next morning, played the cassette. They weren't real snores, only a child's gravelly night-breath. Still.

Ricky threatened to rack up Robby's skateboard if he didn't

erase the tape. "It wasn't me, it was you, butthole," Ricky said. "You taped your own butthole self." Big didn't mention snores again.

There are windows beyond his feet; outside, a huge ash tree, ivy climbing its trunk in thick clumps, past the top of the window high into the tree. Mornings Big likes to study it. Closing his right eye, he looks out the left. Without the contact lens, from that eye the world is a blur. Sometimes a woodpecker comes to knock holes in the ash's trunk, sometimes there are screaming bluejays or mockingbirds, pumping up and down to make songs. State bird, the kids told him. Same in Texas as in Mississippi, mocking mocking state bird. Some mornings a red-bird couple visits, the male a brash scarlet thing doodling his song, his quiet wife a dull scattered brown, a pale-orange beak her only sign of flash.

Friday.

Last day of the week, hotfooting-it, catch-up day.

All the frozen yogurt he has not placed earlier in the week, Big will move today. End of the week means commissions to be figured, quotas tallied, the reckoning: what kind of week it was. If he added it up, over the course of his selling life he is sure he would have sold at least half his combined wares on Friday.

LAST CHANCE CITY, GET THE COMMISH.

Never on salary, never had a desk, a detail man all his life by his wits on the road, his years and time and the places he has lived and traveled are in memory divided up into territories and quotas, mileage and percentages, net versus gross, commissions to get up and go out and get.

IF YOU HAVE A BAD DAY IT DOESN'T MEAN YOU'LL
    HAVE A BAD WEEK.
IF YOU HAVE A BAD WEEK IT DOESN'T MEAN YOU'LL
    HAVE A BAD MONTH.

IF YOU HAVE A BAD MONTH, IF YOU HAVE A BAD
   YEAR . . .
IF YOU HAVE A BAD DREAM?

Forget it.

The bed is too small. In his own apartment, he has king-size, which he sleeps across on the slant, corner to corner, an oversized pillow clutched to his chest taking the place of his wife.

A fake bamboo shade covers the top half of the window, Sears Best plastic bamboo. Sue said it wouldn't mildew and in Houston that was a factor: real bamboo would spot up in a year. You'd have to stink up the room, Clorox it off, soon as you did here would come the mildew back. During the night Big pulled the shade up, careful not to waken Ricky. He wanted to know the instant daylight met the ash.

Five-of. Time.

Hit it.

The cover is in a bunch on the floor beyond the foot of the bed, kicked off the minute he got in. There's a paper sack on the boys' chest of drawers; in it, clean underwear, socks. Toothbrush and razor are in the bathroom. Sue has no husband, Big has no wife. Don't think about it.

In the bathroom, Big reaches for a bottle, the giant economy size Rexall. He buys the cheaper Rexall brand because aspirins are all the same. From being a detail man for drug companies all those years, he knows. Call it Bayer, call it Nopain, call it B.C., a brand name is only snake oil, after all. Something to get people to step up and buy.

Loosening the plastic cap, he pours six tablets in his palm and, two by two, throws them down his throat. Sets the bottle back on the shelf without replacing the cap.

Midmorning the aches will set back in. There is another king-size Rexall bottle in the glove compartment of his car and several in his apartment.

At the Zodiac, he has a stall shower; here, he has to maneuver into the bathtub, and with nothing dependable to hold on to, it's dangerous. In the two-story house he and Linda built back in Ophelia, one of the things he asked for first was a stand-up shower stall. For a big man a tub's a hazard, even with a mat. Sue has yellow rubber stick-on daisies in hers. Sue is always trying newfangled stuff. Whatever the kids ask for, whatever's advertised on TV. Junk. Soybeans.

He holds on to the towel rack as long as he can before letting go, to balance a second before landing on his feet in the tub. Should have ragged off at the sink. Should have taken a whore's bath, wipe off the vital parts and back to work. But he's in, flat feet planted firmly on the Rubbermaid daisies.

A dream hangs in his mind. A different dream, and he has catalogued them, something about a scientist, a hippopotamus, a rhinoceros. The scientist was trying to crossbreed the animals. Make a hipperocermus?

Probably will. The way things are going.

Big shaves while he showers, leaves stubble in the tub.

By the time he gets to the kitchen, he is dressed, down to starched white shirt and collar stays, cuff links, polka-dot bow tie.

WASHED MY FACE, CLEANED MY FEET.
UNDERARMS POWDERED, AM I SWEET.

Breakfast, upbeat. Breakfast is always good. Bacon, two eggs, English muffin, butter. Coffee. Jam. The same breakfast every day.

He had bought Sue a Mister Coffee but he didn't think she liked it. Every time she made coffee she used her old drip pot. But he didn't like to wait around, pouring water drip drip, so he used Mister Coffee. And certainly Sue drank it. Even though he didn't make it strong enough to suit her, strong enough to crawl up out of the pot, that is. Still. She drank it.

HOWZ IT GOING, HOWZ IT GO. FINE, BROTHER, FINE.

Sue will sleep in until everyone is gone. He will fix the kids' breakfast and see them off, a different breakfast for each one, plus his specialty: personalized alarms. Morning Poems by James Eldon Stovall. That'll be his book someday.

RISE AND SHINE, SHINE AND RISE.
EVERYBODY UP. SHOW ME SOME EYES.

No need for her to get up when he's there. Like her mother, Sue doesn't wake up until past nine, not enough to talk to . . . ten, in Linda's case. Cat-eyed both of them: see in the dark. Don't cross Sue or her mother in the morning or expect conversation. Not even a civilized hello.

When Sue got married, Big told her husband, "They're just alike, Muff. Peas in a pod. They might as well be sisters."

It wasn't altogether true but true wasn't the whole story and for a while he and Muff had called one another Brother-in-Law.

Sue had been in during the night to check on him. He was awake, sitting on the side of Robby's bed, but didn't let on he knew she was there. Some nights he looked up and waved her away; last night he hadn't felt like doing even that. The dream had been startling. Hadn't the hippo sweated blood? And fat? Drops of blood ran into the fat.

KEEP THE BEAT. PLAY THE TUNE.

No use rehashing. No good looking back.

He has saved a crinkle of bacon, to go with his last bite of buttered and plum-jammed muffin: sharp and sweet together, washed down with coffee for a last-bite treat.

"Mmmmmh!" Big says aloud. "Good."

It would be better if he had a wife. If he met somebody compatible who liked his grandkids he'd marry her like a shot. He didn't need to horn in on Sue's life like this. Every time he woke up in Robby's bed he felt a quick shot of guilt, the same as when he'd been on a binge and couldn't remember going to sleep. Every time it happens he takes the pledge. Not tonight. He'll go home to the Zodiac tonight.

Press on, that's the thing. If he stayed in bed like Sue, he might never get up. Had to get on up and just do it.

By the day. One at a time.

Clearing his throat, Big shouts. Mailboxes rattle, piano wires buzz, people up and down the block open windows and say, What was that?

BANANA CITY. DOOWAH DITTY.

Slicing a banana over Ricky's raisin bran.

HEART OF MY HEART, MATE OF MY SOUL,
GRAPEFRUIT AWAITS YOU. FROOT LOOPS IN YOUR BOWL.

Big. Fixing breakfast and making up poems.
Me. Glad I don't have to.
Still. It's a rowdy hello.

When Big is in the house, the house is his. He has these sayings that have run through his life: *How's it going. What's the beat who makes the music go. How're you getting along along with your work. Shall we dance?*

And the poems. Even Ricky gets grumpy at Big's poems and Ricky dotes on Big.

"Mom," he said. "I hate Doowah Ditty."

"Shhh," I hushed him. "Don't tell."

"Big duh, Mom, I'd never tell. But I do hate it."

Big told him it was how to write poems.

"It's a breeze," he said. "You just say Something-or-other City then Doowah Ditty and, snap, you're a poet. They could put you on talk shows. We'd be watching you on TV. Donahue? Johnny Carson? 'Mr. Muffaletta,' Merv would say, 'how do you write your poems?' "

"Sure, Big," said Ricky in his best, drop-dead tone. "Sure."

"And you'd say, 'Easy, Merv. Piece of cake, Phil. I just say Snap City. . . .' " Big popped his fingers and, like a buck-and-wing hoofer passing the spotlight on, pointed his imaginary straw boater at Ricky.

Who, in spite of himself, did the expected ball-change.

"Doowah Ditty."

And Big continued his number, hopstep shuffling off to Buffalo.

No one can stand to deny Big a thing. And give Big his due: he brings a lot of life to the party.

Yesterday, Robby was in the kitchen scouring the evening newspaper for money-off coupons and contests to enter. Big was in the living room watching the news.

"Hey, Big." Robby had to shout. Big likes TV loud.

"Say what?" yelled Big.

"What's *expose* mean?" Robby asked, straining his voice.

"What's *what* mean?"

Top of his lungs. "EXPOSE. E-X- . . ."

"Oh," Big trilled, taking a full four syllables. "Expose. Expose means demonstrate. To show."

Silence. Robby reread the article, inserting "show" in place of "expose."

Big interrupted him. "Robby?"

"What?"

"What kind of expose?"

"It says, 'Post Oak Place man arrested for . . .' "

"Well, that's a different story."

"What's it mean?"

"It means—" Big paused. The TV news was telling about a good-hearted mother of five who'd been kidnapped and shot by a sixteen-year-old boy. "SDIP."

Robby came to from his irritation. "What?"

"Don't you know what SDIP means?"

"No. What?"

"You never heard of SDIP?"

"No, Big, now tell me."

Big paused a long moment then chuckled.

"SDIP, Robby, my boy, means Shows Dick in Public."

Silence again. The woman was a twenty-year employee of the Houston School District, a cafeteria manager who loved her work. Robby giggled. He had it. Man arrested for. That was it.

"You get it?" Big asked. "Shows Dick in Public, you get it?"

"I got it, Big, I got it."

Kids call him on the telephone to tell him jokes from school, riddles from *Shazam,* The Teen-Age Magazine. "Can I speak to Big?" they say. Other kids wish they had such a grandfather. Imagine. A grandfather who stages farting and breath-holding contests. A grandfather who always wins.

He taught them a farting ritual: anytime somebody farts, everybody has to say Bulgem. The last person to say it eats the fart.

I walk into a room. They're at it.

Bulgem! Bulgem! Bulgem! You ate it, I did not, yes you did, I said it first, he ate it didn't he, Big?

Hey, Big, you heard the one about? . . .

Week before last, he took Robby and Ricky and two of their friends to Jack-in-the-Box for hamburgers. Dinners in sacks, they came home in stitches, laughing and beating each other on the back. I asked what happened. Big just grinned.

"Big asked Jack for *slaw!*"

Ricky had run in fast to be the one to tell.

"What?"

"Jack. You know. Jack-in-the-Box. The Jack will speak to you machine? It asked for our order and Big said, real loud—"

"He didn't even *need* the machine." (Robby)

"I bet they heard him in the kitchen. He didn't even need the machine." (One of the other boys)

"Real loud." (Another boy) "Like a torpedo. He didn't even need the machine."

Ricky protested. "Will you guys shut up. I got here first."

The others retreated. Ricky's a sometime bully; the block tough guy.

"Okay. We drive up to Jack, see. And Jack says, 'May I take your order?' And Big's over there looking at the menu and then he says, real loud, into the machine—" Ricky paused for emphasis. Looked at the other boys. Giggled again. Big grinned. "Says, 'YOU GOT ANY SLAW?' "

"Slaw." Robby said. "At Jack-in-the-Crack."

"Then what happened?" Having learned to be straight man early on, I moved the story along.

Big shrugged.

"Jack broke up."

"The machine?"

"The machine. Fell out laughing, then said, 'Slaw?' "

Since that day slaw has new life in our house. Every so often Ricky or Robby brings slaw up again and they both get tickled all over again, just saying the word. We went to the Hikoree Pit, for instance. I was trying to get the orders straight but Robby kept laughing. I looked up at the sign: SLAW. "You got any slaw?" Ricky asked the puzzled cook. They were on the floor. Oh, Daddy. A lot of life. Even to franchised intercoms.

He gets out the milk, puts the toaster down.

HOW CAN I GET THEE UP? LET ME COUNT THE WAYS.

I COULD BRING THEE DR. RETAW, I COULD KICK THE COVERS OFF.

I COULD TICKLE THY FEET ALL MORNING,

OR COME IN THY ROOM AND COUGH.

Slices a banana for Ricky's cereal but not too soon, so it won't turn brown.

Pours Robby's milk over his cereal ahead of time so it gets nice and sogged up like he likes it. ("I can't stand it to crunch in my head," Robby says.)

Butters Caroline's muffin to the very edge and fixes her two slices of bacon well-done, the fat nicely browned, never soft or floppy.

Halves me a grapefruit and has my coffee hot, not strong enough or made in the pot I prefer, still. Big says: "You can't have it all, Sally Jane."

Takes Caroline to school, who refuses to walk or ride the bus and snubs the local car pool.

Boosts my solemn middle-child Robby when he's low.

Tickles the giggling piss out of Ricky, playing wake-up games.

In general, jacks up the Muffaletta morning, saving my kids from a fate much worse than Doowah Ditty, namely their mother in the kitchen in a hateful robe, stirring glum hot chocolate, yelling I told you guys to get UP.

Caroline enters the kitchen like Big, fully dressed. Her hair, combed back long and thick, is held in place behind her ears with barrettes shaped like intertwined hearts. She is courteous but aloof, an earnest girl who needs prestige. Big understands this.

"Hi, Big."

"Morning, Princess Grace. How're you getting along with your work."

"Fine, I guess. A little sleepy."

Her voice is high and pearly, nearly a whisper. Caroline nurses a little-girl air. A royal air as well: better than us. People who don't know Big respond to "How're you getting along with your work" literally. "What work?" they say, as if he meant job.

Big sets Caroline's breakfast in front of her. She sips her milk, snaps a slice of bacon in two. Lady Queen. Taking delicate bites.

"Robby-ma-hobby, oh, Robby, I say."

Silently, Robby stumbles up from the couch-bed and staggers, all arms and legs and wheezy breathing, to the bathroom.

Ricky will be last. Like his mother, Ricky lies in bed, fighting the fact of morning every day. He's awake now, no question. But Ricky likes attention, and games of any kind. Once everybody else is up, Big will play him one.

His alarm takes various guises. Sometimes it's a fart. Big backs into the bedroom door, sticks his butt in, and just rips one off.

"GROSS!" Ricky will shout from under his pillow, sneaking his nose out for quick sniffs. "Gross, Big, gross."

This morning it's Dr. Retaw: water, spelled backwards, in a glass, backwards spelling being one of the all-time Stovall games.

Big used to make up horror stories for me and my junior-high

friends, about Dracula and Frankenstein, Alucard and Niets-
neknarf to us. Big told his stories at night in the dark, on the
back porch under the moon. When it was full, sometimes he
switched and told Namflow. Namflow was a decent ordinary
fellow who every twenty-eight days sprouted wolf hair, got red
eyes, and ran on all fours, under the full moon greedy for blood.
We were thrilled. But Alucard was our favorite. Big bared his
teeth telling it, and shined a flashlight under his chin. He devel-
oped a fiendish Alucardian laugh, dangling his hands from the
wrist vampire fashion, as if blood dripped from his fingertips.
Alucard came not from Transylvania but a far more terrible
place. Ainavlysnart. Oh, Ainavlysnart!

We called each other by our backwards names. I was Eus, Big
was Semaj. Steve, my brother, became Evets. A friend, Sandra
Parkinton, participated. She was Ardnas. Ardnas Notnikrap.
Mama's name worked well, though it sounded like medicine.
Adnil. Adnil never played. And Stovalls were Llavots, and to
Daddy and me they still are. A Llavots forehead means broad
and high, and big: when Big played football, he had to have a
special helmet made; I always wore bangs for disguise, to bring
my hairline down and turn Llavots round into perfect fifties
oval. Legs with heft are Llavots, calves so chunky they won't fit
in regular boots. A nose like a button, skin that tans, hearts that
go flooey. When people ask what I did to get such calves, ski or
dance or what, I tell them Daddy's legs. I have my daddy's legs.
Llavots.

"All right, Ricky," Big says. "I have been patient, but your
time is up. You have forced me, Ricky, to call on [*pause*] Dr.
Retaw."

Ricky buries his head.

"I'm calling him, Ricky." Big splashes water. "I've got his
emergency number." More splashing. "Here he comes, Ricky.
Dr. Retaw is on his way."

Big stomps across the floor to Ricky's room. The house shakes.
Doesn't faze Big. Does the world notice when it turns?

"I've got the glass, Ricky; it's cold, Ricky; are you up, Ricky?"

He slurps and gurgles as if drinking. "Mmmmmm, Ricky, nice and cold." Louder footsteps than before. Windows rattle. Earbones buzz. The story is his.

"I'm at your door, Ricky. And Dr. Retaw is with me." He clinks his college ring against the glass.

Ricky burrows in, knees drawn, sheets to his ears. His black hair blooms from the covers like parsley. Who'd have thought it, Jim Stovall with dago grandkids, a name like Muffaletta. From the start who'd have thought it ever would have turned out this way. Sue in this house writing country songs, these kids, no husband; Linda with her carrot juice and Swiss Kriss and herbs living with a Jew photographer half her age; Steve so far away with that sourbutted wife of his. His family. So whacko, so haywire. Backwards would be a pleasure, compared to willy-nilly fruit basket.

Big holds the empty glass over Ricky's head.

"I'm pouring it, Ricky, better get up. Here comes Dr. Retaw."

Ricky rolls to the edge of his bed then jumps to the other side, out of the way of the pouring water in case Big actually has any.

"I knew you didn't have any, Big. I knew you were kidding."

Robby, who has come in the room to see if his brother gets doused, puts in his two cents.

"Sure you did, Ricky, sure. Then why'd you get up so fast?"

"Because it's time to, asshole, that's why." Ricky gives Robby the rod then storms to the bathroom muttering, "Chicken. Dirty crapping creepo farthead. Weirdo suck."

"All right, guys, don't fight," Big says. "Your cereal's ready. Don't wake your mom."

He takes the empty glass back to the kitchen and leaves it on the table next to the jelly jar. Dr. Retaw is Ricky's favorite alarm. One time Big actually poured some water. Not much, just drops in his hair so that from then on Ricky could never be sure if he had any or not, so that Dr. Retaw could be more than an imaginary threat.

"Got to keep him wondering," Big says. "Got to keep them on their toes."

From my bed I've heard it all. The front door slams. That's Ricky. Shuts. Robby. Slams. Big and Caroline.

The house holds on awhile, waiting to see if it's over, then begins to settle into itself, creaking at corners, hunkering down.

Soon it will be altogether quiet. Cheerios will be stuck to the table, leftover milk and eggs will clot up the grout, my feet will make a sucking sound walking through spilled something, Mr. Coffee will not be strong. Still. A dark and quiet house is a blessing. I've got a song in mind to write, "Mama," it's called.

Nearly relaxed, the house, alerted, draws itself up. The front door opens, footsteps race through the front room, down a hall. Caroline. More footsteps, then: SLAM.

Mine. Quiet Friday, last chance day of the week. Houston gunk and steam move through the house, sinking into cracks until every room feels like a cellar. Wet City. Mushrooms could grow through my toes, I wouldn't mind. A dry day lures a girl outside, makes her want to wash her car. In funk like this, I'll get some work done. Doowah Ditty, the house is mine.

Big's Stories:

#1 ALUCARD

By the time you wake up he is at you. The tearing of your flesh happened in your sleep; already there are the two perfect holes; he is at work. You are flowing.

You would have thought there would have been an instant's grace, time enough to protest, to have some say in the matter. But it was not until after the teeth were in that you even knew he was there and by then it was too late. He had pushed the top of your head back against the pillow, your breasts were lifted, knees bent, feet curled. Who'd have thought it. You! You didn't know there would be no time to call out, or that he would be at you so fast, that you would be flowing by the time you wakened, arched up to help.

The next thing you know it is morning. You lie in your bed wondering why you feel clawed and reckless. Something has happened. In the night something came out. You arch your neck, bend your knees, curl your feet. Up to get it, asking. Up to get it. You will never be the same.

#2 NIETSNEKNARF

Junk. Man-made.
Rags and garbage. Nothing.
Tell us Alucard instead.

#3 NAMFLOW

A good man, he lies beneath the trees, his eye on the moon. Full, it mocks him. Nothing for him to do, the hair will grow. His nostrils will turn sharp and canny, his feet become paws. Teeth will change into fangs, hang from his lips.

The eyes go last. They beg the moon's mercy. No such luck. His eyes turn red. There is a kitten, deep in the forest; he can see it. A child playing. Smell it. The good man has disappeared. He is Namflow. Namflow runs on all fours. The smell of flesh, the smell of flesh. Soon blood will fill his mouth. He sniffs the ground.

By morning he will be himself again. He will wake up wondering whose blood he has spilled. His eyes will turn back to blue. He will be himself. Full of remorse.

Little Big and SSS

"Remember the time you let goats in the school?" That's Robby, Big's best audience, giving Big all the opening he needs.

And give him his due, Big can tell one. Telling stories, in fact, Big can dance out your eyes. Jokes stale as leftover toast, tired as day-old pie—people will hear them out, to see how they go. It's the same story, this one—how Big let goats into the school building, not just overnight but on the day before Easter vacation so the goats stayed four full days and . . .

(Like watching rerun TV: not for plot but how you get there. The ride. I walk in on "Gilligan," "Lucy," "M*A*S*H." They're glued. They've seen it seven times, yet no one blinks.

"Watch, Mom, this is a good one. Gilligan eats a frog."

"I hate it when the Professor . . ."

Everything is known. Gilligan's their Rumpelstilskin. In unison, they sing his song.

"The Professor's cheap."

"What about Gilligan? That hat?"

"Skipper's okay."

When Gilligan leaves, Beaver arrives. The Beave.

"I hate the way they say *dear*. 'Ward, dear,' 'June, dear.' Nobody says that."

"What about 'Gee, Dad.' That's all Beaver says."

"I heard Eddie Haskell's a cop."

June comes in, wearing an apron. "Ward, dear . . ."

"See?")

". . . not just overnight but on the day before Easter vacation so the goats stayed four full days. By the time the janitor came Monday morning, the school was I mean hall-to-hall goat piss and dooky. Papers all over. Chewed-up everything. Goats in the library eating books. Baa-ing to beat the band."

"Did you really, Big?"

"I ought to know. Mama beat the living daylights out of me. I told her I was at Glee Club but she didn't believe it."

"What about the principal?"

"Didn't do pea turkey. Mama was president of the PTA. 'Jimmy would never do a thing like that,' she told the principal in no uncertain terms and huffed out of there like Lady Pease. Took me home and gave it to me. She knew."

Everybody knew. Who else would think of goats?

There were three of them. Big, named James Eldon, was the baby. Walt Junior was in the middle. Louise Mildred, called Lou, was oldest. Lou was big-boned, tall, with a strong jaw. Later she'd be said to have the Mrs. Roosevelt look. Lou took after Mother Stovall's family, the Earlys, who tended in some instances toward the rangy, though Mother Stovall herself was square and boxy. The Stovalls—Mother Stovall, Big Walt, and their three children—lived in a big green house in Pine Bluff, Arkansas, on the corner of Walnut and Pecan (Pine Bluff streets all being named for trees).

When I was a girl we used to go there. From Ophelia, we had to cross the river to get to Pine Bluff. There were two ferries. One, the big one, was green and white with a huge paddlewheel and a fine concession stand; it looked like a showboat. We'd get hot chocolate and Nabs. The other one was small and rickety; it came on the in-between trips. We called it The Dinky. Brown river water would lap up on The Dinky's deck. They had to cram cars on, if there were many. I was terrified of The Dinky. "Oh, no," we'd say, seeing it. "The Dinky." I remember the Stovall cellar, gray and damp, smelling of the roots Big Walt stored there.

Walt Junior was a likable boy, pleasant if dull, a good audience for his brother and a born farmer. A proper son for Big Walt, though Big Walt, like most, favored the baby.

Baby Snowball, workers on the place called him, seeing Jimmy Stovall talk his way out of work and blame and every discomfort, putting the story on right and left. *Baby gets the taters every time,* workers said. A bamboozler from the start, in other words, but nobody could resist.

Big was always fat. In baby pictures he's a butterball: three

chins, no neck. Later, he looks more like his high-school nickname, a Chunk. And his eyes are always black and shining. In
every picture, they roll with life and expectation. When he goes
back to Pine Bluff, people recognize him instantly. Remembering those pranks.

Robby wishes he had such nerve. More stories, he begs. Tell
about the time—

When he was thirteen, Big sat down one afternoon at his
mother's upright. He'd never played before. The piano was for
Mother Stovall's lessons, which she gave to Pine Bluff girls
twice a week. Every Tuesday and Thursday, light classical
plink-plank jabbered from the Stovall living room. Jimmy usu-
ally managed to be out of the house. What they played was silly.
Following sticks and dots and lines on a page, what was that?

Had not actually played it but had spent hours at the piano
roll, pumping the pedals, watching keys press magically down.
The last time I was in Pine Bluff, I worked it, playing "Maple
Leaf Rag," faster than fingers can go. Whose fingers, I won-
dered, made the rolls that mashed down the keys, going so fast?
What fingers had such speed?

The Stovalls had a record player too, an RCA Victor crank-up
by the piano-roll chest. But you couldn't buy hot records then.
Only march tunes and weepy ballads. "Nadine," "Valse Ca-
price," "Lilacs in Morning Dew." But oh, piano rolls. Oh,
"Charleston Rag" and "Boll Weevil Blues," "Chicago" and "Hot
Socks." A syncopated beat, emphasis on the in-between.

Hadn't played a note in his life before that day. Sat down, set
his fingers in a chord, BLOM, had it. F# or C minor he hadn't a
clue. Only how it sounded. Like riding a bike: hot was hot, once
you had it you could ride forever.

Dots and sticks on a page. What was that?

There was a dance at the Pine Bluff gym for kids Walt Junior's
age. Uninvited, Big went.

"You invited, Big?" Robby keeps the story afloat. His thin face
shines, imagining Big.

"Naw. I just went."

"Anybody know?"

"Three people."

"Me, myself, and I, right?"

"How'd you know, Robby?"

"Oh, Big."

Stood in the back, eyes peeled for chaperones.

"Used to get big-time bands in Arkansas. They'd be traveling the river, going from Chicago through St. Louis, to Memphis and New Orleans. Catch one at the right time, no telling who you'd get to play. We danced to the big time, right in Pine Bluff. That night it was Cal Caster playing hot jazz and new ragtime, also swing, which was just coming in. Cal had been all over, heard the new stuff and played for everybody, even us kids. Between big-time bands and piano rolls, I mean we heard us some *music.*"

"Cal played xylophone, right?"

"Cal Caster the Czar of the Xylophone. Fast? Quicker than lightning bugs. Then there was my man. You know."

"Fuzzy WhamminBamminMileaMinuteFourString Wilson."

"How'd you know, Robby? You heard this story?"

"Come on, Big."

"Here came Fuzzy."

"Played 'Front Street Jive.' "

"On the ? . . ."

"Four-string banjo."

"Nothing moved but his hands."

When "Front Street Jive" was done, Jimmy came up to the bandstand, tapped Fuzzy on the shoulder, said he wanted to learn the banjo, where could he? Turned out Fuzzy was retired from the road, living in Pine Bluff over Corner Drugs, playing pick-up when bands came through. Imagine Fuzzy. Banjo in his lap, looking at a kid in knickers, his dark shining eyes. Imagine turning down the kid.

"Fuzzy didn't like teaching, so he just sat there. I didn't know if he'd say yes or not. Called me Kid. I thought when I got famous that might be my name. Kid Snowball on the roof of the Peabody Hotel, the Kid King of the Four Strings."

Big wasn't fast like Fuzzy but he had something else, that sense of life and risk he still has, which Fuzzy called The Shine. Said he hadn't seen it in many white musicians. Louis Armstrong had it; Fats Waller, Big Mama Lee; gospel singers, raising the roof.

Fuzzy taught him terminology, augment and diminish, modulate and minor, to flatten a fifth. The Kid learned fast but never to read notes. The Shine, he figured, was enough.

"Kid," Fuzzy said one day, "I'm going to Memphis. Catch a Greyhound, play with Cal at the Peabody Hotel. You want to go you can. Maybe he'll let you sit in; I doubt it. You get the bus fare you can go. Friday night. Maybe he'll let you sit in on a number or two. I doubt it."

Imagine Big. Fourteen years old, invited to the Plantation Roof. Now the Peabody is gone. RAZED THE ROOF, Big says.

It was late spring when Fuzzy made Jimmy the Memphis offer. The Stovall home garden was in full bloom. Vegetables to beat the band. Squash, peas. Jimmy scanned the bounty. Cantaloupes were in the far row. Big picked a red wagonful, hid them for the night, behind the cherry laurel.

"I thought when I came in the kitchen something was up. Lou standing there arms crossed giving me a look. But what did Lou know? And what did I care besides?"

"Nothing. You didn't care for nothing."

"Right, Robby my boy. Correct."

Next morning, before anyone was awake but Mother Stovall, Jimmy took his cantaloupes, hit the streets.

"Sold the whole load before school took in."

"Didn't you think about getting in trouble?"

"I guess I knew something would happen but that didn't mean a thing, Robby. I was going. I don't know what I would *not* have done to make that trip and sit in with Cal Caster on the Peabody Roof. Or not sit in. Just go. I didn't know for sure ahead of time I'd actually get to play."

"But you did."

"I did."

"How many songs, two?"

"Two songs."

" 'Baby Face,' and . . ."

" 'Baby Face' and 'I'm Just Wild about Harry.' "

"Did they tell you how to play?"

"No. I just played."

"Had you ever played those songs before?"

"I knew them. We had them on piano rolls. But I never played them."

"Gah, Big. How'd you know?"

"You know how in the night when you have to go to the bathroom and it's dark and you don't want to turn on the light because you'll wake up Ricky, how you hold on to the dresser, then the chair, then the wall, and don't let go of one until you're grabbing another?"

"Yeah. . . ."

"Like that. I'd hold on and hope for the best, hold on and hope for the best. Reach for the next, hold on and hope. From one part of the song to the next until I got to the end."

"And you did it."

"I did it. They gathered around on the Peabody Roof to hear me play and I can't tell you how I did it, it amazed me in fact that I could, at my age. Sang a little too. A kid. Not even fourteen. Lord. The things I did. Imagine."

"And they found out."

"Already knew. Not where I'd been exactly but what was going on and the cantaloupes."

"Lou told."

"She did."

"Lou was a witch."

"Well. Your aunt Lou has had her problems."

"Then what?"

"What what?"

"When you got home and they already knew."

"Well, Daddy left the punishing up to Mama. You'd think

that would be better but it wasn't. I'd have taken Daddy's licks anytime. Daddy was loud but underneath he was soft. Mama just drew back a razor strop and let it rip. Strong? Little as she was, Lord."

Thought he had it. That was the first time. Thought he'd be a banjo star on the Peabody Roof, Kid Stovall on top of the world, river air blowing through the dancers' feet, across the roof. Mother Stovall nixed any more trips to Memphis until he was at least sixteen, but Big Walt got a kick out of the boy's high spirits and told him on the q.t. if he got another chance to go to let him know and he'd take the bus up too. He'd never been to the Peabody Roof and he'd heard about it. He'd like to see what it was like, of course he wouldn't want Jimmy's mother to know.

When Fuzzy Wilson left Pine Bluff, he wrote Jimmy a note, saying he'd taught him as much as he needed and Jimmy was on his own.

The note went on:

My life is a mess, he said.
I have screwed up every chance I ever had and gone through two real marriages plus I won't tell you how many other near hits (or misses depending on your point of view). It's a hard life, Jimmy. All there is is nightlife. Calloused fingers, people wondering how you do it. Go home, wonder how you got so cut off when you never meant to. I mean to be discouraging, Kid. If I sound discouraging, I mean to be. Because nothing's going to stop you. All I can do is say this is how it has been for me and look, living over drugstores and saloons, buying food by the day, boiling coffee on somebody else's hot plate. It's never going to change. This is it, Kid. This is it. I'm going to hit it now. Time to go. I never like to overstay a place. Good luck. Your friend Fuzzy Wilson. —P.S. Hold on to The Shine.

Big tried to track Fuzzy down. He wrote letters to Cal Caster in care of the Peabody Hotel but Cal never answered, and by the time Jimmy was older and got to the Peabody on his own, Cal —who was still doing engagements there—said he thought maybe Fuzzy had died but he didn't think so. The last he heard he was living in New Orleans with a waitress, playing Dixieland. But he didn't know.

"He might have died," Cal said, "but I don't think so."

When Jimmy was in high school, the football coach saw him wrestling on the school grounds and realized that what he had taken for fat was mass and bulk and pure strength. Jimmy's arms were like a bear's. He could hold six baseballs in the palm of one hand. The coach watched Jimmy hug his opponent around the chest until the boy could barely find breath to call uncle to stop the fight. Jimmy stood up. He had a barrel chest and legs as shapely as a girl's, only big—Llavots legs. His knees and ankles might give him problems, they were small compared to his thighs and calves. But with the strength in his legs he could go a long way on pure acceleration.

Coach called him in.

"You like to play football, son? I know you mess around on a banjo, but this won't interfere."

Jimmy was fifteen and a half then, stars as big as moon pies in his eyes. He was the pearl in the oyster, he got the taters everytime. Babied baby boy. Why not?

He played blocking back, sometimes fullback, or double running back which meant you did whatever the play called for, defend, run, tackle, even throw. Sometimes he switched to the line and played guard for a change, but mostly the coach enjoyed showing him off, watching other people's amazement—especially the opposing team's—that the fat boy could run. The first year, especially, the coach won many side bets on Jimmy's rushing yardage.

"Run, fat boy, run," PBHS fans shouted.

"That boy's a chunk," somebody said.

A *chunk*. A literal chunk. Rolling snowball. "Send in The Chunk." "Give it to The Chunk."

Big had a new name. It would take him to Green Bay.

"Chunk could do it all," Century Milch, a Packer teammate is quoted as having said. "Run, hit, tackle, take your head off. I mean when Chunk hit you, you knew you was *hit*."

In nearby Stuttgart the same year Jimmy was recruited to play for the PBHS Wild Hogs, a small frail girl with blond hair and glittering blue eyes was getting her period for the first time. The girl's mother, Dolly, was tormenting her, and the girl, Linda, was swearing as soon as she found a way she would free herself from Stuttgart and Dolly. Two years later, Linda Shannon Day was a tiny cheerleader with no voice, quietly rah-rahing for the Stuttgart Hawks when they played the Pine Bluff Wild Hogs. At the dance in the Pine Bluff gym after the game, she met The Chunk. He was playing banjo in the band, after having run all over the field during the game to help Pine Bluff beat Stuttgart 28-zip. From the sidelines, she had thought he was just a big hunk of football flesh. Now here he was beating his foot against the floor, shaking his head, and singing. He got up and danced. Light on his feet, he danced their eyes out. Linda loved to dance.

"Don't take it hard," Jimmy told Linda when the band took a break. And he offered her a sip of the whiskey he'd poured into a paper cup. When she accepted it, he was surprised. "We're bigger than you," he said. "Big towns just naturally beat little ones."

"What else do you do besides play football and plink on that ban-JOH?" Expertly, Linda Day lit a cigarette. Jimmy's eyes widened. Stuttgart girls were certainly sophisticated. The smoke curled past her shining blue eyes and into her angel gold hair. The Chunk was entranced. Her eyes were like blue stones. She was five foot two. She smoked like Jean Harlow, but had a soft look, like peaches. Such a tiny thing.

"I'll tell you what, girl. Everything I need to." He flashed her his moon-pie grin. "And more."

Linda sighed.

I met my husband at a funeral.

My musical bent by then was well established. Mama had insisted on piano lessons early, and I had graduated from Thompson's one-note primer, gone on to "Golliwog's Cakewalk," tried "Moonlight Sonata," even "Malagueña." Soon I would hit "Ritual Fire Dance," if my fingers were feisty enough. Ophelia mothers loved all this, or seemed to, their girls in formal net gowns and lipstick, playing recitals for adoring parents on metal folding chairs. Not that we should be nut musicians. Only so when somebody said "Play a tune for me, Melanie," we'd be able to.

My talent, however, was humdrum, rinkydink.

DANCE RECITALS:
"Hawaiian War Chant," "Five Foot Two, Eyes of Blue," etc.
"Pas de Deux from *Swan Lake*," etc.
"Put Down Six and Carry Two"
"Baby Face," "Alexander's Ragtime Band," etc.

You've heard the organ at hockey games?

TALENT SHOWS:
"*Un Bel Dì*," etc.
"Way Down Upon the Swanee River," "Dixie," "Mammy,"
"Danny Boy," etc.
"If You Ever Been a Nigger on Saturday Night, You Won't Want to Be White Folks No More."

Background music, accompanying. The one behind the curtains nodding and-two-and-NOW. My repertoire was the time's chosen stuff. It varied. Bach meant funerals, opera meant Miss Ophelia, "Finlandia" meant the OHS band concert.

CHURCH:
"Oh, Promise Me," "Because," etc.
The Doxology, The Gloria Patri, etc.
"Onward, Christian Soldiers," "Rugged Cross," "In the Garden,"
The Messiah, Bach fugues, etc.

Quietness is scary, makes people feel tense. I was paid to fill in that gap, "It Had to Be You" being less noticeable by a long shot than silence.

COCKTAIL PARTIES:
"Laura," "Louise," "Nadine," "Marie," etc.

"Secret Love," "Sentimental Journey," "The Gypsy," etc.
All of Nat King Cole, All of Perry Como, etc.

It's a trendy business. Tastes go with the times, change month
to month. When Mario Lanza was at his peak, everybody
wanted operettas and opera, even at drunk parties. *Student Prince*
was a big favorite. "Serenade," *Pagliacci:* I hear them now and
I think I'm back fending off drunks.

OLD SOUTH TEAS:
"Dixie," "Swanee," etc.
"Alexander's Ragtime Band," etc.
"Old Black Joe" and all of Stephen Collins Foster
"On the M-I-Crooked Letter," etc.

Movies. One day nobody has heard of "Love Is a Many-
Splendored Thing," Kathryn Grayson, Doris Day. Next thing
you know everybody is requesting "I'm a Lonesome Polecat."

MINSTREL SHOWS:
"Dixie," "Swanee," "Alexander's Ragtime Band," etc.

Whatever the song, you name it—give me the sheet music and
I'd fire away, sight-reading like a fiend, in perfect cooperation
and time with the singer, that is to say perfectly subservient to.

Not every piano player can accompany; it takes a certain
knack. People who can drill the fire out of "Malagueña" get
completely balled up when a singer stands on the far end of high
C awaiting a cue. I could cover over, speed up, slow down. If a
singer held overlong I never rushed. It was their song after all.
Their foolish face to get no applause.

BEAUTY PAGEANTS:
"Lovely to Look At," "Secret Love," "You Must Have Been a Beautiful Baby," etc.

I worked constantly, all over town. My "Blue Moon" and
"Trees" were so smooth you'd think the keys were made of
water. And since Daddy's income was feast or famine, music
assured me I could have the things I wanted, the Coro bracelets

and patent-leather Deliso Debs; Ship 'n Shore from the Smart Shoppe, a mouton coat. All the good things of the time. Cole and Catalina, Fire and Ice.

SORORITY RUSH PARTIES:
  "Chi O My Chi O," "K D Cutie," "Tri-Delt I Love You"
  "Kappa Kappa Key Key Key"
  "I Wanna Be a Good Phi Mu," etc.

Organ too. Weddings, baptisms, funerals. Funerals were the cream. Organists fought over wakes and last rites. Insurance pays and back then twenty-five dollars was healthy fee for an easy afternoon's work of "Old Rugged Cross," "In the Garden," a piece of cake Bach fugue, some Haydn and good old Martin Luther.

I never liked the organ. Too blurry. But I could play one like crazy; I could put on my funeral frame of mind and not even think. I carried my music in a brown leather case, one of Daddy's old sample bags. Wore patent-leather tap shoes, the best for organ pedaling, hated the bag, hated the organ, hated the shoes.

Still. I got my Hanes and Maidenform.

I knew who Paul Muffaletta was and since the lady at whose wake I was playing was named Estelle Muffaletta I might have known, if I'd thought, that they were kin. But who noticed? My job was to play. I already had my mouton coat. Estelle Muffaletta and "I Come to the Garden Alone" would buy me a turquoise Jonathan Logan dyed-to-match cashmere sweater set I'd had my eye on.

I was playing along, eyes closed, in a dreamy kind of trance. And since my bones knew the drill, while fingers performed, I drifted.

Walks with me and he talks with me.

Muffaletta's was the biggest laundry and dry-cleaning establishment in town. Muff had graduated two years before; I was a senior. Muff was a big rough boy, a brawler who played mean football. Not to mention Italian. His whole family had quick nicknames. Mink and Moose, Itz, Mick, and Od. Moose owned Ophelia's only dance hall and nightspot, out on the edge of town. The Moose. I'd never met Muff face to face. I'd heard he'd settled down since high school, working at the plant for his father.

Muffaletta's is gone now, sold out to do-it-yourself Ucleanum. Wash-and-wear polyester and leisure suits hit private cleaners hard—not to mention the onslaught of the one-hour in-out franchise, clean in the blink of an eye. Home delivery, all the trimmings, was everyday stuff at Muffaletta's. "CLEAN-ers," Muff's uncle Od would holler, bringing Daddy his starched white shirts.

Tells me I am his own.

There I was, in my dreamy, organ-playing trance, moving in mind from sweater sets to more fruitful things, wondering what the worst way to die would be, the worst possible taste—liver? brains?—how it would feel to have a boy's tongue in your mouth or be eaten by a bear. There had been a newspaper story that week about a girl who had her period and was camping out in Yellowstone. She'd been eaten by a bear. It didn't say period in so many words but you knew, and Lord . . . Lying there in belt and pad and the bear, the bear.

And the voice I hear.

Muff sneaked up behind me during one of those reveries and from between velvet curtains reached out and swiftly cupped his big hands around my ribs.

I fell over the organ keys, my feet flopped hard on the pedals, I screamed. A man standing by Estelle Muffaletta's head looked up, one hand on the pink tulle of the casket and one to his hearing aid. I smiled sweetly, lifting my shoulders in an apologetic shrug, then went back to my song, breathing fast.

Voice I hear.

The hands had reached nearly around my rib cage, swathed even in folds of robe. A football player's hands?

I prayed for a halfback, fullback, someone who ran with the ball. What I got was a guard. Meat. Paul Muffaletta. Great-Galloping-Huey-the-Duck Muff.

I had seen him in a Golden Gloves fight. A football coach had said if he liked to fight so much, why didn't he put his talent to work? Everybody went. It looked like a rout. The other guy was from a tiny speck of a town, Drew. Nobody came from Drew. Muff was bigger and stronger, with a longer reach, a bigger chest, bigger hands. And he had us, his cheering squad.

Muff was also about half as much in shape. By the middle of the first round he was begging for breath. By the middle of the second he was finished. It was pathetic. The Drew boy knocked Muff from corner to corner and rope to rope and never looked winded at all, bouncing on his toes like he could go on forever. All Muff could do was draw back and lunge, draw back and lunge. And never get there. He never landed a punch.

When the third and final round was over, Muff climbed out of the ring before the winner was announced. One eye swollen shut, he made tracks straight out of the VFW Armory, still in his boxing gloves, his soft white belly hanging over his red drawstring trunks. The football coach chased after him with a terry-cloth robe.

Next weekend Muff was back at The Moose, picking his own kind of fight. A brawl. In the nightclub parking lot where you could push somebody across a car hood and go to town on him without some referee stepping in every other breath to say, "Take your hands off his neck, Muffaletta."

Falling on my ear . . .

I swiveled on the organ bench, saw him.

None other . . .

"Muff," I said.

Has ever . . .

"You scared me."

Known.

The grizzliest of bears turn out to have the gentlest of touch, the kindest caress. See him risk teeth and bones to punch somebody out, see him as soft with me as dyed-to-match cashmere.

Such a good girl. "You scared me, Muff," she said.

I wondered one thing only: When Muff touched me, had he felt my fat? I had not had time to suck it in. That night I tried it myself, sitting at the piano bench hands around my ribs. I couldn't tell. Different with your own hands than somebody else's but: probably he had. Probably there was no way out, the fat was there and he felt it.

He wasn't everything, Muff. Nobody understood what I saw in him, but there were assets. He was a man who was what he was, no June Day shoes or snake oil. We had good times together, loved and lusted, played it out. The works. Later, when we married and I went down on him like he liked, he had this way of putting his great hand on the back of my head while I did it, acknowledging, cradling, telling me. That big paw: it took me by the hand gently and led me down a new garden path where, dew on the roses who'd have thought it, I learned what I could be other than the old SSS. There were definitely compensations for the girl who thought doing it was for the boy only, that all it meant for girls was watch out: you could get pregnant.

He called the night after the funeral to ask me out. I said I had to study, it was spring and there were tests. I was thinking of hands on my ribs, the bear. He said, "Well what about the next night or the next?" It was going to happen. I was going to say yes and the rest of it was going to follow. I just had to resist awhile, in the interests of my well-earned interests.

Like Namflow, I had kept things divided neatly in two. There was the dream girl, me, at the organ running wild, in imagination testing every limit, and there was me in the flesh all body and blood, SSS turned to stone.

<u>SSS</u>

Perfect daughter: daddies remember. Daddies in fact will never forget. In Ophelia, Topeka, Houston, you name it, daddies are still wishing for her return, still trying to convince their own daughters to be like her, still wanting to say the way daddies of other daughters did back then, "Why can't you be more like her?"

Now? Dr. Brothers says sex is an integral part of a young person's life; Dear Abby sanctions birth control; even Billy Graham has loosened up. That their baby girls carry diaphragms in their purses next to lipstick flatly breaks daddies' hearts, however update 1980s they profess to be, wearing beards and chains, buying *Good Sex for All*.

In her yearbook SSS has more honors listed by her picture than anyone. President of, best of, honorary this and that. HER SMILE WAS DELIGHTFUL, HER GRADES OUTSHINED US ALL. She has bangs to cover her Llavots forehead, a pageboy, a white piqué dickey, a constipated smile.

Who loved her? Only every adult. Every Rotarian and Elk and good Lion, every mayor and Mason and Moose, even Ike. In his fuzzy-duck heart of hearts the president himself loved our girl SSS and all like her in every American town.

Oh, daddies.

Daddies took their sons hunting, bought them catchers' mitts but oh that girl. Put a june bug down her ruffled behind, watch her dance, see how cute she runs. Like a girl. A daddy sat beside me on the piano bench to teach me "The Darktown Strutters' Ball." Reaching up to hit a high note he touched me. The point of his elbow punched in the bull's-eye of my target-stitched bra. Did he? A daddy? Dare I believe it? His arm pressed against me. A man at the Delta Theatre took my hand said feel this, and put something in my hand. I drew away but did I change seats? No. Who told? Nobody. Don't say how the thing felt in your hand.

Make me a debutante, Daddy, buy me a cinch belt, get me into Chi O.

We never wanted to be like our mamas. Daddies had more fun.

Meantime none of us knew anything for sure, having never tested, tasted or felt. Orgasm? Meant watch out you could get pregnant, meant he did it till he had it, did it till he had it. You waited. He had it.

Good girls—SSS and the rest—in place of testing, dreamed, gobbling their way through every version of gluttony they could imagine, wondering what the worst thing in the world was, how it would be to find Alucard in your bed, a tongue in your mouth, have your fingernails bent back by Korean crazymen.

What was it like? We crossed our legs, went to Coke parties and in our imagination did things far worse than the actual bad girls who were familiar with the more everyday details, stuff on your skirt, watching for periods, all that. We looked in *National Geographic* not for nakedness but gore: cannibalism, vultures, blood, hyenas after entrails. The bear of our dreams, after us.

And so the bad girl turns into All-American Mrs. PTA Everything while the good one forsakes motherhood and Little League barbecues, church and pie, to lie with one-shot salesmen and boys younger than her son and best friends' husbands and doctors taking Pap smears. The works. The fish turns over, white belly up, scales in sand. All their lives the good girls will be on that crusade, trying to match up real life with the wild wild dreams of their early imagination. Muff could have bragged and boasted. The great SSS with her head back, neck arched, feet curled on his backseat. He didn't. We'd be kissing, he'd be doing these other things, this feeling would come. "Did you?" he'd ask, amazed at my quick-trigger response. Did I what? It was there, that was all, like angel wings fluttering somewhere I'd not known about, down there. Orgasm meant he did it; meant watch out; what this was happening to me I only knew was some treat. It had no name.

A nice guy at heart, Muff made the mistake of assuming girls are good because they believe; because it is their nature, not their opening act. But—enter the snake—they do it for the glory. And because it pays. Hungriest of all, they will hog the whole apple once they get a taste. Skin, seeds, core, stem.

I haven't told Caroline about the star I was in Ophelia, or what fame I collected there. Big doubtless has, but she and I have never discussed it. If she asks, I'll take it as it comes. High school's not life. I want her to respect me now.

Other people hide a sordid past. I put the lid on propriety. My yearbook's tucked away, that honor girl in pageboy and dickey.

The Girl of My Dreams #1

Mario Lanza.

Soft eyes, excessive heart, the great appetite, reaching for notes higher than the throat can imagine.

Beneath the sweet exterior, fire.

Be my love.

The high notes.

His heart burst; mine did. No one knew him the way I did. I was him. Mario Lanza was me.

One kiss is all I need to seal our fate.

I did not want to be his Ann Blyth wife. I was not girl or boy but him. Inside where the fire was. Sweet Sue. Oh the high notes, the passion and bursting heart.

There is no one but you for me.
Eternally.

A tenor not a guard.

The Girl of My Dreams #2

Tina Turner. Onstage making her long fringe shake and shiver, her spangles reflect the light. The secret is the knees, the hips, the flex. Locked knees turn you into a palm tree, no give. Be a willow, be a birch, bend and dance. Flex.
Move.
In the lights your skin is shiny. It reflects the lights. Sweat makes you a glittering blur. Shine!
Do it. Be her. Ike bub-bubs and Tina shakes her hips and the drumbeat never stops. Perform. Perform.
This is it.

Daddy was so disappointed.
Of all people—Muff. A dago, a launderer's son, a spaghetti winder. His Sweet Sally Jane. Grandkids with dago names. If he'd made more money it would have worked out. I wouldn't have been playing the organ because I wouldn't have needed the money and Paul Muffaletta wouldn't have had the chance to sneak up behind me through the curtains and grab my rib cage like a bear and hear me sweetly say to the tune of "In the Garden," "You scared me, Muff." It would have been different, if only, what if. If there'd been one more down to play!

It happened at the First Presbyterian Church. I wore white satin, lace around my face. The choir's star soprano sang "Because." All the right stuff. Breasts in strapless Merry Widow, waist cinched to there. On my face, in wedding pictures, I have a wondering look . . . what will it be like? I had jacked Muff off and jacked him off, into handkerchiefs and Kleenex, against my palm, on my skirt, my thigh, my arm, in my mouth. The works, except. It ran down one leg into my sock: I walked in after a date to say good night, toes stuck together in stuff. Still. I had followed the rules. Watch out was the byword: you could get pregnant. He'd done the things to me as well, with hands and the rest, except, except. I wondered. What would it be like, look like, how would it feel? The real thing. Which had to be different or there wouldn't have been all the fuss. The real thing was ahead, altogether new, not like Muff's backseat. Soon we would do it!

Meantime, down the aisle in white.

On Daddy's arm to the altar, technically unfucked.

Cowtown: Jane

Jane was a technical virgin when she got married too, a Pi Phi from Tennessee. Six months into her marriage, Jane found herself on the floor of a bookmobile with a dazed and bespectacled young librarian, humping between bookstacks. Not long after that, she got naked with a neighbor from a downstairs apartment whose wife had just given birth. They showered together; the new father showed Jane tricks with soap. Within the same year, she met a boy with hair to his waist, who sang songs of freedom in small vegetarian cafés. That was in those days.

Jane:

"Sometimes I pass some seedy boardinghouse, some tumble-down place in Montrose you know is crawling with roaches the size of your ear, and like a flash it comes back. And I can't believe it. You know? It seems like somebody else; some dream. Somebody I remember and can tell you about but not me. All those places. The couch, the bed, floor, table, the other people there. Me, Jane Stone Bartholomew, Freshman Honor Girl at Vanderbilt. Knocking on ratty doors, walking the streets, out to get some."

Jane and her husband, Lewis, moved into Post Oak Place when their baby was a year old. Before that, they lived in an apartment complex Jane calls "The Projects," a place of government sameness and one-foot-and-then-the-other occupants. A place just tacky enough to help Jane pry herself loose from her Pi Phi ways.

"Think about it. I'd worked during college and every summer in high school, I was used to being busy. Then pow I was a wife and that was that, wife was it. Lewis didn't want me to work. 'No wife of mine is going to work so long as Lewis Bartholomew hauls ass.' That was his motto. I was bored. Edgy. Nothing to do. We lived in a small apartment. Hour and a half and the corners were toothbrushed. Then what? I tried artsy-craftsy shit, gluing colored bits of tile and glass on a board to make a picture of sailboats in the breeze. Never saw a sailboat in my life. I felt like a kid at camp making lanyards.

"There was this book, *My Eight Weeks*. It was the rage that year. About a woman getting into an S-and-M relationship with this normal everyday guy, a bookkeeper as I recall. The book was passed around the Projects, the topic of every clothesline conversation. Gags, ropes, whips, the works. Things changed fast. First, *My Eight Weeks* in hand, I masturbated, in every room of the apartment, with every utensil appropriately shaped and some not so appropriate but chancy, fun. Stood in front of full-length mirrors and watched. Saw what I looked like and, Lord, what a shock. I kept thinking Lewis would sniff the handle of the plumber's friend, the candles, pens, pencils, the Water

Pik, doorstops, wine bottles, Dr. Pepper, Lone Star, Wink, and detect a familiar aroma. Fat chance.

"Upward and onward from self-abuse, I hit the streets for real. Convinced Lewis I needed a car . . . to get the best grocery buys, shop the specials. I'd have said anything. Once I was married, it seemed like, after protecting the thing all those years, the contest was over, Miss America was crowned, roses gone to dust. The only rule I had learned was DON'T, DO NOT, SAY NO. No morals, no standards, just no. How could I think for myself? Suddenly no turned on every occasion to yes. A hundred was the same as one: if I wasn't the virgin princess, well shoot the moon city, try them all. I tell you I know Houston like the back of my hand. Did it all over town, Third Ward, Heights, Montrose, Memorial, you name it, when I got pregnant and after the baby came, as well. Used to drop Liz off at the baby-sitter's. Left her crying her head off many a time. Said, 'Oh, she'll be all right, soon as I'm gone.' And I'd be out the door while she screamed, sixty miles an hour to some dump, off with the clothes wham bam. So much for motherly instinct."

Jane's divorce came not because of her affairs. As far as she knows, Lewis never found out, though she suspects he always knew. The divorce was a result of the usual things: the marriage wasn't working, he didn't feel like being married anymore, the spark the spark, love turned to friendship, all that. Because nothing. Either it works or it doesn't.

Jane's done well since her divorce. She's got a good-paying job at Houston Vital Parts, a drilling bit firm. Practically runs the office there, gets good money. Jane's got the old-fashioned kind of body you don't see much anymore, big bosoms, narrow hips, straight back, long shapely legs, great ankles. A Joan Crawford/suit kind of shape. But her wisecracking air hides the facts. Jane has fallen, utterly, for three different men this year, two of them newly separated from wives they went back to—one pleading children, the other his wife's health—the last and most recent a fly-by-night Cajun mud salesman she met at Vital Parts. She has just gotten loose from the Cajun.

At present Jane is fasting. No men, no sex. It's been three and a half weeks and so far she's stuck to it. Still eating her heart out over that Cajun.

Marrying Muff lost me some station. How could I stoop so low? Easy to explain. I could not get past him, over him, until the rest of it had happened and since I could not get to that until we were married, the fix was in, tune up the organ, buy the rice. I finished college, four years at Mississippi State College for Women, four years running back and forth from the "W" weekends to see Muff. Just past the middle of May—two days after my last exam and three weeks before formal graduation—Muff and I took the big step.

Then what? never entered my mind.

Nine months and some weeks later, Caroline was born.

Two years later, Robby.

One year after that, Ricky.

Three babies in four-and-a-half years.

Like mamas had warned: watch out. Orgasm in Muff's backseat had been such a surprise. Then it left. In all that time, between getting pregnant with Caroline until my second affair, which came between Robby's birth and Ricky's, that lovely backseat flutter disappeared. The magic left. I kept trying but deep in marriage and babies, my nervous system had simply lost the knack.

We moved to Cowtown. Muff caught the drift fast how it was going to go with laundries and began scouting for a new place with more action, some hotbed of opportunity everybody and his brother hadn't already found. Houston. Snake Oil City. Wildcatter's dream, new money shoot the moon. Houston was waiting for us, heaven on earth for ribbon clerks and medicine men. Back then everybody was saying Dallas Dallas Dallas but Muff had a wise eye, settled on Cowtown instead, then went and looked for a business. By the time he told me we were going, he had signed a contract with Mother Rancher's Ho-Maid Salads: chicken, potato, and pimiento, sold in your dairy case. Jalapeño pimiento came later.

The year we moved I was pregnant with Robby. Caroline was a baby. Nervous, tired, I had begun to feel regretful, anxious for change. I was happy to leave Ophelia. Robby was born in Texas.

Soon after we came here, Jane and Lewis moved next door. When Jane kept dumping Liz off to go run mysterious errands from which she returned looking like a nest of bees had set up housekeeping in her hair, I caught on. Muff traveled a lot and when he went as far as, say San Antonio or Dallas, he spent the night. And so the blessing of time fell upon me. Step one.

Cowtown's tacky, Big says. Music to my ears. Rougher, rawer: doesn't know which side the fork goes on. Fine with me. In jeans you take a wider stride. Boots give your footsteps that terrific click. Beneath your cowboy hat your hair is wild and loose.

Taking Jane's lead, between Robby's birth and Ricky's I received into my body stuff from a man not my husband. It wasn't an affair, we didn't go to bed, and certainly there was nothing of love in what we did. But we did it. He put it in and we did it.

March on Cancer had called, looking for block marchers. "One block?" they had whined and, feeling hectored, I gave in. A man came by with M. O. Cancer badge and collection envelopes. He admired my piano and left.

I didn't march. Cancer was worthwhile, but I could not march on it. I put my own money in the envelope and sealed it, my neighbors listed as contributors. The man came back, admired the piano a second time, listened: Caroline was at Jane's, the baby was asleep. The look passed. We went to the bathroom. He sat on the john and took it out. I sat in his lap and we did it, him

49

in sport coat and shoes, glasses, towel on his lap to protect his pants. Up and down, off and gone. He took the M. O. Cancer paraphernalia. I never saw him again. Didn't see much of him at the time.

I told Jane. We had a beer. This was also new: talking to women. I had thought doing it was the great secret and once you got married you shared intimacies only with the one you did it with, that that properly separated you from anyone else, especially other women since all of us were so quiet about ourselves anyway, and knocking on strange and ratty doors was not, we said, in our repertoire.

After M. O. Cancer came Al Theater. After all that boring churchy plink-plank in Ophelia, I had sworn off music for good. In Houston, I decided to take up acting. Good outlet, I told Muff, and joined the Post Oak Players. We performed weekends at the community house, a cozy group, discussing exits, motivation, and makeup. I tried out for *Separate Tables*. Al Theater was the director. After auditions, Al asked me to stay.

"Have you had acting experience?"

"Not much. The senior play in high school."

"Incredible. Turn your face to the light, please."

I lifted my chin.

"Fantastic."

He cast me in the lead as the lonely old maid. Rehearsals began. I quivered my chin to show how lonely I was, meantime postrehearsals doing another act altogether.

Center stage there was a parlor couch, part of the set; a scratchy thing. Late nights Al Theater and I took to it. Al was a flowery type, all drama and the grand gesture. Short was the problem, too short to play leading roles, not to mention bald. Al turned to directing. The theater was Al's passion, thus his name. Night after night we stayed late; night after night, one leg on the couch back, the other dangling to the floor, spread-eagled center stage.

"Sue," Al would say. "You are so good." Naked on a stage set was such a thrill. Like being in a TOTALLY NAKED REVUE.

I wasn't sure if good meant as an actress or on the couch, but I was willing to take either. It was as important to think I was as adept sexually as on the stage; after all, I wanted to be a going girl, good in bed, and the times were going in that direction.

With Al magic returned. My nervous system relearned its old tricks and with him I came, again and again. Angel Wing City, what a relief—I thought they'd left forever. Al had a way with his hands that was quite special. Also he did a number with ears It was all a little practiced and I knew it. Still. After a while I lost track.

I'd go home with red places on my behind, bumps and indentations from the couch. I'd finger them and sigh.

Muff saw the play. Boring, he said.

I said, "You don't understand."

Muff said, "So I'm a clod, still. Boring."

Me: "You're not a clod, don't say that."

Him: "I'm a clod. I don't care. It was boring."

Me: "You don't understand."

Him: "See? A clod."

He was right, it was boring.

"Nothing happened," he said. "People sat around. Blah-blah."

Al Theater had cast two genuine English ladies in substantial parts, a noble experiment, but they couldn't remember their lines and through the final performance had to be cued from offstage and reminded not to ask What? when they couldn't hear the prompt.

"I played Bo-Peep in a skit once," one of them said. "I was six, I think."

"No action," said Muff. "Give me *Guns of Navarone* anyday."

By then we were far apart. Muff was ready to settle in for the rest of it and I wasn't; by marrying him I had become even more saintly than the holy SSS, as the mother of his children, had turned into the same as his own mother, more to be adored than stars. In time, we might have pieced things back together but we weren't to have the chance. We weren't people to let go of things easily. We'd have held on a long time.

Muff and I still made love often and it never was bad, no matter my no-show orgasms, which of course Muff never knew about. Matter of fact, once I hit the couch with Al Theater things got magic again with Muff as well.

And I did treat him like a clod and he didn't see the red bumps because he didn't want to, an old story: we conspired.

I got pregnant. Ricky.

Move the circle around one notch. Same circle, same routine. Different hat and gloves; still.

When I did that play in high school, Daddy gave me a new name. Sarah Stage. During the rehearsals of *Separate Tables*, Daddy told Muff about the name and on opening night Muff sent a telegram addressed SARAH STAGE, POST OAK PLAYERS, INC., HOUSTON. I don't know how but it got there.

Daddy and I have terrible dreams. In the night we fly, are naked, come to on some street with no clothes on, on some stage in the middle of a play we know not a line of. There's a red-eyed donkey that comes at us teeth bared, a road we get on that's not wide enough for the car. We slide and are smothered. The children, in the back, are foolishly depending on us, believing in us, our skill. Fat chance. In dreams, our babies die and die.

Sometimes we wake up and have had the same one.

On the same night we will both try to drive the bridge that goes straight up, knowing if we make it to the top, the other side will be a horrible fall. We wake up falling. The little ones in the backseats, screaming. We wake up in a heat.

What I haven't figured out is whether Big steals my dream or I steal his or if dreams are maybe autonomous things, nothing to do with us. If maybe we only think we're the one doing the dreaming, while in fact they're the ones passing by, making social calls, dropping down to get two birds at once, Daddy then me.

Actually, however, I think Daddy steals mine.

Mama One

There's a nightmare stretch of highway between Houston and Texarkana, some eighty to a hundred miles just this side of the Texas-Arkansas line on Highway 59. Not bad daytimes, a plain ordinary straight road, timber forests on either side, small towns along. Nothing fancy, but not bad.

But oh night.

Just outside Loop 610, after the towns that are only satellites to Houston, you hit it. Somewhere between Cleveland and Diboll, due north.

We drove 59 going to Ophelia, for visits and holidays. Going up, we'd leave Houston in good time, be in Texarkana by noon, Ophelia by dark. Coming home to Houston, however, there would be a hundred delays—snags and last-minute meals, long good-byes—and we'd leave hours later than we planned. Fine for a while. Fine across Arkansas. Then we'd turn down 59 into Texas.

Middle of the night loony, 2 and 3 a.m., the nightmare stretch.

It's the same the whole hundred miles. Same straight road, same pines. The towns are all small and close up not only early but altogether: pitch-black, not a flicker.

You sit up straighter, stretch open your eyes, spit on a finger to wet them, open the window to let the cold air blow, turn up the radio. Not even a blinking EAT sign in Diboll, no all-night Lotta Cuppa Café.

How can cafés and stores close up completely, leaving rooms pure dark all night for burglars to ransack? Muggers and rapists, loose wild dogs. Where are the lights?

The road closes in. Cars brush by too close. Trees move toward the road. Trucks threaten to suck you under. There are traffic loops now, skirting towns. And so it's worse than it used to be, even with four lanes. On the road the whole time, you don't have even shut-up Carthage to wonder at. There's nothing but road.

Eager for Loop 610, anxious for familiar blight, you pass on. Short hop at a time, spitting on your eyes, watching for the city.

When I drove, I'd take it as it came, by the mile. If a sign said Lufkin 16, I'd think back to familiar distances; remember how long sixteen miles was from another town to Ophelia. Lula, for instance, was nine and that was nothing, the Indian Mounds seven in the other direction. Put them together I'd be in Lufkin. Piece of cake.

Muff was a good driver. It wasn't his fault. Somebody going north on 59 got caught up in that nightmare cloud of East Texas disorientation and, suddenly convinced Muff's car was going his way, veered over into Muff's lane to pass, just as Muff's car got there. They met dead straight head on, headlight to headlight. There were only two lanes then. Muff had no place to go and no time to get there.

I was in Houston, fat as a tub, waiting for number three. Muff had gone to Ophelia to get Linda, who was coming down to take care of the children while I was in the hospital. Big wasn't supposed to have come but he pouted so they let him. The three of them had had barbecue in Texarkana then crossed the state line, heading south. It was past midnight when they hit. Big was in the backseat. Muff and Linda sat up front. They had passed Nacogdoches. They were on the dark part of the highway, approaching Lufkin.

"I swear," the man in the other car said. "I could swear I was passing a car in my lane. I still think I was. I mean, don't get me wrong, I know what happened, but in my mind, you understand, I still remember it the other way. Like I was two places at one time."

He had just left Lufkin; Big, Muff and Linda were on their way, heading toward it.

A crisscross embrace: his sleeping wife smashed into my husband, he collided with my mother. One husband, one wife dead; the other two survived, though Linda by a hair. Big, relaxed as a cat, snored in the backseat and was not hurt.

In between Nacogdoches and Lufkin, ambulance drivers

debated which way to take the dead and injured, north or south. Wreckers came from both directions, to fight over the cars. There was heated conversation.

In the end, they flipped a coin. Tails. Lufkin won. And so by that narrow a margin Linda was taken to a hospital instead of the morgue, a hospital where a doctor named Lon Creekmore would happen to be on call that night, a doctor who would, by some coincidence, decide she was not dead, not yet.

Fate, says Linda. Karma, essential Shambala.

The point is, she's alive.

Linda: "I knew I was alive, I could hear Jimmy's snores. Things were dripping, lights going in funny directions, I could hear a tire spinning. I knew it was bad by the sound we made when we hit. I still hear that sound in my dreams. But your daddy? Snoring, same as before. How could I be dead?"

Still. She was.

"I went out awhile, then people came. Sirens, more glass, and spinning lights. I hadn't moved but I was there. Somebody touched me. I felt it. Somebody did something to my eyes. *She's dead,* they said. *Let's see about the other one.* I heard it plain as day. Dead? I was alive and dead at the same time. I was myself and body was something else again. How could I be dead if I wanted a cigarette?"

No vital signs: they took her into Lufkin for dead. But one attendant thought he saw something so they put her in the emergency room. Took the other wife and Muff to the morgue.

"I could see the whole time. Creek came, stood over me, took one look, and said, 'We'll operate.' And that was that. I knew I'd be all right."

No mama anymore. Patient, survivor, a plastic name-tag bracelet on her wrist. If she would live, she had to be fixed only on herself. Had to leave the rest of us out or die.

Lon Creekmore's a crusty old fart who bucked the odds and opened her up. She was a mess. Everything ruptured and cut apart, not an organ whole or intact. She had fallen against her buckled seat belt then went through it, breaking the belt. Her organs were ripped and torn, her back broken in two places. She was always small. Now she's even lighter. Half of her is gone. Battling poison, they took out everything she could do without.

"I just wish you hadn't eaten that barbecue," Creek told her. "Fried chicken would have been easier." Lon Creekmore never talked of miracles or gave Linda's new occult beliefs any weight. He simply fixed her body as best he could, like a plumber setting in new pipes. She was in Lufkin Memorial a year, dying, coming back, going under, coming back. Fourteen times no vital signs. Fifteen times back. I had a dead mother, no a live one, dead, alive, which?

"I just would not die," she says "I wanted to, but something wouldn't let go. I'd get blood poisoning and hurt so bad, I'd say good-bye, tell Creek what I wanted everybody to know and let go. No pain. Dead. I thought of the self of me as being like an old stray dog you try to get rid of. Throw him on the road thirty miles from town, here he comes back, wagging his tail. I'd die, wake up the same old me. Hurting again. It was, most of all, tedious and infinitely *boring.* "

My brother, Steve, went to see her, eighty-five pounds and smelling of death. Soon after, he married and moved to Morgan, Virginia, with a fancy wife named Brook.

It's a miracle. Rot sloughed off, skin grew back. Not pretty but alive. Why? is a question no one can answer. Linda's never gone far from the spot of the wreck. Her house is maybe thirty miles from there, an hour and a half north of Houston. So we're all in Texas now except Steve, who fled. He studied engineering in college, but he's a gun pro at the Morgan Club, a prestigious shooting club you have to be invited to join. Steve and Brook have two babies, Shannon and Priscilla, ages five and three . . . Salt and Pepper by Daddy, or simply, Ess and Pee.

Mama's esoteric now. She's big on yoga, herbs, reincarnation, and the moon. Lives in a lake house with a pretty boy younger than me. Has a Houston astrologer, named—I ask you—Sasha Moon. Imagine. Mama. Who used to be a den mother: cheese straws for the troops, fudge and lanyards; blackbottom pie.

She calls her lakehouse Nalandya: *peace* in some far-off dead Eastern language nobody else ever heard of. Linda comes to Houston occasionally. She went to Stuttgart when her brother died and once flew to Virginia to visit Brook and Steve. But mostly she stays where she is, next to her hotshot lake, close to her hotshot doctor, with her hotshot young beautiful boy.

Joseph. Slim as a pencil and half her age.

Joseph. A boy I swear I can hardly keep my hands off of myself. Even I would be an older woman to him and I am the daughter in this; yet there she is, my mother, a grandmother, Mama One, nuzzling flesh younger than her own son's.

Sometimes it puts me in a rage. I could cup his ribs between my palms he is so thin, wrap my fingers around his waist, hold his thigh all at once, make a circle of thumb and forefinger about his knee. There is a perfect flatness at his middle, the skin there stretched taut with no yield. His chest is smooth and tan and often smells of coconut oil from lying face-up in the sun; he has coin-round nipples the color of clay. No bigger than pennies, his tits. An indolent boy, he's Jewish, has money, went to an Eastern classy prep school with sons of great sons. There is no hair between his nipples. His chest is like a child's. Ah, Joseph. Jewish prince from Connecticut, come down this far from your home to lie with my mother, Mama One, twenty-six years your elder, and capture my Mama Two, her daughter's, lust.

I do love men's tits. Like erasers to gnaw.

His face is lovely, particularly from a three-quarter view. There's a shadow that falls at that angle, across the slant of his cheekbone down to the corner of his mouth.

Research, Mama says with a wink, watching as I fix on Joseph's chest or resolutely don't notice when he sasses past. Tax deductible.

Mama writes stories of a certain nature and taste; she's quite successful and gets much mail, which she reads and diligently answers herself. She uses a pieced-together name, her middle and maiden ones which side-by-side come to Shannon Day. And wouldn't Mothers Shannon and Day roll over in their graves if they knew. You may have heard of her if you read that kind of thing. If, that is, in newsstands and certain unadvertised stores you go behind certain well-guarded swinging doors to browse, or ask for certain brown-wrapped publications kept safe beneath check-out desks guarded by suspiciously accented clerks whose hands rise only to ring sales.

The phony name protects her identity, of course, in case she decides someday to write other kinds of things. Also, she says, by using a pseudonym she is saving her grandchildren from unexpected humiliation, from parents and PTA folk who—this is Linda talking—know no better than to attack her work as immoral.

The children, she insists, might not relish having it known that their Grandmother Day sells stories from the woman's point of view to *Erotica Monthly* and *Ero-Fantasy Digest*, not to mention a new and very fancy one just out, called—beautiful simplicity—simply *Skin*. *Skin* exists, so their ads say, to prove that erotica can be art. We'll see. Mama specializes in fantasies and revised fairy tales and adventures of the marvelous tending toward sci-fi and dreamlike tales; surrealistic, futuristic sex, where hairless, androgynous beings search for new and different ways to get off. Her latest published story was in *Skin*, last month's issue. On the cover, two body builders, male and female, were together on a beach, hamstrings and quads entwined, the woman's meaty behind grinding into clean white sand. They looked buttered. Like chickens before the roast. Mama's story was a new version of *Sleeping Beauty*, set in the sixties. "A Parable," the cutline read, "for the Times." The Princess's name was Leni, a leftover fifties child, asleep all that time. The story began, "Leni was a good girl. . . ."

It took my breath. I'm scared to death she'll write about me. She says everything's always about herself, but I don't know.

Most of the mail Shannon Day gets is from women, asking how in the world he knows what he knows if he is a man the way his name sounds, and who it was told him so well how it feels to a girl, and how long to do what in which place, and when to take another tack. Reading Mama's mail is very educational. She is carrying on a particularly interesting correspondence now with a woman who signs her name Mrs. Edmund Grant, about an underground housewives' sex group, made up of respectable pillars of everything, MRS. license plates, Cadillacs, beauty-parlor appointments, the works . . . getting it on the side while the kids go to Montessori.

People write all kinds of things to Mama. Confessions of adultery, questions of the utmost intimacy, marriage proposals, obscene suggestions, the works.

Used to be in the garden club. Floated gardenias in a crystal bowl. Was a whiz at azaleas.

Then: a DOA on 59, resurrected in Lufkin.

They tried to call, again and again. Three a.m., nobody home. Where could I be? By 3 a.m., I was cradling my new ten-pound baby boy, born the night his daddy died. Caroline and Robby were at Jane's. It was August. I had just turned twenty-six. A widow and a mama at once. It was steaming hot.

I'd taken a course on natural childbirth at Methodist Hospital, bending and squatting with other pregnant ladies in slips. I'd read the books—Dr. Grantly Dick-Read and Betsy Palmer—learned proper breathing and how to relax in labor. Had it going. My big moment. I lay on a table knees up, watching in mirrors as Ricky's great Llavots head slid out. Amazed and wondering: was that me? In the mirror lit up, draped, and shaved? Such a sight; I'll never forget it. I'd gone to camp once, between the fourth and fifth grades with a group of friends from Ophelia. At rest hour we'd gotten out a compact, sat bare-assed on a bunk in a circle, passed the mirror around, looking over one another's shoulders to see. We were amazed. Was that us? The girl who had the biggest won the contest. Size was the only criterion we could think of. Afterward, I put the episode out of my mind. That couldn't have been me. SSS would not have such a thing. But on the delivery table was different. Clean, like a picture. After the baby came out, there was a drop of blood, clinging, one tear. It held. Nurses were busy with the baby; I watched until the blood dropped onto the bleached white sheet. Then the placenta slid out, shimmering and silky, red and silvery gray, the cord twisted and wet. The nurse caught it, palpitating, in a dishpan and after the cord was cut, set the pan on the floor. The afterbirth shivered there. *Natural Childbirth* had spoken of its wonders but never said how beautiful it was.

The doctor came between me and the mirrors. "He's a big one," he said, and handed Richard Stovall Muffaletta over.

I'd been so brave. It wasn't fair. There was nobody to tell. No one to comment, or boast to. And Mama was dead, then alive, and Muff was perfectly dead. The swap, while clean, didn't seem even.

Muff left a healthy insurance policy, not enough to live well on but a solid amount for which I'm still grateful. We got by for a time, on his benefits. Muff's pride was his ability to take care of people and he did a good job. When you were sick, in fact, he drove you crazy. Such a nurse. I'd wake up to find him standing over me. Just standing there looking.

I still get checks and there's a college provision for the kids. My first truly selfish purchase was, a few years after the wreck, a white Mustang convertible.

I still drive it. Boys stop me on the street, ask what I'll take for it. Grocery sackers, bringing goods to my car, offer to trade me their 280 Z's. No deal, I tell them, not for sale or trade. I take it out west on the I-10 for repairs and parts, to a shop called Absolutely Mustang.

Things come around, go around, never stay the same.

Daddy went to Muff's funeral, representing the family. I said not to hold services up for me, wondering if they'd put him in the funeral parlor we met in. I was in the hospital with his new son; I insisted they go on without me. Recovery from this loss was slow. Time took on a new, dragged-out beat. In a few years, after Jane went for Barn Red, I decided to pep up my own spirits by painting my house that intended Clay. Was writing songs by then. The circles don't match up but they do go around.

60

Robby doesn't like bacon. Never eats it. One weekend morning when we got up late, I fixed some. Two pieces each, except for Robby. Put the plates out, turned around, went for coffee, came back, there sat Robby, eating my bacon.

"I thought you didn't like bacon," I said.

"Who said I liked it," he said, reading the latest issue of *Shazam*.

"You're eating it."

He shrugged. "Sometimes it goes away and sometimes it comes around."

My piece of bacon crunched between his teeth. He turned the page to an article on a new rock group called Tail.

The circle turns. With us or on its own.

I wrote "Mama." I think it's finished. Short, but they can drag out the end with a tag chorus. I'll sing it for Daddy tonight, get it notated then send it off. I'm hoping for Tammy. Maybe Crystal or Loueene, but it feels more like Tammy to me.

After June Day does it, that is. Me first.

MAMA

She tells the children not to worry cause their mama'll be
    home soon.
That she'll take her bow and rush right home at the end of
    her last tune.
"Go to bed right now," she tells them, "don't forget to say
    your prayers.
"When you wake up in the morning, you know Mama will
    be there."

She is her babies' darling mama and she's doing what she
    can.
Making the best of what she's got, living without a man.
Their daddy up and left them and never sends a dime.
Mama does what Mama can and Mama's doing fine.

John Junior zips her up in a tight red dress, there's a kiss
from little Sue.
Jimmy says, "Make the last song short and, Mama, we'll
pray for you."
She stands before the bedroom mirror, holding back her
tears.
A mama with her three children, kissing away their fears.

She is her babies' . . . etc.

She does not tell them where she goes each night in their
old beat-up car.
They thinks she sings country music and soon will be a
star.
They dream of moving away to Nashville, Mama singing
hits someday.
They'll never know how Mama pays the rent if Mama has
her way.

She is her babies' . . . etc.

Mama's doing fine.
Mama's doing fine.

M. S. Sue

After Muff died, I stewed a long time, doing nothing. I was
nervous all the time. Had the jitters. Couldn't sit still. Had
trouble breathing; the doctor said it was anxiety, leftover grief.
I learned to deep-breathe, to get through the day. Devoted a lot
of time to Ricky, who didn't need it; he was a sweet baby, the
first to take long naps and play by himself in his crib. He'd been

a pistol before he got out, kicking and punching my spleen. Once in the world he seemed content. I'd check him periodically, wondering how he could be happy just sleeping; watch him, nap with him, daydream while he slept. He was also the first I breast-fed. At night, I'd bring him to bed with me. We'd drop off to sleep together on our backs, my breast still out for him, caked with milk. For a while he took up enough time and jitters that I could get by.

Then Ricky got older. He'd rather play with Robby than me. Then what, get a job? Money wasn't a big problem, because of the insurance. And in my book, a job never was hot stuff. There had to be better. There was that other me, that limelight in the back of my mind, still shining. Something to do so people would once again say, oh, *her!* I know *her!* Why can't you be more like *her?*

Married to Muff, all that got lost a little but not altogether. Go to his grave, shake his shoulder, ask him. He'll tell you how arrogant my ambitions kept me; how high-toned and haughty. How, thank the Lord, discontent.

But when babies are little, time for mothers turns gray. They don't understand it themselves. I didn't. You don't know who you are. I see young mothers now, pushing grocery carts, a baby in the cart's papoose. Check their eyes: nothing; pure zero. They may smile but the smile yields nothing. It's pasted on. The baby starts to scream; they deal with the screaming, shushing the baby, saying no you can't have jelly beans, I told you last time I wasn't going to buy you jelly beans, you didn't eat your bananas when we got home all you wanted was jelly beans, you'll have to do without from now on. Clever as a mutt, the baby screams on. The mother has canceled out the world, except occasionally to make apologetic noises about the screaming. Finally, she slams a bag of jelly beans into the baby's hand and pushes on.

When I think back over that time there are huge blank spaces I can't fill in. What did I do all day, how did I feel, wasn't I miserable staying at home doing nothing but baby care? I don't know. I don't remember being miserable. I have no idea. It's like somebody poured hot wax over the clocks, melting hours into a flat plane of no time, a huge gray momentless wash.

When Ricky was three Jane insisted I send him right away, part-time, to the Methodist Church Day School. I did. Three hours a day three days a week. Robby was in nursery school every day, and Caroline was in kindergarten. Ricky's first day at baby school marks the exact moment when things started to change.

I'd drop them all off, come home, get more coffee, sit, think. What? What would I do? It had to be something fancy. There was the limelight; my noblest self.

I started with the fanciest of all. Poetry. After all it looked easy and I had a lot to say.

I wrote poems all year. Typed on a portable Smith-Corona I'd won in a Community Fund essay contest in Ophelia, poems about how sad I was, what terrible things had been done to me, how awful it was to sit in the back room of your house writing poems, how lonely.

I didn't write about Muff, motherhood, or marriage. No mundane everyday stuff. I shot the moon.

The next summer I went to a writer's conference at a local university. Paid $150 to attend a few classes and have my poems "critiqued." Snap, I was a poet. Doowah.

The conference turned out to be chiefly a gathering of writing conference groupies: lonely old ladies spending retirement funds and Social Security checks on travel and hotel expenses, going from one writing conference to another; lonely old men writing about Germany and Pearl. "I was fucking a nurse in Pearl when the Japs struck." Their manuscripts were as brown as the spots on their hands from so much time on the road. I figured they figured it was a better thing to do than staying home to baby-sit grandkids, but still . . . The schedule of classes featured less noble versions of the art than I had anticipated: how to write fillers and headlines and jokes; articles for *My Baby Times;* TV commercials, and quickie travel tips; how to protect yourself from plagiarists. (That was a good one. People over-flowed with what if? questions, who hadn't yet written a word to plagiarize.) Selling was what the conference was about, not writing.

I did, however, meet a poet in the flesh, a tall, swivel-hipped young man in a shaggy boat-neck sweater, bleached jeans, and bronze-colored zip-boots. His hair was blond and curly, his eyes baby blue, and he had this look, sweet as pie, unrippled as cream. This was Houston, understand, in August, but the boat-neck sweater, the poet was right, gave him a certain look. He said my poems were special, that they had an appealing sense of, quote, the naïveté to which more established poets long to return, unquote. Had I never published? Like Al Theater, the poet professed astonishment. He checked my finger for rings, said the only reason he agreed to attend the conference was they paid him well and he had some friends in Houston he wanted to visit, having just arrived there from Taos on his way back to Soho, where he lived. Otherwise: he rolled his eyes and said—well you know.

The poet had a soft look about him I have never been attracted to; something that if challenged I sensed would automatically roll over and yield. I like men to move against, some flint. Grit. I don't know: friction. Somebody you can tell is *there*. Other-wise, why bother?

Still. The poet had that look.

We went to his room. The conference had set him up in what in regular school session was a dorm for the handicapped. There were ramps to all the doors; the elevator buttons were thigh-high. For some reason, when we got there and took off our clothes we lay in his bed swapping masturbation tales. I have no idea how this got started, whether it was the poet's standard line, or maybe a way of gathering material for his poems. (Since the conference I have waited and watched for a book of his to come on the market, to see if I'm in it, lying in a low bed telling about one time in the bathroom with candles and a mirror. So far nothing. I've never seen his name come up anywhere.) The poet told about how his grandmother caught him fucking the vacuum cleaner when he was little and how it felt when he did it, the wind sucking at his cock.

Whatever the reason, the prelude worked. Fired up, we got into it, fingers and sucking. He went down on me for a long time. And it was all working pretty well for a while. Then he switched back around, and I was right about the yield.

"It'll just take a minute," he kept apologizing and I'd work him up again. It was no big deal except in his mind which meant of course it was a big deal. Our concentration lagged. We began to press. I lost the thread.

The poet had a pretty body; I remember every spot. Ankle-bones that went up a long way into shin before turning into calf. A sweet ass, a long spine. Freckled collarbone. Moles. Chest and underarms smelling of wet wool.

After going to the bathroom to clean himself (grateful if you ask me to have the thing over and done with), the poet tossed me a copy of *Ultra*, a big-time literary magazine he said—no: *important* was what he said—in which his work had been published. The poem seemed to be about piano keys. I couldn't make head or tail of it and had no idea what it was about, other than piano keys which didn't seem likely. But *about*, I figured, was not an appropriate question and so I said the poem was wonderful and didn't bother mentioning a mistake he'd made about a C# minor chord he used as a metaphor for I could not tell what. After all what did I know? The poet nodded when I said wonderful and we lay side by side in his bed sweating, feeling virtuous and snooty. He got a copy of *Ultra* for himself. Together we read his work. His toes wiggled in delight. The world may have been too much with some. Not us.

At least I can say for myself, at *least* I did not go back. Once I took the downhill ramps out of the handicapped dorm I did not see the poet again, except at a talk he made on Poetry Is a Quality of Life.

I also went to a moneymaking seminar, in which a woman with dyed black hair and lips bright as wet vinyl told us how to write stories for *True Romance* and *My Real Tale*.

"A virgin," the woman instructed. "You have to have a virgin."

I thought her lesson more useful than the poet's "Poetry is a quality of life. It is *the* quality of a life well lived."

I ask you.

I came home from the conference basically uncheered. But I sent my poems to *The New Yorker* and *Ultra* as the poet suggested. The poems came straight back. I still have them, rejection slips attached, a rusted outline of a paperclip engraved in a corner.

Meantime virtue wore thin. I bought my Mustang, started to ride around, moving my body, feeling a new itch. Jane helped. Got me dates, insisted I not mope. I went places now and then where country music played. In Ophelia we'd been uppity toward hillbilly music, preferring bop and boogie and black rock and roll. But I started to like it. Danced to it. Started to pick up the one-two beat. Tapped my nails, rocked, felt the beat move inside. I'd twitch my calf muscle to the beat, when a country song came on.

I missed Muff. Missed him a lot. His size, and spirit, that Great-Galloping-Huey-the-Duck version of himself in the world. Like at the Golden Gloves. It never occurred to Muff the Drew boy's skill would outdo his bulk and punch. Who could whip him? Entering a restaurant or movie, I kept turning around, thinking Muff was there. I'd say to people "we," meaning me.

There were stories to tell him. I'd think, Wait till I tell Muff this, something inconsequential that went on at the store, a prank the kids had pulled he'd have gotten a kick out of. That he was not there to share stories with honestly took my breath. And I'd have to deep breathe; concentrate.

Muff used to do this act for the two kids, Creepo the Clown.

Creepo did a trick where he took off his thumb, a trick passed on to Muff from his uncle Od. They both had double-jointed thumbs. Muff would bend one down at the knuckle until it tucked into his palm then substitute the top of the other one and, wrapping a finger around the gap, lift off the top. The kids would be amazed. He pulled quarters from Robby's ears and brought them balloons. That sense of high times; that outsized spirit: it was cheering; I missed it. Life shrank, possibilities lessened, a day became a matter of eight o'clock then nine, what to have for breakfast, then dinner. Not to mention lunch. It wasn't until Big moved to Houston that size returned to our life, and eggs for breakfast became, again, just part of a day, only food. After Big came, M. S. Sue was born.

I went to The Poor Man's Country Club one afternoon with Jane, to sip beer and share stories. We heard some country tunes. I came home humming one. It got stuck in my head. And then it changed, became not the tune I had heard but a new one, hatched on my own. I'd been clipping out newspaper stories for a while, human-interest feature articles, dealing mostly with impossible feats and depravity, amazing stories of how people got through their lives: the tale of two sisters who, when the third sister died, committed suicide by looping a sheet over a door and double-hanging themselves. Humming my new tune, I remembered an article I'd saved from the *Houston Post*, about a woman named Sylvia Brown who had "left home to enter a life of crime" and loved it. "I'd recommend it to anybody," Sylvia said. "It was a natural high." Sylvia, mother of two, was tiny; had served in her hometown PTA; once hijacked a family camper, which, with her boyfriend, she tied a tricycle to the top, to look on I-10 like an All-American touring family. The story was a natural. I set it to my tune.

All I had to do was lift out phrases and catchy lingo already in the paper, fill in the beat. It seemed, in fact, too easy. I wrote it at night while the kids watched TV, my first song. Picked it out on the piano, played it for Daddy and the kids. They liked it. Played it for Jane. She liked it. Went to the library, checked out *Songwriter's Market, '75.* Figured how to peddle it.

(The phony name was a concession to Caroline. She's a picky girl. By the time I got "Sylvia" published, she was old enough to understand and she's a girl who needs prestige. She'd have been mortified; country songwriting is not Post Oak proper. I should have been doing volunteer work in Red Cross shoes and panty hose. I think now it wasn't such a good idea to make that concession, but I've had a hard time all my life denying my kids what they out and out ask for. I keep softening edges, prettying up the world. My mistaken assumption is: if they ask for it, they want it. A gift for the overview doesn't seem to be a talent of mine.)

And the rest of it, well you know. In time, "Sylvia Brown" became a hit. Later, June Day was added to my repertoire. One June day, in fact, wouldn't you know it. How cornball can you get? Shameless as June Day and M. S. Sue.

Because a lot of my songs are stories, people are always coming up to me in the joints where I sing to tell me theirs. "Girl," they say, "if you only knew. You would not believe it, girl," they say, "the things I know. What I know would curl your hair. Would make Snake Pit look like Lassie."

And I always agree because it's always true, the stories are all good and bad and strange and boring and wonderful and terrible and true. Most of all amazing, the least among them, even the ones that seem so tame. "I never would have believed I ever would have stayed in this one hick town all my life," a shift-worker at an oil refinery told me. "Pulling shifts, graveyards every three weeks, forty-odd years and then some. Lord," he shook his head. "The things I dreamed of." Over our heads as we talked, a beer sign with fake waterfalls turned and sparkled and the jukebox flashed red and yellow as brown long-neck beer bottles went up and down. Then came the clincher. "Lotta pathos," the shiftworker said. "Lotta pathos."

All those dreams. Now look.

Mama's Boy

Two minutes in, two out, on the last tag of the last exhalation, she is nearly finished. There is a tiny tunnel behind nose and throat that feels like a glass tube, thin enough to shatter. Breath makes a sound there, inside her head. She has never been to a class or met a real yogi, but learned on her own, to records bought from Sasha Moon. When her lungs are empty, she pushes again, a light snort to expel any leftover cigarette smoke. Feeling heavy enough to have sunk through the mattress, she opens her eyes.

Joseph. Beyond her bed at her mirror he stands there, naked as grass and slim as a pencil, admiring his face.

His back is to her, the long bony curve of his spine, his curly dark head. He has a kind of swayback stance which, naked, he gives in to. It lends him a girlish look.

Something between them is neither man nor woman but the same. It had startled her, at first, that there could be something other than difference but there it was. The midpoint between, neither sex.

"Joseph?"

He answers to the mirror without turning.

"Would you hand me my robe?"

He turns to profile, runs a finger across a mole on his cheek-bone, inspecting. Raising his chin, he peers down his long, aristocratic bones. As if he had not heard. Preening, pretending. Pretty pretty boy.

She keeps thinking she has got past astonishment and disbelief—that he is here, this pretty young thing, living in her house, living out with her whatever they have to its end. Yet look. There he is.

And her. Who once was. Don't think about it, it will never come together or make sense.

There is not an ounce of fat on him. His buttocks are slight nearly to pathetic, like a panicky adolescent girl starved into fashion, down to bones and beyond. There is space enough between his thighs to see a landscape through, his knees fleshless and knotted as wood. He studies himself constantly. She has seen him catching quick glimpses wherever they go, eyeing his reflection in store windows and gum-machine mirrors, as if what he looked like would tell him who he was.

Spoiled baby, rich boy, still trying to find out what it is he wants to be.

Finally he turns. The robe is on a rocking chair beside him. He stands there naked, accepting attention as his due.

"Why do you want it?"

"I'm cold."

"It's not cold."

"I am."

This is the in-between, languorous and playful. Just up from sex, they are teasing as cats, all questions and sassy jousting. He pouts, challenging her request. He wants her naked. This is baby self, double-dog daring. On other men it would seem spiteful, on Joseph it's only a pose. Hands on craggy hipbones, he moves to stand at her feet, taking his position: I am still the man in this. You may be older, this may be your house and bed and mirror but make no mistake there are ways in which I am still the man.

Oh men. This boy. Younger and older, she has learned from him. Twice his age nearly but he knew things she didn't.

He takes pills, experiments with powders and drugs, tests limits she had been frightened to admit even existed. Smokes his precious weed, wakes up, smokes it, goes to bed, smokes it. He is slightly stoned now. She had shared that kind of experimentation with him for a time, to see, and something in her had been loosened; some tight wire in her mind allowed to slip free; she had become all skin and sense of skin then, and suddenly was adrift. Too free, she thought, and gave it up. If the wreck were to happen again, she is not sure she would have the will to keep coming back. The loosening, it seems, has a carryover effect: more patience, more drift, a quicker responsiveness. Yoga comes easier, memories flood quicker. Good news and bad.

With one finger, Joseph lifts her robe, holds it out. She will have to raise up to get it. The sheet falls.

"Bully."

From this side of it, it seems always to have been going to happen, the wreck or at least something terrible, if not actual death then something. The year before, she had had several small accidents. While peeling apples, a small paring knife had fallen from her hands and sliced into her foot, causing problems for a year. It shouldn't have been so bad, such a small cut, yet infection kept recurring. Jimmy driving, they had had a less serious car accident. In the yard she had slipped and, that quickly, cracked a rib. In retrospect, there seemed to have been warnings. Jimmy took her to Hawaii. There was a volcano, said to be hexed; if you took away the balls of lava lying about its base, you would receive its lifelong curse. She had not dared even to touch one, though Jimmy thought lava would be a terrific gift to take home to the kids. Still, it was after the trip, seeing that great gray mountain, that the troubles began.

Now, when doctors unfamiliar with her case looked at her body, her X rays, and charts, and said to her, "What are you doing in this world, girl? How in the world are you alive?" she had nothing to say. There she was. Linda. Herself. What more was there?

It was not a gift, however; survival has had its price. Loneliness for one. People live inside a track she no longer shares, her death having come in the center of her life instead of at the end. She sits like a curled cat watching. The terribleness and the certain knowledge of what the very end is like has freed her from normal time, set her at a remove.

There is, in recompense, however, this: she now lives inside her skin, one with it, the same Linda Day in name and flesh. It allows her time to be with this pretty boy, to admire his slim nakedness for as long as it lasts. Life is inside itself now, in mind and name together. *I am the named self.*

In the bathroom, she combs out her hair and freshens her makeup. Not so old, not so. There are lines around Joseph's young eyes too, from the drugs, she suspects. Certainly he is not old enough to have them.

He won't stay. Daredevil, thrillseeker, looking for risks, he is trying this for a while—her, her house, the older woman, new pleasures—and will at some point move on. His current occupation is taking pictures; with his expensive Nikon he snaps the world to a black-and-white standstill measured by F-stops, available light, shutter speed, composition. He curls thumb and forefinger around one eye, scanning the landscape, searching for frames. "Look at this," he will say, showing her a photograph of a tree as if he were the first to see it. She is one of his studies, real to his life as long as he records her. Once thoroughly snapped, she will become old hat.

Still. Her attention, that silky erotic thread, is caught up. It takes her breath to think of his dark eyes, how he looks at her, what he sees. He keeps so much of himself private. She can barely tell when he comes. Once he had whispered in her ear, "I think I'll come now," and she had been amazed.

So there it is, him, her, what she has. And whatever it is for however long it lasts, she will take it and when he leaves she will crack for a while. Not forever. But it will take time and she will always miss him, their times together, the loosening and patience she has discovered. Fact: some things you get past but not over. Time's a famous healer but there are limits. Never's a fact as well as someday.

He will always be in her life.

She will never get over losing him.

She has told him so.

"If you left this minute," she said, "I'd miss you forever."

Joseph said nothing. Joseph was not much on conversation.

"I wouldn't be bitter, you understand. I'd go on with my life and be fine. All the same I'd be missing you and loving you the whole time. The whole way, however things turn out. Do you understand that?"

They both were quiet then, and finally Joseph said, "Linda. One thing is . . ." and reached for her and that was it.

He didn't understand and it didn't matter.

She raises her chin to smooth the skin beneath the jaw, down the neck. The first place it shows. There and in the hands.

Her eyes are a clear glittering blue, movable as water.

Sex eyes, Dolly said.

Men have always been attracted to her eyes. So trusting and with that blue shine, they look like mirrors. Men like to see what they look like in her eyes, find themselves reflected back. It wasn't her fault, was it?

Dolly had dark eyes with no center. As a girl she had jet-black hair. *Indians in my past,* Dolly used to say, as if the family history belonged exclusively to her. Linda never could make out what her mother was saying. There was always something between the words. Something fierce; a threat. The real message.

She rubs Vaseline into the skin around her eyes and over her mouth. Since the accident her skin is always dry. The medicine and transfusions and IV's took out some ease and oil, leaving her skin crackly and dry. She is light as a leaf.

Little toy, Dolly said. *Made for sex.* She was only a child then, but her mother instructed her early, telling her nothing in the meantime about what it meant to be born for sex, what to expect, what her body was up to as it changed.

She tried to destroy the evidence when it happened. She thought she was dying. She threw her soiled underpants down the well, bloodying the water. More came. It would not stop. Finally her brother, seeing how she was carrying herself, watching as she crossed her legs then looked down at herself, asked if it had happened and when she would not say yes or no but only turned her head, told her what it meant.

To hear it from your brother. It wasn't right. There was no one to go to. It was a curse. No one to tell or explain or give her the facts exactly. It all seemed a blur. She had never known the whys of things, throughout her life.

That night Dolly brought her some rags and told her what to do. As she left the room she said, "Just don't come home if you miss one."

Joseph has said she is the first true Gentile he has been with beyond one-night stands. Have they all been Jewish? she asked. She met him at a party at Sasha Moon's. Most of the men there were gay; she had assumed he was, so thin, such a pretty boy. Not all, he said, but some Gentiles are Jews under the skin, particularly city girls. But you. Linda. You are true Southern goyim, Arkansas pure white.

Her hair is slippery. Up in a knot, some of it falls loose about her face in feathery wisps, as casually provocative as the golden chain Joseph wears, which lies in a coil against his collarbone in a calculated S.

Passing him, she brushes his shoulder. He takes her place in the bathroom. More mirrors.

From the kitchen she calls him.

"Joseph?"

"Yes."

"Want some carrot juice?"

A standing joke. She swears by carrot juice and he will not be converted. He was at Sasha Moon's because there was a party and he thought pretty girls might be there, not because as he says he believed any of that astrology crap. Joseph likes beer and Mexican food. He makes *chili con queso* with melted Velveeta and Ro-Tel, into which he dips Frito-Lay's cheese-flavored Tostitos. The kind of food her grandchildren adore.

Lifting a carrot, Linda Day presses its root end against the extractor's wheel and watches as orange liquid collects in the clear plastic container below. The machine whines, a high crying sound as familiar a noise as the mailman's approach, the night owl's song, the evening frog, the whirr of boats on the lake nearby, whizzing across.

Linda's Notebook

NEW STORY: TO BE TITLED "THE FROG
PRINCE" BASED ON ORIGINAL GRIMM.
CONSIDER FROGS AND HEXES. THE VIRGINAL
PRINCESS, HER LIFE. HAVING TO STAY A
VIRGIN, YET: STILL HAVE FUN.

How to write such stories: once you have bottomed out in some way, seen the worst and best and gone full out for what you need—life and not death; Joseph—it comes easy. Once you have a clear idea just how far you will go, to what extremes, at what cost. Cost is important. What a person is willing to pay. Humor comes later, much, if it will. After you've been dead a lot of things turn comic. A way to get through. (Keep one secret. *Always*.)

II.
Post Oak Blues

Big at the Table

Look at him: you'd think he was sleeping. He's not. Big does this every night, pretending not to be going to sleep at the same time acting like he already is, a double-fisted deceit. Fact is, if he says sleep, he wakes up. So he sneaks up on it. Acts like he doesn't care if he never sleeps again, sits there resting in his chair. Reading his eyelids, he claims.

Bed's the enemy. Nighttime; dreams.

Witches come then. Hags and night things. Old and angry ghosts, to hex his sleep.

When Big's left eye stops twitching I'll know he's truly gone.

I fixed him his liver. We just ate. It wasn't bad; I'm just not much on liver and if Big didn't love it, I wouldn't fix it. I'd eat it. But I wouldn't cook it, even though I do it pretty well. Once a month, about, I cook it for Big: his treat for letting me sleep.

There's a Bama jelly glass by Big's plate with a sip left in it, maybe even two. Imagine. A slug of roogle and he's left it. Gone but not forgotten, guaranteed. Big may lose track of where his shoes are but roogle? Hide and watch. He's got a plan.

On a slug of roogle the eye of Big never shuts.

Me, I've got it going too. With my afterdinner black coffee and red jug wine—my version of roogle—I'm sitting here sipping, before the night moves on and things need doing. The table's still littered with dishes and scraps. The pan I cooked in, the family-size ketchup jug. The kids are in the living room watching TV. They ate earlier, on trays, Hamburger Helper Mexican Style, which they love, second only to boxed macaroni and cheese you make with a powdered orange stuff mixed with milk to make fake cheese, third only to taco-flavored anything, fourth only to cheap pizza and Pop-Tarts and Little Debbie Oatmeal Cakes. Brand names are their Bible. The same as knowing to listen to AC/DC and not Wayne Newton.

The kids hate liver.

The leftover sip in Big's glass is sherry, Almadén Pale Gold, which he drinks at my house by the jelly glass. At the Zodiac he doubtless still guzzles hard stuff; to avoid my huff at our house he sticks to sweet sherry, puny 16 percent. No matter what we eat, Big Macs to tamales, Big has Pale Gold. By the Bama jelly glass. And the Bama jelly glass.

DOCTOR'S ORDERS, he announces every night and like it was medicine, bolts the first glass down. Sighing—AHHHHH—he pours another before the first has gone down. Every night he does this, gets a foxy look, goes through this Think-I'll-have-a-drink routine. My part of the dance is to be Eve just born, new in the world, ga-ga at apples. Oh, Daddy: having a drink?

The second glass he nurses through dinner, a nightcap to ease out on, sip by loving sip. Daddy's doctor may know arteries but about Daddy he's a fool.

Two glasses of sherry a night can't hurt anybody. That's Big's rendition of what his heart man told him and I believe he said it. No one wants to deny Big his portion.

If it helps, feel free.

Feel free, I ask you. The doctor ought to come see what kind of two glasses . . . Bama plum, Bama grape, Bama strawberry preserves; Big is not choosy about fruit. So long as we buy the Econo-King Size. His hand is curled next to his glass in case I try to take it. Never mind forgotten, he knows.

Six weeks ago he had a cataract removed from that left eye,

the one he keeps pinching, because his contact's still in. He calls his contact lens his eye. Just after the operation, which took hours longer than they had predicted, the surgeon came to the hospital waiting room and announced, "He's quite a man."

I looked up. He was cute for a doctor; bouncy. He gave me a look, checking my hand for rings. I have made this vow: No more married men. Not as strict as Jane's chastity oath but still. If it isn't going to be married Sam Moore, I swear it isn't going to be married anybody; I have done the married man waltz and left the floor.

"We couldn't get him out," the surgeon said.

I asked what out meant. He had changed from operating clothes into a golf outfit, knit shirt, placket pants, those fancy leather loafers with pom-poms. Sharp stuff, color-coordinated. He turned his wrist, limbering it for the links; bounced on his toes. Shook his head. Made a click with his tongue.

"The anesthetist. Every time we thought we had him, *blip*, here he came." The surgeon snapped his fingers to accent *blip*. "Asking some question about work."

"How're you getting along with your work."

"That's it."

"It's not a question."

"At any rate." He smiled. "We had to keep feeding him pentathol. Anesthetist said he'd never seen anything like it. It may take him awhile to come to but everything is fine. No problem. The eye is a beauty." (Pause) (Look) "Your husband coming by?"

No rings but he wasn't taking a chance. I said no and he left. I waited for Big to get out of the recovery room. So far I have stuck to my vow: since Sam Moore not one. The eye man was, I know. I'm a wife expert. Doctors need one. Like politicians. When in trouble, on trial, in a jam, drag her out. Take her to the party in a fancy dress, introduce her: my wife (fill in the blank).

As for Daddy and the dope, how was a surgeon to know? Charts don't measure Big. All that whiskey? His liver's soft as gravy. Eggs every morning fried in grease, liver once a month, yet his cholesterol count for lowness challenges toes. His own father never brushed his teeth in his life according to Big, but only rubbed them at night with a washrag yet look. Big Walt died with every last tooth, not a filling. A heart surrounded by fat, it's true. But no silver in his teeth.

I still don't love liver. But sometimes I crave it. Something back behind the tongue. You never can tell, can you, what you'll end up having a yen for, what dark, dingy taste will turn to cream-cake in your grown-up mouth.

Daddy's apartment at Signs of the Zodiac is huge; it's in Pisces. Caroline says it's disastrous for Big, a Gemini, to live in a water-sign house but I don't know.

No pets are allowed at the Zodiac, or children. It is an Adult Complex. SECURITY, TENNIS, the sign says. A ski room, hot tub. Computerized haircuts, classes in scuba and stained glass, lessons in the Cotton-eyed Joe. Caroline says Daddy should be in Sagittarius instead. Or Capricorn.

Fact is, he shouldn't be there at all. His apartment has more space in it than my whole house, his den by itself large enough for him to live in. The Zodiac leaves flyers advertising Sunday Meat Shows, where drinks for women are free. Word is, disco's out. Country's coming in. Soon, fiddles and dobroes will tune up in the Wreck Room. Maybe me.

Daddy won't move. Says he likes the floor plan.

There, I think he's going; no, he's not. Big's head jogged then popped back up. Not yet. The left eye just twitched. Not yet.

Big and His Wife

Sue's watching; he knows. Behind Big's eyelids, consciousness winks and slides. He feels wide awake then drifts, comes to, then is gone. The contact bothers him, makes his eye itch, inside his lid feels as big as a plate. But if he wakes up enough to take it out, forget it. Start-Over City after all this work. Never mind. He can get there with it in.

Linda keeps slipping into his mind. Sue took him once to Hermann Park to see free Shakespeare. The park was dangerous; he went to see she got home safe. He fell asleep. Sue woke him up to see the end. *My wife,* the man in black face said, then stopped short, remembering he'd killed her. *What wife?* He won't turn Linda loose, he can't, she's his wife. *Alas, I have no wife.* A name meant something. A wife wasn't supposed to up and just leave.

Waking up is a blessing; that twitching left eye. Waking up disrupts his dream about Linda.

Three men are around her. She is naked on a table, her bright glittering easy blue eyes shining. Flecks of silver light up the blue, like sunshine on a lake. Her blond hair lies across her shoulders unpinned. It was whore hair to wear it down. She had let the blond grow out in the hospital, to a no-color straw. He liked it blond. Whores wear it down to advertise.

Her eyes are too easy. Sex eyes, like Dolly said. When they drove to Stuttgart and announced they had gone to West Memphis and got married, Dolly tore a switch from a peach tree. As if Linda were a child. "She's mine now," Big had said. "She's mine." And checked Dolly's rage, holding her wrist with his big hand. Dolly had jerked away from his grasp and gone away, throwing dark looks back over her shoulder at Linda, as if hatching hexes.

"Did you see her eyes?" Linda said. Big said to forget it, she was married, Dolly couldn't touch her anymore. But Linda shuddered. "You don't know her," she said. "You just don't know." And her darling blue eyes looked ready to fly from her skull, like rockets.

More men come. They are like small animals. Her hair fans out over the table, hanging over its edge. She lifts her hips. He could not stand it when she lifted them, it was whorish but he wanted her to: it got confused. Whore, wife. He married a whore? No. Married Dolly's girl, Linda Shannon Day. Barefoot easy blonde, eyes bright as stones. His wife. Whore hair, but still. What wife? He has none.

Drift and slide.

You know what they say about Jim Stovall? They say Jim Stovall could sell broken light bulbs if he put his mind to it. Sell cockroaches to housewives. Tails to a lizard. Venom to rattlers.

In the night remorse strikes. All the nagging rees. Recapitulation, remorse, regret. Reliving his mistakes. Restoring blame and guilt where it belongs, on his head.

Money he has gone through would send his grandchildren through college, with enough left over for island vacations all around. Bankruptcies filed, judgments against him from hot deals in pork bellies and the future of soybean oil. Nothing is in his name anymore, not wife or money. Everything in Sue's. Big rents. Leases. Pays in cash. Safe from clerks and agents, small-minded pencil-pushers working for the IRS.

At the Peabody he had it. The Shine. Dancing while the people clapped and the river air blew. Gave that up, went to Green Bay, got hurt, gave that up, hit the road.

Gave the road up once, for Bats by The Chunk, a surefire scheme: a baseball bat factory in Ophelia, in a deserted hangar out from town. Spalding nearly in on it; signatures on the bats from top of the line players.

In Ophelia they called him Chunk, from his glory days playing football, All-American at Ole Miss and, in 1942, a brief member of the early Pack. Those days, Green Bay was a golden team, the one to root for. To claim membership in its ranks, however brief, held some glow in Ophelia.

He wore starched white shirts with French cuffs, gold cuff links with stones, pale and perfectly tailored suits and, in the summer, spotless white shoes. Every day he pinned a flower in his lapel, a red carnation on flawless sharkskin. He liked Florsheim wingtips and polka-dotted bow ties. Every Wednesday he got a shoeshine. His handkerchiefs were clean and white, his hair clipped just so. Up or down he did these things, even in bad times when the sheriff was calling and creditors at his heels. Spanked his face when he shaved to give his cheeks a rosy glow.

Christmas he was Ophelia's Santa Claus. Had a red velvet suit trimmed in real bunny fur. Looking into Chunk Stovall's black eyes children saw the dream come true. It was real: the beard, the North Pole. The eyes sparkled: life, expectation, possibility, the long odds, go for it. Even parents lost their heads. "He convinced even me, and I hired him. I forgot he was Jim Stovall, I thought Santa Claus was in our house."

WHOZ ON FIRST, WHATZ THE MUSIC SAY? SHINE, BROTHER, SHINE.

Banks backed him up. Spalding's interested meant Spalding was a sure thing, no question. Big put the story on. Wanting to, his audience believed. He wanted his family to have everything. Castles, Buicks, dreams come true. A T-bird with a removable top, the trip to Florida they'd planned to the minute in their minds. Hawaii on credit. Hula skirts and luaus; that blue blue surf. The romance was in his head. He believed he could do it.

They went to Florida. All the way to Destin and back on hot checks, Big with $16.30 in his pocket and an unbalanced checkbook, heavy on the side of the bank. The sand in Destin was white as sugar and as fine. Sue ate fried shrimp; her skin turned nut-brown. Linda got water blisters on her chest from staying out too long in a cloudy day that seemed undangerous. *Would you mind if I made this for ten dollars more, my friend?* Service station operators, NO CHECKS signs in their windows, said yes. To Big? They said yes. When somebody finally said no he had to change his tune. It was a relief, in a way.

But at least they got to go. They had photographs of Florida to prove it. And memories. That was what a daddy was for: to provide.

Linda took one look at the airplane hangar and, hearing Big's plan about Bats by The Chunk, voiced uncertainty.

"I don't know, Jimmy," she said. "I just don't know."

Big pouted. "Aw, Mama," he said. "Don't hang the crepe on me now."

He must have said hang the crepe to Linda a thousand thousand times. It meant draping the house for funerals, calling the hearse before the dead had died.

And Sue was there in the airplane hangar that day, and little Steve. Stars in their eyes. Bats. A factory. They yelled out their names to hear them echo back. Big yelled his. SUE. STEVE. DADDY.

Linda stood apart. But she would do her share. "Well, all right, go ahead and do it."

Big staged a gala to announce the factory's opening.

"Got to have a gala," Big said.

The open-faced sandwiches arrived late. The caterer at the last minute had balked, wanting cash. To convince her she would get her money, Big finally signed a contract saying if the caterer didn't get paid by a certain time he would pay the stated amount plus that sum half-again as well. He'd think of something. First things first, he couldn't open up without a party.

The sandwiches were cut in shapes, bats and balls, paprika on the round ones, for stitching.

Sue and Steve handed out tiny bat-shaped pins at the door, flat on the side where the safety pin was. On the front were the letters BBTC. Sue wore a plaid jumper and long socks, Steve a short sailor suit and white leather shoes. Steve was crazy for sailor suits and pants with pockets. There is a picture of them in front of the hangar holding hands, squinting into the sun. Steve has his hand up. They have on cardboard party hats with pom-poms.

Oh that day—anything was possible. Even a desk.

The bat factory didn't last till the water got hot. Big had hardly got the machinery in, and the wood, when things started to fall through. Spalding never signed. He had got some two-bit company to back him. And so the signatures on the bats were of second-string players who rode the bench. Who wanted a bat with a nobody's name on it. Gus Loomus? Who in the world was Gus Loomus?

The trouble was leverage; leeway; margins. Big had to be right every time, he could not afford to lose or be wrong, there was no margin for grace or mistakes. A gambler has to have some cushion. To bet high and roll fast, a gambler has to count on some loss, have a fat enough bankroll to cover his high-stake ass.

Other people enter Linda's room. Hippies and whores, Jews, Negroes, the black girl from other dreams, after his billfold. She has followed him for years, sliding a dark swift hand into his pants. Big Walt had had the same dream. *Nigger gal,* he used to say, *after my hard-earned cash.* People are all over the room Linda is in, doing it everywhere. On the floor, the couch, the table. Linda's eyes look like neon. Around her neck there is a locket. Near her tiny foot, an ankle bracelet. Whore jewelry. In the dream, he begins to run.

Could sell broken light bulbs. He sells frozen yogurt now, for a company called Simply Good. Rackets are everywhere. There is no professionalism anymore, only rackets. He calls on junky people in foul-smelling stores, selling wheat germ and seaweed as if by virtue. He despises their smug self-righteousness, that look in their eyes as they mark up raw almonds and alfalfa to ridiculously inflated prices.

Ginseng? Ginseng used to grow on the ditchbank in Ophelia. Chinamen who lived there would collect it, send it back to relatives for processing. Now there it was in packages, "Pure Ginseng from China." By way of Ophelia ditches, is what. Snake oil. The hippies' game is not to show it but it's all the same.

Still, it is Friday and he has had a good week. He has broken all records for Simply Good and is now placing frozen-yogurt machines in ice-cream stores and at ball parks and high-school gymnasiums, selling school districts on the idea of a virtuous, so-called *organic* treat. "Will take the place of ice cream," is his line. And they look into those dark, rolling Santa Claus eyes and, knowing it's a shill, find a way to believe he's reciting facts. What else can they do in the face of such size and faith but submit?

His own father had warned him. He took one look at Linda and said, *Son, she's a dish. You better watch her. You put black lace next to her pretty white bohunkus, she won't ever go back to cotton again. You got to watch her. Pretty little sassy thing.*

He might have given her too much.

A wife was not supposed to just up and go.

Phony baloney health-food crap. Simply's ass. Rackets and snake oil. All over.

The dream changes. Linda is gone. He is still running but he is naked now. His toes seemed to have grown together, making webs, like frog feet. The hippies have disappeared. Only he and the persistent black girl are left. She slips her hand in.

The Married Man Waltz

Sam Moore owns a joint, an icehouse on the Post-oh border, named Zoe's for his wife. I sang there once and didn't do well. Zoe's is too close. There was a POP border sign staring me in the face the whole time.

Post Oak Place is square centered in Houston, the eye of the eye, a tony address in fact. Houston's gone so loony sprawling huge, any street address inside the Loop can be high-class these days and high-rent means good value, a lot of money when you sell. Outside the Loop's the suburbs: winding streets with names like Lochness Heather and Enchanted Mesquite: apartments/town houses/apartments/down the road a 7-Eleven/farther away a shopping mall. Whispering Huisache means built-in gas grills and intercoms, a long drive to work, apartments/town houses/apartments/down the road a 7-Eleven/farther away a shopping mall. Skunks, raccoons, and armadillos have hit the road west, leaving FM 1960 to newcomers looking for jobs and opportunity and golden streets, running with oil. An optician's office out on I-10 is named Eye Ten. I've seen it. It's on the way to Absolutely Mustang. Eye Ten.

Post-oh, however, has its own sewers and taxes and dogcatchers and mayor and garbage collectors. A CITY OF HOMES, our boundary signs declare. All single-family dwellings, we have no NEKKID GIRLS, BOOBS, AND BOTTOMS—COME SEE, no BOOBTOWN BAR, no bare buns on public parade. Tastee Dawgs don't clutter our skyline, Food City's beyond us. Let Houston get the raunch and sprawl; Post-oh stays the same. No apartments. Our border may be ringed with dirty movies and peep shows and beer joints, pool halls and fleshpot emporia; you will however have to cross POP's hem to get there. Sin's hot marketplace skirts our signs.

Sam Moore is thin thin thin. He has these hollows in his flank, a scooped out place into which you can lay your hand, feel your fingers curl, your palm sink. Oh leanness. A flat middle, long and muscle-stretched. His thighs, loose at the joint, a long way to his knees. I think of Joseph, bored and princelike in a bony boyish heap. I think of Mama. How we both go for thinness. Married bulk, go for leanness on the side. What to make of that I don't even want to ask.

Until a few years ago, POP was all white. Then a black mortician put down an earnest money contract on a house, and with real estate so high the group formed to deflect such an instrusion was hard pressed to buy first, so his earnest money got him in. Down the street from us are two frankly homosexual men, in one house. We're on the lesser end of POP but still . . . It means things are loosening up a little, not that somebody sold, but that they wanted to get in. There is also one black dentist, whose wife has never been seen. The black families are borne. Their sons add clout to our teams.

At the heart of Cowtown then is us: POP, this incorporated community. And at the eye of our eye?

Look to the calendar: early March, a Friday. Men are there

now. Tryouts are finished; the season's yet to begin. No boys are there; only the men; the dads. Sam Moore himself may be in on it, this seasonal taking stock. Counting catchers' cups, fingering bats, inspecting balls, the men make plans. POP hearts beat high this time of year. POP hearts feel full absolutely to bursting with utter righteousness and All-American pride.

It's the season.

A diamond is at the center of Post-oh, our version of court-house square, flag, and monument to war dead: the elementary school and next to it, our Little League field.

Fact: Houston is King City in the Little League department. More teams per numbers of daddies and boys than any other city in the country.

Our history will be written in tabulating language: scores and numbers, ERA's, RBI's, batting averages, at-bats, standings in the league. Percentages tell us who we are, DP's, errors, times picked off.

Field Day Sunday will be the one-year anniversary of my introduction to Sam Moore—which means Sunday I will see him again. He'll be manager just like he was, and I'm Team Father again.

My job that Sunday last year was to pull up roots of Saint Augustine grass, which in the offseason had grown in thatches, clotting up basepaths and home plate and the pitcher's mound. I was to shake off excess dirt, deposit roots and grass in a plastic sack, move down the baseline, cleaning, sifting. Third to home was my assignment.

A green-capped man had given me instructions. There were three white stars on his bill. Men in green caps are or have been Post-oh All-Star managers and they wear their caps with pride. The man who instructed me had a clipboard, and was stationed at home. Meanwhile Jack Auhl, POP's field manager, also in green cap, drove a small tractor-tiller around the field, coming behind us lowly field hands to turn the earth we had sifted. Some dug, others swept, a few painted and caulked. Good parents, decent citizens, a member of a unified community, each doing a share. Legions of Red Cross workers rolling bandages could not have felt a higher sense of calling.

Shirtless and tan, Jack Auhl wheeled his machine about the field with great flair, roaring and terrorizing like Marlon Brando come to town in a gang. Recently divorced from POP's PTA Program Chairman, Jack had some new stuff: a barbershop mustache, longer sideburns, a bubble-top Porsche, which home-run hitters, he had announced, would get to ride in. Jack Auhl drove his tractor half naked. Nice back. He knew it.

I was on third base when Sam Moore appeared, on my knees, a half-filled Big Boy sack at my side.

"I hear you sing," he said and I jumped, and that was the first I knew he was even there.

Sam Moore waited.

We were knee to knee. It was warm. I remember sweating.

"Do what?" I said, as if singing was a new one on me.

Sam Moore wore that white-starred green cap. Not a point in his favor, but Sam Moore wore his back on his head at an angle more fisherman style than baseball.

A lean and sandy man, there's a suppleness about his upper thighs, the way his legs fold under. Belly flat as a floor.

Jane likes men with heft. Her Cajun was a walrus type with generous lap. Not me.

He held out his hand.

"I'm Sam Moore," he said. Lean as a fish.

I knew who he was. The kids had pointed him out. Ricky told me he was the Yankee manager. I wiped my palm and shook his hand.

"I understand you're Team Father," he said, shifting the tilt of his cap.

"Nobody else would do it."

"Well it's nice you would."

Robby's thirteen and for him that's a blessing: he can drop out of Little League without having shame heaped upon him by men in green hats. In sports, frail Robby wishes for what he'll never have, namely easy toughness and muscles, a winning attitude, heart for the game, a decent BA, to field balls with grace. To be a part of the team. Robby, however, is all speed and lightness, air, zip and quickness, no bulk. Every spring, he gets asthma instead of hits. His Superlite Adidas, forty bucks a pair, barely skim basepaths, his feet fly like the wind, he can steal his way home, execute a perfect slide. Getting on base is the problem. Making bat meet ball. Robby has, in green-cap parlance, no eye, no arm, no heart for the game. Yet, rather than be tagged a sissy, he played ball five seasons, from age eight on, and all five years sat the bench more than played. Every team has its ragnots; Robby was high lama on that squad. He is only fast. And so he lies, making up percentages and adventures that elude him.

Ricky, on the other hand, is our everyday neighborhood kid. He lives on the block, by the block, the block sets his goals and disappointments. Ricky likes cutthroat games and roller coasters, has season passes to Astroworld and Skateboard City, is king of cupball at the Little League field, cupball being a game of the kids' own devising, played with a wadded up paper cup. The rules of this game are highly sophisticated; any number can play. Cupball has been officially outlawed by the POP Little League executive board, citing the dangerous sharp edges of the cups, the velocity with which they are thrown. Still, the kids play. On the legal diamond, Ricky's successful as well. Unlike his brother, Ricky doesn't lie: he hits them out. Last year four cleared the fence. The Team Mother gave him a bakery cake for each, four white cakes saying OVER THE FENCE, RICKY. His BA was .345, his RBI's impressive, his defense a joy: assists on six DP's, third to the lowest ERA in all of Post-oh. His selection as an All-Star was a cinch. To Ricky the game is simple. You aim bat at ball and, expecting to hit it, you do. Ricky's twelve, and a Yankee. He wants to be like Graig Nettles. Wearing pinstripes, he has read *The Year of the Yankee*. Robby, who never made it to the majors, was a Beaver his last two years. A Beaver.

At the preseason Yankee get-together, two lists had gone around, one for women, one for men. Sam Moore hadn't been there; Jack Auhl did the honors. Volunteer mothers were to work the concession stand, collect money from candy sales, handle group picture sales. I considered the choices and passed the list on. Many mothers were present and in fact the sheet filled up fast.

Not so the Daddy List. Serious fathers were already committed, to manage or coach. Lesser positions went unfilled.

"Okay, you guys," Jack Auhl said. "We have to have a Team Father."

Nobody. Coughs and shuffling.

Team Father oversees clean-up of the stands and field twice during a season. Two Sundays. Not as bad as cookies. I raised my hand. Big laugh. Eventually they signed me up.

"Well, look, TF," Sam Moore said, giving me a nickname straight off. "Like I said, I hear you sing."

"Who says?"

"People I know. Club owners. They tell me you're June Day, tell me you wrote 'Sylvia Brown.'"

I shook a clump of Saint Augustine. A drop of sweat ran around the lip of my ear.

"They say you're good."

Such an easy air, sweet as a breeze. There is no push to Sam Moore; he has this sense of, Whatever you want to give, my dear, it's up to you. And so you shower him with attention. Whatever there is, is the answer. You'd suck his toes.

"No," I said in spite of having never intended to admit to his first question. "I can't sing really. But I can carry a tune enough to sing my own songs. And sometimes I do."

I lifted some hair off my neck to cool it, held it against my head with the back of my arm. Sam Moore watched. If I'd taken off my T-shirt I wouldn't have felt more bare. I let the hair fall.

"And you did write 'Sylvia Brown'?"

"I did."

"I have a place, you know. Zoe's. Just outside Post-oh?"

"I know." I'd seen it, also Zoe. I'd heard Zoe's was his, as well as the wife.

"Would you sing for me some time? Fridays we have a live band."

"I doubt it. I don't do it close to home."

Sam Moore took off his green cap again and rearranged it closer down over his eyes.

"Do what close?" he said.

"Sing. My kids don't love it that I do it at all. So I use the name June Day, drive outside the Loop. Pasadena, Jake City. When I sing, that is."

"Meaning?"

"I don't much."

"Why not?"

"It's not my deal."

"Mostly you write?"

"Mostly I write, yes."

"Songs?"

"Songs."

"When you're not team-fathering."

"Right."

The baseball diamond was gone, the parents with their rakes and shovels and Ajax and Clorox and Big Wally, their clipboards and giant-sized boxes of Glow. Gone my Big Boy sack, gone third base. Conversation was a bypass. Sweat clouding my eyes, there was only Sam Moore and me, on our knees. He touched my leg.

"Keep it in mind, will you? This coming Friday maybe, or the next? I can keep a secret."

About that time Jack Auhl came roaring by and that was it. But between Sam Moore and me a look had crossed. Recognition, confirmation; yes. We were at the top of something the only way to get down from was to slide . . . just let go and slide.

Caroline's fifteen. She's waiting for her period. Whatever else it looks like she's doing, homework, watching TV, forget it, her mind's got one track only. Everybody else in her group has it, Caroline wants it too. I've tried to tell her a late start's a blessing but you can't tell her. She's an all-star honor girl, straight A's, Major Works, the rest. Another SSS, holier than stars.

When I went to sing at Zoe's, I thought of Caroline, and how close I was to home, on the border in my singing dress doing "Sylvia Brown." Afraid she might drive by, or one of her friends, and see me.

Zoe's is on the corner of Times and Prospect, facing Times. Across the street is one of those POP, A CITY OF HOMES signs. You can see it from the jukebox. Like most icehouses, Zoe's has garage-type overhead doors that, in good weather, are rolled to the ceiling, leaving bar and customers open to the street.

It's a raucous place, especially Fridays when truck drivers and stockbrokers come by to drink beer and swap lies, shoot pool, hear some tunes, watch whatever ball game is in season. We did it in the parking lot, the band wired high to compete with traffic. It was a good band. Too good for me that night. I couldn't sing at all.

"I don't think so," I told Sam Moore afterward. "It makes me too nervous."

"It's that sign," he said, pointing at POP's city limits.

I said, "Yes, probably," and he sipped his long-necked bottle of beer and complimented my songs, saying he guessed he'd have to come outside the Loop to hear me properly. My hair was pinned back just right. He lifted the gardenia out and sniffed it. Cornball: it slays me.

"I guess you will," I said. "Yes."

He took my hand and led me down the Prospect sidewalk, to the alley behind Zoe's. There's a gray metal door there, inches thick. He opened it. The room inside was utterly dark. A shot of cool air whipped by my face.

"This is where the ice was," he explained, "back in the days when Zoe's was a real icehouse." He took me by the elbows and steered me in, then closed the thick metal door. I couldn't have seen my hand, it was so dark. "I used to have a lamp," he said. "But there's a door leading to the bar and even though the jukebox is in front of it, people would see the light and cause trouble. Bang on the wall and stuff. So I leave it dark. You mind?"

I said I didn't.

There was a bed, actually a cot. He'd brought us each a beer.

Not ten feet away, beyond the barricaded door, salesmen in company cars drank beer and ate barbecue. The band had gone home; music from the jukebox rocked our love nest like a heavy hand. The low notes vibrated our door.

"People drink more when there's music. I figure it pays in beer to let it play free."

The jukebox is wired to play without charge and so it goes all the time, playing the same songs again and again. That night "Blue Eyes Crying in the Rain" played and played. If I hear it now I'm back there again, in the dark, adoring Sam Moore's bones, the hollows of his flank, that spare caving middle, his drifting hands, here there, doing this and that. The skin across his palm is drum-tight, his fingers come to delicate tips. I couldn't see him at all. Pure songs and feeling. And drifting fingertips. Willie Nelson's baritone.

I shivered. Trembled. Curled happily beneath him.

Two o'clock afternoons became our time: after the lunch rush and before the kids got home. "Love Is Just a Game" played, and "Good Time Charlie's Got the Blues." "Do You Want to Make Love? (Or Do You Just Want to Fool Around?)" We rocked to a country beat in the dark.

Leaving Zoe's, sunlight would stab my eyes. I'd stand in the alley until I could bear the light, then cross Prospect. The Mustang's easy to spot. I parked in a lot over there, to be safe. One day I found a note on my windshield: PLEASE DO NOT PARK HERE. PRIVATE—FOR BUSINESS ONLY. I looked up. In a watch-repair shop a large man sat on a stool, a glass in one eye. With a tiny instrument he poked at the insides of a watch. The sun was blazing hot. He looked up. He had very black hair, cut around his face in a bowl. A Mexican perhaps, or Oriental. His look ran through me. Like he knew. I wondered how many other Yankee mothers had parked there, and run across the street to the alley behind Zoe's, and come out blind and blinking into the sun.

Meantime Little League season began. The Yankees got off to a slow start. The Red Sox beat them, the Orioles, the Phillies. By midseason they were two and nine. As patient with the boys as with drunks at Zoe's, Sam Moore never ranted, never brought up the Yankee winning tradition but sat closer, tried to figure out what was wrong, gave advice. For the first time in his career, Ricky went several games without a hit.

"I hit it," he said.

"Not a hit," Robby corrected. "A pop fly."

"I hit the ball, farthead."

"And Scott Auhl caught it."

"Asshole. You don't even get to play."

"It wasn't a hit."

"I hit it."

Big interceded. "That you did, Ricky. You did hit the ball."

"See?"

Sam Moore's legs. When he walks they stride out in front of him, as if connected by threads. He wears moccasins. Games, he'd laze out onto the field to give the scorekeeper his line-up card. I'd watch that high point, where hipbones gather and legs begin.

It seemed impossible. There had to be two. One Sam Moore in the dark whose legs I was so happy to be wrapped up in, the other this calm fatherly manager consoling my baby boy. He asked the Yankees for nothing they could not give. Same with me.

In the bleachers, Zoe sat between us. The black cap of her hair. Her pale skin. Like a thorn, Zoe sat apart. Zoe knew everything.

———

Sitting here now in this easy afterdinner mood I'm wondering if I shouldn't have just taken what I could get and gone on. It's been six months since I've seen him. There was no big breakup, just a quiet split, the sound of my heart, tearing. There was something I had to get past and could not.

Wife, not wife, married man: the blues.

The last time I saw him was at Phil's Café, a restaurant not too far from here. It was a Saturday. I'd been out running errands and decided to treat myself to a secret meal. Went in, there he was. I went to his table. He was alone and, after all, we were Yankee Coach and Team Father, what harm? But Sam Moore was uncomfortable. His sweet easy air deserted him. I'd crossed a fixed line. Phil's was a family restaurant, Phil's was not Zoe's. Post-oh married means solid fixed, for the long haul. And in the end I have found, married is married first and last.

Still. I was there, wasn't I? I ordered. He had tongue and I got gumbo. I tasted his tongue; it wasn't bad. Like pressed ham, but meatier.

He ate one dish at a time. All the peas. All the beans. All the tongue. I'd never seen him eat. In the light I noticed his hair had a faint red cast.

When it came time for dessert, the waitress said, "I don't suppose you want dessert."

Sam Moore said he didn't and the waitress said, Well she'd have been shocked if he did, tore off our checks, and left.

He drained his iced tea.

"No pie?" I said.

Sam Moore turned to me, giving me his breeze easy look. "I never eat sweets," he said.

So much I didn't know. Only his hands in the dark. Never saw him at it, how his eyes looked when he came, when I did, where it took him. We could be anybody.

We said good-bye and I left.

———

Now Field Day's upon us again. Sunday I'll see him and sitting here drinking black coffee and cheap red wine I feel moony and I miss him. That scooped-out place in his flank, his easy drifting hands. Us in the dark, to country music.

The Ballad of Sylvia Brown

In Bryan last year policemen stopped a Mark V,
Because it was a stolen car.
They didn't know what they had, till they opened the door,
"Lord," they said, "look at that, she's set for war."

A .38, a .45, a sawed-off shotgun they found,
Stolen goods and dope by the pound.
Behind the wheel, the mother of two.
Little lady who are you?
    My own boss, write it down:
    Sylvia Brown.

She was just five feet tall, 110 pounds is all,
Had two kids and a life that seemed real fine.
But PTA and scrubbing floors, a working husband to adore,
Cramped her style, she'd get out, wouldn't walk that line.

Independence her cry, Sylvia stole a car one night,
Drove it off and felt a natural high.
"This is power," she said, "I can do what I want.
Don't tell me I'm just a gal, I've set my sights."

(Chorus)

She could aim, she could shoot, she could strip down a car.
Her daddy taught her everything she knew.
He was a hero to her but he wanted a boy.
Sylvia said, "Okay, Dad, I'll show you."

She stole guns, wrote hot checks, took a family mobile home,
To fill up, with stock of her trade.

Put state stickers on the sides and front, tied a baby tricycle
    on the top,
Drove scot-free, a touring pop and mom, down the interstate.

(Chorus)

But she made one mistake, got tied up with a boy.
He chickened out, got caught as they fled.
"I should have known," Sylvia said, "but I've got not one
    regret.
I've been free, had a ball, made my own bread."

Now she's going to jail, her hands are cuffed, she's not so free.
Thirty years, said the judge, put her away.
Sylvia Brown does not cry. She says, "Judge, I'll serve my
    time.
I'd rather be locked up in jail than at the PTA."

(Chorus)

She'd rather be
Locked up in jail
Than at the PTA.

Copyright © 1976 M. S. Sue

Princess Grace

Behind a closed door, Caroline sits on the bed with her books.
Beside her are four soft stuffed animals: a furry Persian cat, a
pink bear, a gray-and-white cat, a brown owl. They are lined up
precisely in a row, like soldiers.

Sometimes she feels like she was born into the wrong family.
Is it possible? That the moon went on strike the night she was
born and canceled out signs and made her someone she was not
supposed to be, living in the wrong house?

Everyone else was born in a hot month. Aquarian, winter child, Caroline feels like a snow queen, watching silly sporting animals run tree to tree with no purpose, laughing at their own jokes, making a to-do over every single thing.

Friday night: she's doing homework for Monday.

She will tackle geometry first, her least favorite subject. She is better with algebra, puzzles to figure, mysteries to solve. Geometry depends on neatness. If the drawing is incorrect or sloppy, however careful your figuring is, it does you no good.

She is a light-skinned girl, like her grandmother, with blue eyes and blondish honey-colored hair that hangs down her back in current fashion; it tends to be wiry and to frizz: a throwback to the Days, Big says.

There is something slight about her, though she tends to run to flesh. Something frail inside the extra weight.

She picks up a protractor, pencil, book, notebook. Her bedspread is white with ruffles, matching her curtains. On her dresser, perfume bottles and a collection of ceramic cats are carefully arranged. Everything is clean; Caroline keeps her own room; it is the neatest in the house.

She draws the angles first. Afterward she will go on to the better part, the analysis and figuring.

After geometry, American history, and then biology.

Between history and biology she will bathe.

A pink-flowered robe hangs on her closet door.

She erases the third angle and redraws it.

She was supposed to have taken her plate to the kitchen after dinner; she left it on the TV tray instead; she will say she forgot. Or maybe she won't have to. Maybe her mother will sigh and complain, then take it to rinse herself. After all, she keeps her room neat, her clothes folded, does her schoolwork well and is honored for it. She does her part . . . more than her brothers, who live like pigs. They should not expect more. It's not her fault if they do.

The brown owl's name is Lester. Big gave it to her. Her legs are crossed tailor-fashion, her open notebook across her lap. She looks up from her work. A certain twitch in her concentration has broken her train of thought. She makes sure her door is tightly closed, then, moving the notebook aside, pulls down her jeans to her knees and bends her head down.

Not yet. She is fifteen years old, the last of her group to get it. The doctor has said nothing is wrong. Her mother makes remarks: "I don't know why you're in such a rush. Wait till it happens. You'll see." Nobody understands. She doesn't want children; it's not that. But it matters. She was the last one to get hair, the last to get breasts, the last to shave her legs, now the last to get her period. Even now, what hair she has is so pale it hardly needs shaving; she did it because it was what you did, what girls did. Everybody should do what they are supposed to. In this family, everybody seemed to feel called upon to be weird in every possible way.

She pulls her jeans back up but does not button them. Flinging a strand of hair back over her shoulder, she returns to her work.

Don't worry, her mother said. *It's bound to happen soon.*
What did she know.

Robby and Ricky

"Did you see that?"
"See what?"
"He gave him the finger."
"Who?"
"Oscar. Oscar gave Felix the finger for cleaning out his closet."
"He did not."
"Yes he did. You were looking down and I saw it. He gave him

the finger. He did. I saw it. Yes, he did."

"Aw, Robby, you lie. You always lie. Nobody gives the finger on TV."

"Bull. They forgot to cut it. I know what I saw."

"Well, I know what I know and you're a liar. Nobody gives fingers on TV. You lie all the time, you know that, Robby? You're a buttface liar."

Robby sulks but does not answer. He has no real power. He cannot fight, or argue. He can only appeal, then suffer being called other names. Chicken. Tattle-tale. Worse.

Ricky sneers: "I bet if somebody asks you your name you lie."

Ricky loves to fight. Squat and tough, he is built close to the ground, while Robby is reedy and slim. If he allows Ricky to bait him into fighting, Robby will be hurt; will cry, will go to bed ashamed.

"Look." He laughs, trying to distract Ricky's attention.

On the TV screen, a funny-faced red-haired child is singing about hamburgers. The child's name is Wesley and he is well-known, a child star.

"Messy's singing about Jack in the Crack again."

Ricky turns back to the TV to watch the boy.

". . . gee-ja, Jack, gee-ja, Jack in the BAH-AHX!"

"Jesus!" Ricky says.

"What?" Robby is hopeful.

"I hate that guy."

Robby sinks down in his chair in relief. He would like to stop lying but, however he tries, can't seem to. The real stories he knows are never good enough, so it seems of life-or-death importance to make up new ones in their place.

"All in the Family" is next, then "Bonanza," a favorite.

Ricky likes Hoss, Robby Little Joe. They both liked Adam but he died. And Ben, until he started selling dog food.

Robby rests his head on his pale, bony wrist.

Ricky—a Chunk, like his grandfather—switches channels. His fingers are blunt at the tip; his nails bitten to the quick.

Thin, skittish Robby waits for another chance to comment. If trouble is all he can get, he'll take it.

You Know

Big's awake.

"Hello, Sue," he says, blinking. "How're you getting along with your work."

He lifts his glass, turns it up.

"Good dinner," he says. "Good liver." He always says this. "Builds up the brood."

Did he say brood? Blood. He meant blood.

Holding on to the table, he pushes his chair to the wall and, left eye shut, rises. Palming the wall for a guide, he knocks against it as he goes slowly to find the way. He has fallen once in this Almadén half-stupor and hurt his knee. He is more careful now.

"Good night, Daddy. Don't forget to take out your eye."

He puts his free hand behind his back and flutters his fingers.

" 'Kay," he says.

Not going to bed is his fancy, just heading off down the hall. He may not even take off his clothes, may fall across Robby's bed hoping the next thing he knows it is morning.

History. He can't match his up—what he knows with what he always thought would be. Me neither. How it has gone. Sometimes it amazes us both too much.

Without Big, the kitchen is quiet. Other things are more defined; nasty plates and pan loom. On to the sink and where is the cap to the ketchup keg? Should have done it sooner. The stuff by now is stuck fast. It will have to be blasted off to come clean.

At least I got a song from my Sam Moore affair. A waltz. I just sold it last month so it hasn't been recorded yet. Imagine: my song about Zoe's husband playing on Zoe's free jukebox while another Yankee mother swoons in the rear.

Here's the chorus:

The Married Man Waltz

Don't tell me, I know it, it's time now to go.
The children are waiting, your wife's on the phone.
It's one-two-three, two-two-three, leave when she calls.
Three-two-three I'm a fool, doing the Married Man Waltz.

Copyright © 1979 M. S. Sue

"Mom."

"Don't come in if you don't want to help."

"*Mom.*"

Her blond hair flies from her face in unratted thick waves, her face is pink and flushed, her eyes lit up like neon EAT signs. Such wondering. She hugs her pink-flowered Neiman-Marcus robe closer. Her blue eyes look like Linda's.

"I got it. I was in the shower and when I got out I had it. My . . . you know."

"Caroline—" Caroline what? What do I think about her getting her period? She's barefoot. There's a puddle around her feet. She didn't take time to dry off. And she's got it. Her, you know. What do I tell her, to watch out?

After things got heavy, when Muff would ask me out, I'd resist, remembering stuff on my skirt and how scared I'd get. I thought we shouldn't date for a while. "But we don't do anything," Muff would plead. "I mean . . . *you know.*"

Hands in suds to the wrist I move from the sink toward her. She backs away. Watch out, Princess. Things will never be the same.

She was eight when I gave her a book explaining it all. I'd ordered it from Tampax, Inc. CONGRATULATIONS, the manual hailed her. YOU ARE A WOMAN. There were cutaway pictures of wombs and tubes, fingers inserting tampons, eggs floating, blood sloughing off. Things I hadn't known of myself.

Caroline, however, won't use tampons; she insists on belt and pads. Same as I had, same medicinal smell, same belt to rub you raw. There she stands, wearing them.

Her baby-blond pubic hair. That clasp of the sanitary belt will rub her unmercifully at her tailbone, the way it did me. She will walk carefully, sit carefully, straight as a rod so the clasp doesn't move from the place it has already blistered. It will hurt and she won't say. It will hurt and she'll never say. It will all be the same. She will walk down the halls of her school as if tiptoeing on eggshells so that nobody knows, nobody, that she is in pain from a salt red triangle down at the base of her spine. She will come home, sit on the toilet, pull it away, feel the hot red place cool for a moment while she pulls its tormentor away. The curse is silence. I got it: you know. Don't say the words, not this, anything but this, this is too embarrassing to talk about, say fell off the roof, find some other way. It hurts.

I move toward her. She backs away.

"Did you—"

"Everything is fine."

"Are you—"

"I'm fine. I just thought—"

Be careful, I want to say. It will hurt. You could get pregnant, watch out. But Caroline turns and flees, leaving a wet spot on the linoleum, me in the middle of the kitchen mouth open.

A book from Tampax saying YOU ARE AMONG THE MILLIONS TO ENJOY THE FREEDOM AND COMFORT OF TAMPAX TAMPONS was not such a hot idea, I think. Still. Better than curses. Better than underwear down the well. At least she's got some facts to go on. There are only so many options.

I'll mop up the wet spot. Mother Stovall had it right. Boys are easier, she used to say. Boys I can deal with, even Little League.

Time to shut down the kitchen, turn on the dishwasher, switch off the light. Friday's easing out of itself. No more food tonight. Liver's all gone.

I'll tap on the Princess's door then see what the boys are up to. Maybe I can convince them to switch from "Bonanza" to a decent late movie if there is one.

Later on, dreams.

The Girl of My Dreams #3

Sits on a table legs apart.

Lights make her sweat.

A camera is between her legs.

She performs.

Herself inside herself not reaching out but feeling it all inside letting it happen for the great I that is her essential only self not moving out but fixed. Fixed fire. Burning for herself. She is doing herself, herself. The camera lens is straight on her there, like the pocket mirror passed around. The camera is amazed. It can't take its eyes off her there, it is what everyone still wants to see. Still? Yes. Show us. Hold back the curtains so we can see, really see. Pull them back, show us. Lord! Those flaps and knobs and pearly-pink wrinkles. In this businesslike idea of what the world is. Then this. All that time. It was there. Like nothing else. Show us. From inside the camera comes a whirring noise. She is being recorded. She will be able to look at herself in movement, in full color, in the dark. Will sit back and watch as the screen flares up with color and she apart from herself is on it. Up there on a table, on the wall, on the screen on a table, with her legs spread. Pulling back the curtains for the world to see. Touching herself. She watches herself in the dark do herself.

III.
Mother Stovall's Revenge

Field Day

When the phone rang Sunday I was still asleep.

"Mom!"

Caroline poked my shoulder with brief fingers, as if not wanting to suffer the touch of me overlong. A dream of sea and sharks receded, and my bleeding baby girl stood over me, swathed in pink, looking martyred and sleepy not to mention annoyed.

"The phone."

She held it out, giving me a look. "It's long-distance," she sniffed and disappeared out the door trailing clouds of pink and utter righteous Neiman-Marcus.

On elbows, I raised up.

And look: a perfect day. Sun up and out and sparkling, humidity so low you could dry socks. Even dew, and spiderwebs leaf to leaf, like silky spit. A sky blue enough to break your heart. We don't get many of these. A day like this I want to wash the Mustang; get out the Turtle Wax and X-14, go out and rub my whitewalls.

Fat chance.

I answered.

"Sue Stovall Muffaletta?"

Person-to-person, long-distance: my head cleared, time returned, facts filtered through.

"Yes," I told the operator, "this is Sue Muffaletta," and at the same time that the operator was telling her party to go ahead, her party was saying, "SuhUUE?"

Pine Bluff. The accent was unmistakable, the pitch dog high. My mind fishtailed. Who was it?

"This is Louanne Graustark? Your cousin? Lou's girl? I called your daddy's number three times, Sue, but no answer."

"Louanne," I said. "Hello. Daddy's here. Is something the matter?"

Louanne's voice dropped a notch. "Sue," she said, "I have bad news. It's Mama, Sue. She died."

"Oh, Louanne! I'm sorry."

Louanne's voice quavered. "It was her hip, girl. Mama fell in the bathroom and broke her hip then laid there, girl, just laid there. Her heart went."

"Louanne. I'm sorry."

"I hate it she was by herself, but how was I supposed to know?"

She waited for me to answer. It was a real question.

"Well. You weren't. Of course, you weren't."

Louanne is an only child. As a girl she was puny. I remember her pale face in Mother Stovall's window, watching us play. Louanne had spells in her chest, she couldn't run or play strenuous games, had steam in her room at night, a boiling kettle. At dusk playing hide-and-seek if you hid behind the chinaberry tree against the house, Louanne would be there, watching from the window, her breath making fog on the glass. She had pale broomstraw hair and long feet. Her clothes and sheets smelled of Mentholatum. I never saw her in anything but pastels, ribbons in her hair.

"When is the funeral, Louanne?"

"Tomorrow," she said. I told her we'd come.

"Oh, Sue," she said. "I'm so glad, Sue."

I asked if Walt Junior would be there and Louanne paused,

healthily. "I don't know," she said finally, her voice gone Protestant steel.

"Well," I said.

Louanne brightened. "Don't be surprised when you see the house, girl," she warned. "You won't know it, I bet. Mama did such a renovation. . . ." Again she paused. "Sue?"

I said, "Yes?"

Louanne waited. Expensive pauses, person-to-person. She started to speak then caught herself. Something was up.

"Never mind," Louanne finally said, "We'll talk about it when you get here." And I knew. The pauses had made a speech. We hung up—but not before Louanne made one more remark about how Lou had changed the house. That was it—the house and who would get it now that Lou was dead. The other hesitation had to do not with Walt Junior but his wife, Bootsey. Bootsey's a tiger.

Big Walt Stovall had come to Arkansas from Ohio, where his family had been in beer until, so the story goes and is and has been endlessly told, a Jew partner took the stocks and money and ran . . to California, where he was never heard from again. Big Walt's uncle went to find the Jew. He too was never heard from again. Sucked up in California.

So Big Walt got a job with the railroad, which one day he rode south. In Arkansas, he got off. He liked it. Rivers and lakes were plentiful and prospects looked good. A friend of the family who'd moved to Arkansas earlier got Big Walt a job as county road agent.

Meantime Mother Stovall was running a millinery shop in Cincinnati with her sister, Mabel, called Hats by the Early Girls. Both sisters were past proper marrying age and so when Big Walt sent word for Mother Stovall to come, she didn't drop a stitch, but laid down needles and feathers, went running. Mabel ended up crazy, a victim it was said of menopausal breakdown. Mother Stovall became Big Walt's wife.

By the time Big remembers, Big Walt had some farmland east

of Pine Bluff proper, near the river, a fertile black bottom section he'd managed to condemn for roadwork, then buy himself when the road was canceled. Big Walt knew nothing about farming and so he hired Negroes who did. Big Walt farmed by sitting in a big overstuffed armchair at the end of a row, pointing a cane at Negroes or his sons.

Lou was assigned women's work, at which she was an utter failure. Her purple hulls burned, her pie crust wouldn't make, shirts she ironed came out tattooed in scorch. Mother Stovall berated and browbeat; still, Lou would not pay attention and did not learn.

"Give me boys anyday," Mother Stovall would say. Said all her life. I remember.

"Useless as tits on a boar hog," Big Walt said about Lou.

"You can't have it all, Sally Jane." Mother Stovall must have said a thousand thousand times. "You better learn to cook or you'll never make a wife."

Mother Stovall's will, drafted in secret from Big Walt's, provides that the Stovall house go from oldest child to the next down, circumstances permitting—meaning if her children live and die in order of their birth, and if they have living children at the time. An heirless Stovall gets leftover Early Girl costume jewelry and some dishes. When all three die, the house goes to the first child of the oldest and, if that one has no living offspring, to the oldest of the next and if . . . the will is a thatch of complications, threaded with *ifs* and *in the event that's* designed to prove nobody could make out exactly what, except that Mother Stovall knew how to rile up her children. The lawyer who read the will was the same lawyer who went to Pleasant Valley Convalescent Inn to help Mother Stovall write it, but he wasn't talking. When the questions got hot, the lawyer left.

Bootsey said Mother Stovall could not have been in her right mind at the time; there was evidence of other madness in the Early family, witness Mabel dead in the crazy house, menopausal breakdown having run its course and finally taken her. Bootsey has no tact.

Lou, however, much as she wanted the house, was not inclined toward gratitude. "It's not me she's giving it to," Lou said. "It's nobody. This is still Daddy's house and she's still running it. Go look in the kitchen. I bet she's back there making biscuits." Nothing's changed, Lou said, not one iota; it's the same old same old.

Bootsey's position was that as Walt Junior was the farmer in the family, he would hold on to the land, keep it in the Stovall name, that he would in fact have been working it all along except for having served in the war, therefore he deserved to get it. "I hate family disputes," Big said; Walt Junior was silent. "Walt Junior deserves this place," Bootsey said. They went on and on, like squalling turkeys. What it came down to was, Lou got the house. Mother Stovall's will was served.

Cagey Mother Stovall. Knowing how full of rage Lou would be all her life, living one day to the next like renthouse trash.

The door to Robby and Ricky's room is open a crack. Daddy's awake, lying in bed staring out the window. It's an off day. Normal Sundays he's up early fixing pancakes.

"Daddy?"

He waves me over. "Quick."

"What?"

He points out the window toward the ash.

"In the trees. A monkey. Quick, come look. It jumped from that long limb over to the magnolia and back. There. Did you see it?"

He pulls me to the bed.

"It has a black face and pink eyes, one of those monk-ugly red behinds."

"You've been dreaming. It's a dream monkey. I woke up with sharks."

And it comes to me: in the dream, I actually *was* a shark,

swimming underwater, swift and dangerous. And there was another one beside me, a fellow shark. Jack Auhl? Yes. Field Manager himself, in my dream.

Curious. But then, dreams are cagey. Probably it was the liver that did it. Put such a meaty man in my night.

Big squints, closing one eye.

"Daddy. I got a call from Pine Bluff. It's Lou. Daddy? It's your sister, Lou. She died yesterday."

His attention slips from dream monkey to me.

"Lou?"

I explain it was her heart, saving hip and bathroom floor for the road.

"Lou?"

His brow furls, his face collects. Sometimes he up and cries. At the least thing; you can't predict it. Tears gather and he blubbers.

But the crying jag does not develop. Like that, he's gone again, back to the window and the ash. Too much Almadén perhaps. A brown mother redbird wings out of the tree, followed by her fancy soaring husband. Doubtless Big put the two together and in sleepy hangover turned them into a monkey.

Closing the door I leave him looking. It will pass. He needs time.

You won't know the house, Louanne said. It used to be green, as dark a shade as green will go—a shade made to seem deeper by the offsetting glare of the white white woodwork, the crisp shine of the windows. The house faced Pecan Street, a wire fence surrounding both it and the vacant lot next door, where the home garden had been. The home garden was all weeds by the time I remember. Barefoot, however, you could still feel the rows.

Steve and I once buried a bat by the fence. It had been hanging on a wire, asleep. A cousin was there, Walt Three. He found the bat. *Look,* he said. *What? A bat. Where?* We scanned the sky. Walt

Three was younger, but Steve and I had never seen one. *There.*
Was it a vampire? *No,* Walt Three explained, *just a bat.* We
poked it with sticks, to dislodge it from its perch. We hadn't
meant to kill it but the bat died. His tiny claws curled and he
was dead. With a soup spoon Walt Three dug a small hole and
we had a ceremony. I hummed tunes and Walt Three said
mumbo jumbo; we anointed the body with oils. When the bat
was in the hole, Steve dabbed its belly with mayonnaise, then
opened the shaft of Mother Stovall's pen to leak out a stream of
bright-blue ink. Walt Three stirred the ointment, then smeared
it the length of the tiny body, covering the bat to its ears. I
remember the look of the red Arkansas dirt falling into the
blue-white swirls as Walt Three said ashes to ashes. That might
have been that same day we sat in somebody's—whose?—car in
the Pine Bluff driveway burning leaves with the cigarette
lighter. It's all hazy, thick with shades and senses: the fog of that
day, hatching secret ointments, watching smoke rise as the
lighter scarred green leaves. And Louanne, in the window,
watching.

Remember perhaps some of it, some of it not, time and cousins
get confused. Walt Three, for instance, had a brother, Halstead,
who I hardly much remember at all. When Big Walt died, Lou
stayed on. *To keep Mother S. company.* No one asked if she wanted
companionship or not, not to mention the particular company
in question, that is to say, the dreaded Lou. *Mother S. was never
the same.* No one asked; havoc would call. Lou stayed. Mother S.
got worse. Crazier, meaner. And then Mother S. let go.
She is soiling her bed, Lou reported—this was years later—*I am
sending her to Pleasant Valley Convalescent Inn* and Big and Walt
Junior agreed. No one checked Mother Stovall's suitcase to see
that what she was taking with her included Big Walt's papers
and will, a Pine Bluff telephone book, a lawyer's name circled.
Imagine hatmaking her, gone to Pleasant Valley. Imagine
Mother Stovall breathing a sigh of relief: no Lou.

———

It might have been another visit when we burned leaves. I see us so clearly, three cousins on their haunches anointing a bat. I feel us there, in the car, edgy, thrilled. Each took a turn with the lighter. Memory melts events into a fog of senses, shades; shadows of the mind.

There was an L-shaped front porch. It went around the front of the house and down one side. There's an old picture of Mother Stovall on the porch steps in a long dark skirt and Gibson Girl blouse, on her head a no-doubt Early Girl hat, flop-brimmed and lavish, a cascade of ribbons down her back. Hands on hips, she is posed on two steps, looking altogether snappy. I couldn't imagine Mother Stovall such a girl, head tilted, ribbons cascading, ankles cocked like a model's.

On the Walnut side of the porch there was a porch swing; facing Pecan, a glider. When worked, the glider squeaked. We would send it back and forth and back and forth to hear the rusty sound, until some adult would say, "If somebody doesn't oil that thing . . ." Then we'd let the cat die. The windowpanes were large, two to a window. Light seemed to ripple inside the thin glass in wavy rainbows. All this may or may not be true, may or may not be in fact remembered at all. Sometimes things get conjured up from pictures and stories and after a while you become familiar enough with reports to think you were there. I remember, for instance, or think I do, a stove in the cellar that fed the furnaces and somebody—Walt Junior?—stoking it. I see a man open the door with a poker. He comments how hot the handle is. I see the flames. Maybe none of it happened; it's only one quick picture, a shred. I could have seen such a stove in some movie or read a book in which there was such a man stoking a furnace fire. The Pine Bluff cellar is the only one I've ever been in. In my mind I may have transferred a storybook stove into memory, a fictional uncle into Walt Junior. I could have moved the scene from Russia say, to Arkansas. Hard to tell. All of it is possible.

There was a cellar, I do know that. The floor and walls were high and there were rounded humps on either side of the steps. Big Walt made root beer there, grew mushrooms, stored corn liquor he bought by the barrel from a still on the White River, made root beer, grew mushrooms, stored corn: stories. The floors and walls looked like clay. Light came from a single ground-level window in a sharp and dusty slant.

More than stoves and pictures, though, I remember smells. Coal oil in the kitchen, witch hazel in the bathroom, Louanne's Mentholatum. There was a gritty hand soap that made your skin feel like gravel. The upright piano was brassy. The pull-out couch Steve and I slept on was cobweb musty, our noses in its pillows found the smell of Mother Stovall's hair. Furniture polish was strong. The towels smelled like hand soap.

When I played the piano in Mother Stovall's house, she'd never let me be. "In my day," she'd begin and I'd tune her out. *We had to put quarters on our hands to keep them high so that only the fingers moved. I was quite a piano player, Miss Sally—*

"Mother," Big would interrupt. "Let her play. Do 'Malagueña,' Sue."

Mother Stovall's jaw would set. Tick-a-lock.
You can't have it all, Sally Jane.

I want to see it. Surely the house has not changed so much that it's gone, despite Louanne's warning. If Lou has not had the cellar cemented over, I'll see if the stove is there.

When I get there, that is. If I can figure out what to wear.

Collecting weeds: legs are the problem. A skirt is proper, but what about feet and legs, appropriate shoes? Shall I wear a June Day number, up to here, strappy high heels in the bumpy graveyard? Probably fall in. Jane's no help, her feet are bigger. Pants will have to do, then my strappy high heels won't show. I'll have to chance the cemetery lumps.

And what about Steve? Should I call? Will Louanne? Oh Emily Post. Manners, ritual, what one-two-three to do. Baptists have a Grieving Committee. Official grievers who go into action when a member of the flock passes on. I'd welcome Madam Chairman of Mourning Drill today.

WHATZ THE BEAT, WHOZ SONG?

There's Team Father to deal with as well. I'll have to call Sam Moore, tell him I won't make Field Day. That can wait however. Eight's too early for Sunday phone calls.

On the Wednesday before Thanksgiving in 1941 Big Walt and Mother Stovall sat down with Lou and her new husband, Buck Hart, to noontime dinner. Linda and Big were in Oxford, Mississippi. It was Big's senior year and he was all the rage. Linda was his secret wife, hidden from football conference rules. The Saturday after Thanksgiving was to be his last game as Chunk Stovall the All-American Ole Miss flash. Saturday, they would announce their marriage. Big didn't know I was in the works; only Linda knew. The tiniest baby secret, curled in the belly of the sassy girl Big had taken to West Memphis at the end of a double-date and secretly married. We, Big and Linda and the floating seed of me, were due Thanksgiving Day. Big had a chemistry test that Wednesday. Hidden Linda had her own secret. Big tucked us away.

The reason they were having chicken and dumplings was, Mother Stovall liked to boil a hen a day ahead of making turkey so she would have extra stock for her dressing. Anytime turkey was in the works at her house, chicken and dumplings came the day before. Mother Stovall would have boiled two hens, saved the broth, made a cream sauce to simmer the dumplings in.

"Now, Daddy," she would have said. "This is cream sauce, not gravy. I'm saving my stock for tomorrow."

Jimmy was coming. Big Walt's heart was high.

Walt Junior was in New Jersey at boot camp, learning to fly. Things had not been going well with the farm, and Big Walt had sold a lot of his land, despite Walt Junior's advice that they hold on to what they had, and despite Walt Junior's wanting to keep the farmland and work it, because farming was what he loved to do. And so that September, after the measly amount of crops they had were picked and put by, Walt Junior had enlisted in the Army. Things were heating up overseas and it seemed an appropriate thing to do, although Big Walt hardly seemed to care. Walt Junior was not particularly patriotic, but enlisting seemed easier than some other things. Flying, however, was not. It was a choice he would come to regret.

Lou and her new husband, Buck Hart, lived with Mother Stovall and Big Walt . . . temporarily, they said, until Buck found a job, which was taking longer than they thought but then there was Buck's health. Buck claimed to have had every dread disease known to man, scarlet fever, TB, rickets, thrush, worms, whooping cough, the works; he was not a well man. They were all supposed to tiptoe around Buck Hart, who came from over on Mulberry on the other side of Pine Bluff, who it was said married the dreaded Lou only to get into the big green house on the corner of Walnut and Pecan, which he had no intention of leaving no matter what he said about jobs and temporarily. He wasn't much, Buck Hart, but then neither was Lou. Big Walt had thought she'd never get married. Couldn't cook, looked like Mrs. Roosevelt. What a combination. Useless as tits on a boar hog.

Big Walt liked Linda, liked *gals.* Liked them young and sassy, with a walk. Liked Linda's yellow hair and how her temper flared when he lifted her skirt with his cane.

As usual, Mother Stovall served Big Walt the first and biggest helping while the children waited their turn.

"I'm sure it's good, Mother S.," Big Walt would have replied. "You haven't disappointed me yet." Watching as Mother Stovall heaped dumpling after dumpling on his plate while Lou fumed and Buck sucked his teeth and coughed.

Would have because he said it every year and she did. Traditional pleasures, Thanksgiving style.

Buck wouldn't have complained. Lou did the griping; Buck got sick. Mention a job and his legs gave out, his chest rattled, his throat closed up. He would tie a wet rag around his neck and Lou would say *Buck is not a well man.*

Big Walt was obese by then, three hundred pounds and more, nobody knew exactly because he refused to weigh. He had mild sugar diabetes and was supposed to cut down on sugar but he loved cookies and Mother Stovall loved to make them. In the breakfast room there was a jar shaped like a clown; its belly was always stuffed with date-nut bars or butter-crescent cookies. Big Walt's hand was always in the jar. What did doctors know? It was constitution that mattered. Genes. He was never full.

Mother Stovall took a baby-size helping. *I'm not hungry,* she would have said and would have picked at her food through the meal. Mother S. was never hungry at the table, having tasted and sampled her cooking all morning long to make sure it had the right flavor for Big Walt, rich enough with butter and cream and the taste of salt and pork. *Mother S. eats like a bird,* Big Walt might have said. *I don't know why she's not a rail.* Might, might not have. It was standard, dinnertimes.

And so on the 1941 Wednesday before Thanksgiving they ate, not knowing about me, the Sweet Sally Jane grandbaby Big Walt would miss out on. And wouldn't he have adored dark-eyed Llavots me. Mother Stovall would have jumped up a number of times during the course of the meal to get more jelly, another pan of rolls, some lemon for the tea, more ice, and Big Walt would have eaten and eaten, and Buck and Lou Hart would have exchanged dark glances, comparing the size of their helpings to Big Walt's.

"I can't help it," Big says. "I'm not one to hold a grudge but in Buck Hart's case I can't help it. Every time I think about it I get mad all over again. And Lou. Sitting there puking in her plate. If I'd have only been there."

Mother Stovall had already brought in the cobbler. "Now this is hot," she said, and she would have set the pan on a tree-shaped trivet. Big Walt had one more bite of chicken and dumplings to go, before moving on to peach cobbler with butter and ice cream. The one bite was half a breast. He folded it over like an envelope on his fork, to get it in.

Buck didn't see the rib bones.

Lou didn't see the rib bones.

Mother Stovall was dishing out the cobbler, so she could not have seen the rib bones.

In Big Walt's outsized gullet, white meat unfolded, bones were unsheathed, chicken breast filled and clogged his throat. He began to choke. Chicken spewed.

There wasn't much life left in the green house anymore, what with Walt Junior off in the Army and Jimmy in Mississippi playing football. Big Walt had sold half the farmland and so he was home a lot now, to hear Lou and Mother Stovall battle it out, to listen to Buck cough and whine, to hear Lou in the night beg and plead with Buck please to do it to her, it was her time and he had to, trying to get his wormy self up in her to put a baby there. The Philco was a comfort. Gabriel Heatter, Murrow, the news from overseas. He reserved space in his heart for Jimmy and his wife. When they came, life returned. Otherwise, food was his only joy.

That gal, such a walk. One foot in front of the other like a thoroughbred. *Got to watch her,* he told Jimmy. *She's saucy.*

When the rib bones began to hurt him, Big Walt stood, gasped, threw his napkin down. Mother Stovall stopped dishing up cobbler.

"Help him!" she screamed as Big Walt's face turned a bloody blue and Lou said *Oh my god* and began to be sick and Buck Hart sat there hesitating. "Help him!"

Lou jabbed Buck and Buck went and reached his arms as far as they would go around Big Walt's chest and tried to squeeze. Lou puked in her plate. Big Walt, gasping, pushed Buck away. Buck fell on his ass by the table. Between heaves, Lou protested. Mother Stovall went to Big Walt, took him by his great shoulders, began to shake him hard.

The Thanksgiving turkey's neck had been axed. Plucked and scalded, it lay without its head in the kitchen, waiting to be stuffed and trussed. Cornbread for the dressing was made and yams were boiling. The yams in fact would boil dry, ruining Mother Stovall's pot. Seeing it afterward, outside, used for a dog's water pan, Mother Stovall would always be reminded of that Wednesday and the yams, of Big Walt choking at the table, and Lou puking, and Buck on the floor.

Big Walt's head flopped chin to chest and back like a rag. The choking eased. He took a clearer breath. Mother Stovall stood back. Big Walt frowned as if he'd just had a thought. The color in his face mellowed and he looked like himself again. Big Walt swallowed, looked straight at Lou, Lou blanched, Big Walt did a full turn on one heel and fell dead on his face.

"Right by the wicker daybed," Lou reported. "I can still hear him. WHOP. It shook the china in the breakfront."

"WHOP!" echoed Buck.

"It wasn't the chicken," the doctor told Big. Mother Stovall had rattled the meat and rib bones loose and sent them down. "It was his heart. It was enlarged in the first place, twice the size it should have been, and there was a mass of fat around it in the second, thick enough to choke a horse. Old fat. In the X rays you can't see his heart for the fat. When his wind was cut off and the blood got hard to pump, that was all she wrote. It was too much to ask, outsized as his heart was, with all that fat to boot."

Choked to death on his own fat, aided by rib bones and hesitation, size and appetite.

"I never expected Daddy to go first," Mother Stovall said. "I'd as soon go with him." The funeral was Friday. We came from Ole Miss, them and secret me. Walt Junior got leave and came in his uniform.

Afterward, though his heart wasn't in it, Big went back to Mississippi to play his last game. Linda stayed through Sunday and while she was there, to comfort her, told Mother Stovall about me. Lou immediately announced she was pregnant too, and gave Buck Hart sharp looks.

Buck and Lou stayed. *To keep Mother S. company in her grief.* That was the line. It never changed.

For how long nobody asked or thought. Nobody suspected Lou would never leave until she was scraped off the bathroom floor, dead of cracked hip and heart. That December, Walt Junior went overseas. After serving in the war he came back to Pine Bluff thinking he might stay and work the land but there was no place for him to sleep, what with baby Louanne needing her own steamy mentholated room, so Walt Junior took to the wicker daybed in the dining room, which in time became known as Walt Junior's Bed. It was short but so was he. In the night when the furnace came on, Walt Junior from the daybed listened to the sound of his mother's hand-painted china rattling in the breakfront. Walt Junior felt uneasy in the house he was born and grew up in; his sister gave him such looks, his mother was pitiful, and Louanne: he'd never seen such a stringy child. And so, lying in the daybed contemplating it all, Walt Junior made Lou a deal. In return for a certain amount of cash, he would, in writing, negate any claim he might ever have on the Pine Bluff house and land. Lou, who by then of necessity had her hands on the purse strings—after all she had to run the place —snapped up the offer and Walt Junior used the money to go to school to learn to be a CPA. The war had changed him; flying had. All he wanted was to settle in somewhere, be quiet, find a way to get through without any more disruptions than were absolutely necessary. He wanted peace; stillness. The war had made him feel even more cut off from the others than before. After he got his CPA license, Walt Junior married Bootsey Halstead and moved to Hot Springs, where there was an opening for a CPA.

Lou licked her chops. Dumb Lou: they'd see. And they would and so would she.

The next August in Memphis, where Daddy had a job at the Peabody as banjo player and bouncer, I was born. Sue Shannon Stovall: Baptist Hospital, 2 a.m., six pounds four ounces. One of

Daddy's flashiest songs was "Sweet Sue." He swears he was playing it when I came. I got there faster than first babies are supposed to so he didn't make it to the hospital until after I was already out. He named me. Sweet Sue.

Full name Susan? No. Plain *Sue*.

Linda had thought Carole, she said, for Carole Lombard . . . or Lauren. But Big had his way.

In September we went to Pine Bluff to live until Big found a place for the three of us in Green Bay, where he'd gone to play pro football.

Four months later Louanne was born breech. Lou claimed nearly to have died on the table; nobody knew except her and Buck Hart's sister, Mona, who drove Lou to the hospital. Only the two of them knew the details, and Lou and Mona, thick as thieves, weren't saying. Despite coughs and spells, Buck got drafted in September. By October Big had moved in with Linda and me, in the green house, having made his trip to Green Bay to play with the Pack and come back, his professional football career at an end. That made it a houseful: Lou, Louanne, Mother Stovall, Linda, Big, and me. We stayed nearly a year.

THE HISTORY OF PROFESSIONAL FOOTBALL AS TOLD BY THE MEN WHO MADE AND PLAYED THE GAME: VIEWS AND INTERVIEWS.

Edited by J. T. "Sandy" Grierson.
Copyright, Grierson & Co. 1976. Pp. 133–4

JAMES ELDON "THE CHUNK" STOVALL

Ole Miss, 1938–42. DB, BB, RB, FB.
GB Pk'rs, 1942. DB, BB, RB, FB. Injured '42.

THE CHUNK: I heard from Clare Hruska the summer of 1942 I was in Memphis playing banjo at the time, thinking my football days were over. I'd graduated from Ole Miss, got All-American, that was it. Pro football wasn't what it is today. People just didn't think about it. The war was on but I couldn't go: flat feet. So when Coach Hruska called, I thought I might as well give it a try. Wasn't any training camp then, no big preparations, you just got together and played. Rough? I mean. You could get away with anything you had nerve enough to try. It's a different game today, different rules, a different mood in the country. Rules were loose then. If we'd have had today's uniforms I wouldn't have broken my leg, and that's a fact. But like I say, it was a different time. 1942. I went to Green Bay. Never been north of Walls, Arkansas, in my life.

HPF: Tell us about the Bears.

CHUNK: Bears were king. Like the Yankees got to be in baseball. Always big-dogging it. Laz Maynor was a big star. You talk to Laz? Mean tackler, runner, blocker. Laz did it all. People said he put steel between his shoulder pads. Nobody knew for sure but it was said.

HPF: No one checked?

CHUNK: Wasn't done. Anyway by the Bear game we'd won two. Won big. We were feeling spunky. I'd done my part. They said the old Chunk couldn't do the same tricks in pro ball but I did my share. Set a new league record for yards rushing first game out. It was a time, I tell you we had a time. I met some fine men in Green Bay. Century Milch, Shoeshine Leffert, Scooter Biles, Granny Goforth Jones, good men. Didn't see us squawking about contracts, we just played. Then came the big game. The Bears. I didn't wear thigh pads because of my legs. Regulation pants were so tight the pads bunched me up so I took mine out. First half, the Bears defensed me one-on-one, choked us down. It was ten–zip and I was minus yardage at the half. In the locker room, coach and I figured out what to do. I'd set up willy-nilly first one place then the other, moving during the count, shifting right and left. Scored a touch right off. Defense couldn't keep up. Time they'd shift left I'd be gone to the right and left them off-balance there. I could do that. I was big but I could, I mean, move. So it's the end of the third quarter, ten-seven. We get the ball, I start my act: set left, set right, move to the middle, take the ball straight from the center. Soon as the Bears thought I was playing Right Running Back I'd switch to Left Double. One thing I could do was keep my feet moving. Too flat for the Army but they sure fooled the Bears.

HPF: And Laz Maynor?

CHUNK: We were on the fifteen. I went straight up the middle, got ten, saw six clear points. Nobody there, nobody. Feinted left, moved right, nobody. Then Laz got me. On the two. WHAP! Blindsided me, dove into that thighbone with those pads. Now I'm not saying he had the steel but I never felt a shoulder pad hit like that. It was like being whacked with the backside of a hatchet. You could hear the bone crack. Clare said he heard it from the bench. Cracked the femur, I mean in two, and split it, so it was broken both ways. I had bone splinters all in my leg. Had to go to Chicago to have a pin put in. Took four hours. It still gives me the blues.

GBP TEAMMATE CENTURY MILCH: Chunk? The Chunk could do it all. Run, block, hit, take your head off. Too bad he got that break. It wasn't the same then, though. Today Chunk Stovall would be a star, selling light beer on TV. But that's the way it was.

CLARE HRUSKA: Best potential of any player I had. Lord, but I hated losing him. The war was at its peak and players were hard to come by . . . any players, much less a guy in his class. Attendance was way off even at championship games. It was a bad year for the Pack, and pro football altogether. That trick Laz Maynor pulled was a disgrace. And you know he didn't stop? Even after he did that to The Chunk. Runners would come to a dead stop when Laz even threatened to tackle them rather than be hit by that steel. Took a long time to stop that kind of nonsense. By then he'd racked up quite a few.

HPF: Did anybody register complaints?

HRUSKA: It just wasn't the same. Who inspected? Pro ball would never make it, people were saying. It was thought of as a boy's game. When the war was over people would go back to cheering for college teams.

HPF: You never played pro ball again?

CHUNK: The leg took the entire '42 season and then some to heal. It changes you, something like that. You get to wondering if it's worth the risk. When Clare called the next summer I'd already decided to go to UT Med School in Memphis, get on with my life. I never would have thought pro ball would be where it was today or I might have done it differently, but then those things are easier to see looking back. But, Lord, that hit. In damp weather, I mean I can still feel the pin, sharp as fire. When it rains? Gives me the blues. I mean.

In his cast Big went to Pine Bluff to heal. Linda and her baby —me—had moved there temporarily, until he found a house in the freezing north. Buck died that winter in Paris of complications. He got the red measles, which went into his digestive system then his blood cells and he died a terrible death. Lou was satisfied: she had baby Louanne, a medal from the president, money from the government, martyrdom. *It isn't easy being a war widow,* she would have said, raising her Mrs. Roosevelt jaw. *Ya'll just don't know.*

When Big's leg healed the next summer, we moved back to Memphis, leaving Lou, Louanne, and Mother Stovall in the green house.

Walt Junior would come, stay six months, and leave them: Lou, Louanne, Mother Stovall, the green house.

No one to eat her dumplings and cobbler and butter walnut cookies, her cream gravies and double-rich mashed potatoes with cheese and extra butter, only Lou and what did Mother

Stovall care for Lou? Boys. Give her boys over girls anyday. All she had for grandchildren was more girls.

Imagine that fierce housekeeper down to her last broomstraw, the final string in her mop, making the best of what she had, planning a housewife's revenge: shit in her bed, havoc in the house. Thumbed her nose at us all.

Caroline's begrudgingly allowed me to borrow a blouse. With dark pants and jacket it should do; pantyhose from Jane; June Day strappy shoes. Willy-nilly ragtag weeds.

For the road, comfort: jeans and Etonics. A button-up blouse that doesn't show tits.

Big called Steve. Said he couldn't make it; after all it's so far and anyway, Pee, his daughter, has a bug. Suits me. Up and back is all I'm interested in.

Hit it. Up 59 to Texarkana in Big's LTD.

If the weather holds I'll wash the Mustang next week.

PICTURES

Big on the front porch of the green house holding me on one knee beside the stone urns, looking gleeful as Christmas, dark eyes shining.

Linda and me by the birdbath, her in a dark crepey dress, me wrapped in a crocheted blanket. She looks down into the bundle that is me.

Lou scowling. Louanne clutched to her chest, looking smothered and thin, not Stovallish.

Mother Stovall on the front steps holding me in the same crocheted blanket, a smile on her face—not seen in other pictures.

Mother Stovall on front steps holding Louanne, a forced smile on her face, an abstracted look.

Big on the glider in a cast from toes to groin looking serious. The only serious picture ever, of Big.

Linda sitting on the front steps alone, her legs crossed provocatively, her shoulder cocked. Lipstick and pageboy. A saucy look.	Big squeezing Linda, his face over her shoulder with his hugest mile-wide grin. Holding her tight. Her head cocked beauty-queen coy.	Big in his cast on the glider, me on his good leg; Louanne propped against the cast. Forced smile.
Lou on the front steps looking furious. Alone. Mrs. Roosevelt–jaw high. Arms down by her side like they don't belong to her.	Mother Stovall and Linda side by side, shoulder to shoulder, lined up as if in uniform. Squinting.	Big and Lou on the glider. She is at one end, he is at the other, the outer edges of them out of the frame.

59: Jack Auhl

Daytime, 59 is not so bad. Not friendly but no nightmare stretch. On both sides of the highway, pines make a solid shaggy curtain, impossible to see beyond or into. Against the perfect blue sky they sway, tall and stately and utterly indifferent.

There's a moment where they begin, just before Diboll. South of that line you won't find a cone, and now? Needle City. Snooty pines; guards, a wall.

Dwayne Loudermilk's on the radio, a Sunday favorite of mine. He has a weekly show: "Loudermilk's Top Hot Forty as Reported by *Hit,* the Showbiz Weekly."

We're down to the top five. I'm waiting for "You Make the Stars Shine Brighter" by The Questionnaires, a sweet soul group who've just made their first crossover hit.

One thing about Jack Auhl: no wife. She got the house, a

high-class two-story affair on a double lot in the better section of POP. I don't know where Jack moved but it's not far. In his Porsche he drives his son through the neighborhood to deliver the *Post Oak Times*.

Here: The Questionnaires, number four.

You make the stars shine brighter. You give my moon a glow.
Honey, promise to stay with me. Say you'll never go.

I LOVE YOU!

The song rocks easy, a sweet sliding beat. Can't live without you, Baby. I LOVE YOU! In Ophelia we danced to the music of the Re-Bops, the Red Tops, the Shammies, and the Be-Bop-a-Loos. I favored the Re-Bops. They wore pink tuxedos and red bow ties and played hot music. We were in pastel strapless gowns and Merry Widows, our hoop skirts out to there. "One Mint Julep" and "Maybellene," "Hearts Made of Stone," "Don't Let Go." White girls in hoop skirts boogeying to a hot black syncopated beat. Nightingale Norris was the Red Top's lead singer, a tenor well-known for his show-stopping, up-an-octave "Danny Boy."

The Coasters, the Spinners, Nat King Cole. Johnny Ray and Elvis were the only white ones we liked.

We pass Lufkin, Nacogdoches. Farther east is Nalandya; Linda and her boy. Romance? Does Mama have it? I wonder.

Oh Questionnaires, shiningest star. Is it possible? Not to have to put on a swingy skirt, sneak out to the redneck boonies, knock on strange and ratty doors wearing secret names?

Play it again, Dwayne. But Dwayne's moved on to Pink Floyd and Blondie. A new Paul McCartney's the Week's Hot One to Watch.

The pines sway against a flawless blue sky. Heading north, we'll soon be out of their territory, east into red clay gumbo and boring interstate, same blue FOOD GAS LODGING blue same government signs, over and over, same REST AREA NEXT EXIT, until after we turn toward our destination, where some pines will return.

Maybe, to get in a funeral mood, I should switch to church.

Onward, Soldier. In the Garden. Oh Pine Bluff. Dead Lou.

And wonder about Jack Auhl and June Day, secret lovers in the cool and unmarried, the swift dark and sharkish night.

Pine Bluff

"Is this it?"

"What?"

"Wake up."

"What?"

"Look."

"Where? What's the score? Did he get it?"

"Daddy, please. Are we there? I've been around the block twice and I think this is the corner but it doesn't look right."

Big sits up, stretching. He has slept more miles than not, waking from time to time in this dreamy state.

"Says who?"

"Daddy. Help me. Isn't it Walnut and Pecan? Facing Pecan?"

"Nuts. Nuts. Nuts."

We are on Walnut; Pecan is ahead. On Daddy's side of the street there is a brick house I in no way recognize, the flat sprawling Colonial kind of house you see in Whispering Mesquite. It has columns across the front, a circular drive filled with a number of cars—all of which have seen better days. A swag lamp in the shape of a grape cluster hangs between the middle two columns and casts a greenish glow. Bushes clipped to look like swanky poodles outline the porch. Flanking the front door are two slim amber-colored windows with X's of wire inside the glass. The glass, like bottle bottoms, is bubbled. On the front door there is a knocker shaped like a hand. The roof is flat, the front porch a slab.

"Sue?"

"Wake up. Is this Mother Stovall's house?"

"Certified. Cotton in the hypotenuse."

"Louanne said we wouldn't know it." The brick is tawny-colored, like sand.

"She didn't say it was bassackwards." Suddenly, Big's back in the world, wide awake.

We pull into the circular drive behind a beat-up station wagon with a car engine inside. In front of the station wagon is a light-green year-old Chevrolet with no chrome, an earnest, company-looking car. Big takes note of it, patting the hood as we walk past it.

"Preacher's here."

The house is lit up like daytime, the only one on the block not dead dark. We've made good time; it is not yet ten o'clock.

Daddy goes to the front door, starts to turn the knob.

"Daddy!"

"What?"

"Knock."

"It's my house."

"*Knock.*"

He pouts. "All *right.*"

His house: is he planning to claim it?

Big lifts the brass hand as high as it will go and lets it drop. The hand clutches an imitation glass ball. The ball hits a metal plate, bounces, hits. He lifts it again, lets it drop: hit, bounce, hit, echo.

"That ought to do it."

Tip-tip. Somebody's coming.

"Sourbutted heifer," Big says, as if it were Lou.

A short, steel-haired woman answers the door, frowning. She looks questioningly at me and then turns to Daddy.

"Well, Jimmy Stovall, I'd know that face anywhere, how'd ya'll get here so soon, fly? You have not changed a bit, Jimmy, not one iota and you must be Sue. I'm Mona Hart Mullen, the late Buck Hart's sister—come in the house, girl, come in this house."

Mona Mullen ushers us into a foyer. Overhead is another

swag lamp, shaped like an upside-down tulip with several layers of flared and cascading petals. The petals are dashed with color, swabs of yellow and brown. Inside the cup of the tulip, like an eye, is a bulging white globe. There is a white double door ahead of us and rooms to either side. The double door has a vinyl accordion-pleated closing, folded to one side. The walls are painted pale champagne. The woodwork, high gloss white. The floor in the foyer is marblelike linoleum.

Paint Card City, a thousand versions of off-white.

"I bet ya'll didn't know the house," Mona chirps.

Daddy and I stand in the foyer wondering. Is this where the porch swing was? The glider? Where *are* we?

I start to answer then see it's not necessary. With or without us, Mona moves on. "Didn't Lou do a job? Isn't it something? I tell you it's a crying shame she didn't get to finish it. Every time I think about it I just cry, don't you?"

To our left is what seems to be the dining room. There is very little furniture, only an Early American style drop-leaf dining table and on the wall a gold-framed mirror with an eagle on top, wings outspread. Otherwise the room is bare: gold carpeting two shades deeper than the walls, no chairs. An overhead chandelier drops within inches of the table. Made to look like a hanging arrangement of candles, the chandelier has an orange, flame-shaped bulb screwed into each fake candle base, giving the room a faintly Halloween glow, like light from hollow pumpkins. In the center of the table, just beneath the chandelier, there is a cut glass bowl filled with plastic fruit and imitation dried pussy willow. The bowl looks familiar. Standing in the foyer, I catch our reflection in the flying-eagle mirror: Big stands there frowning. Phony candle flames glint off the fruit bowl, casting a small yellow glow in his dark eyes. Like a moonwalker he's trying to figure out which end is what, now that new air has set him upside down.

The room to our right is nearly empty. The same pale-gold carpeting stretches without interruption to the room's far pale-champagne wall, where there is a fake fireplace with gas logs.

Hanging under the mantel is a fireplace set: bellows, tongs, poker, shovel, all made of gleaming polished brass. The fireplace broom has pure black bristles. The only furniture is, by a window, a Samsonite card table and matching folding chair. The chandelier in this room is fancy. Crystal, or a good copy, it drips with dazzling globes and blue-white pyramids. Miniature hurricane mantles cover the bulbs. There are heavy champagne draperies exactly matching the wall and tassle-adorned cornices covered in the same fabric. An open deck of cards is on the card table. The folding chair is pushed back at an angle, as if feet have recently pushed through.

"Lou played Sol," Mona whispers as if Lou were there. "We haven't had the heart to move the cards. She lost, but you know Sol. Every time I come in here and see those cards laid out on that table and think about poor Lou getting up deciding to take a bath in that old bathroom, well it just about breaks my heart doesn't it yours? And, girl, did Louanne tell you— What is it, Jimmy?"

"Is this the dining room, Mona?"

"What, Jimmy?" Mona is slightly deaf. She tilts her right ear toward Big, keeping an eye on his lips.

"Is this . . . never mind. Where is she?"

"Who?"

"Lou."

"Jimmy, did you say Lou?"

"Where'd they *take* her?"

Mona gets it. "Buford's, Jimmy, *Buford's!*" She yells, as if he were the one couldn't hear.

"Buford still in business?"

"Buford? Not Buford. You mean Buford?"

"You said Buford."

"Not Buford, Little Buford. My stars, Jimmy, you have been gone a long time. Buford's been dead now, what, seven–eight years. You didn't hear about Buford?"

Daddy says no and Mona rolls her eyes, looking over at me

as if to say can you beat that, didn't know about Buford. Then, straightening, Mona Mullen shakes back her hair, crosses her short arms across her chest, takes her stance, eyes shining. Mona is built like a tree stump: even the whole way up. She holds the side fat of each arm and stands there, stolid as a gas pump.

Buford, it seems, fell out of his attic while on his way to check the heating: "Stepped on a weak place and fell through the ceiling flat out of his attic WHAP to the floor, WHAP like that." Daddy says "Mmmmh!" in response to the sound of Buford hitting the floor. Satisfied, Mona tells him again. "Flat out of his attic WHAP to the floor. Concussion of the brain, couldn't speak, went blind, just laid there a plank of wood. Ruby? You remember Ruby? Sat by his side in the hospital. Day and night and night and day. Waiting just waiting, wouldn't leave, would not, girl, move an *inch*, hoping Buford would wake up and say something. But Buford was a plank of wood." Mona waits. Daddy says "Mmmmh!" again. "Did not know his own wife, and them married forty-three years. We'd say, 'Now, Ruby, there is no need for you to sit here day and night and make your own self sick when we could hire you a private nurse and Medicare would pay,' but would she hear of it? You know Ruby, the answer was no. Ruby sat there and do you know it came true?" Daddy says what came true? "What Ruby was waiting for. Buford came to like a light bulb: SWITCH." Mona snaps her fingers. "Saw Ruby, said, 'Honey, we got to see about that central heating,' swung his legs over the side of the bed and was ready, honey, to leave that hospital then and there; get up I mean and go!" Again Daddy says "Mmmmh!" "Died anyway though. Went home, had two good weeks normal as anything, fell over dead. Stroke they said but we all knew. You can't fall like that out of your attic without something happening. Can't tell me. And Ruby did have two more good weeks with Buford. Ruby, to this day, is grateful for that—but can you imagine, can you feature it?"

Daddy says no.

"All that and he died anyway."

Daddy looks around. If this was the side of the house, then we must be . . .

Somebody yells from beyond the dining room. "Moh-NAH?" It's Louanne: I recognize the pitch.

"Cry?" Mona continues, hurrying. "Girl? Cried like a baby."

Daddy yields Mona one last "Mmmmh!" allowing as how crying like a baby was terrible too, then turns from the story to the front door. He makes a curious gesture. Holding his left hand stiff, palm out, with his right index finger Big traces the ninety-degree angle he's made, index fingertip down, then across to thumbnail and back . . . like a carpenter with T-square, evening up corners . . . trying to figure out where he is, if this is where the dining room was, where Big Walt fell on his face that Wednesday, WHOP. Or was it WHAP? The finger slides up; into the angle, down. He closes his left eye, as if looking through a scope.

"Who is it, Moh-nah?" Louanne's coming.

I tap Mona's shoulder. "Mona, why is there no furniture?"

Mona stiffens, giving me a look. "Didn't you see the piano?" She slaps the wall by the living-room door. "Didn't you see it?" She slaps it again then, knotting her hands into fists, jams them on her hips.

Sure enough, there it is: Mother Stovall's upright, against the wall Mona slapped. No longer black, the grain of the piano's wood is now reddish and beautiful, with swirls and turns I would not have dreamed were beneath its black bubbly exterior.

"I tell you what," Mona says. "Lou paid a pretty penny to have the Steinway refinished."

I set a chord. BLOM. The piano's been serviced and tuned. Mona says, "See?" I try to push open one of the two small sliding doors above the keyboard. They seem stuck.

"Took it out."

"What?"

"Lou had the piano roll do-hicky taken out."

The pumping pedals have been removed. The sliding doors are glued shut. It is an ordinary, if beautiful, piano.

"But why?"

Mona turns, speaks to Big—still tracing his hand—as if he had asked the question.

"Lou Hart lived in the present," Mona says. "Not like some."

At that moment Louanne enters. "Jimmy," she says. "Sue. You're here."

What some? Like who? But Mona's moved on.

Louanne is the same girl I remember, pale in Mother Stovall's window, only she is heavy now: poor fat, we used to call it. And her hair. Yellow as butter, it is piled in fat curls on top of her head in an upsweep the likes of which you don't see much anymore except on women from those other side of the track nut-churches which disallow loose hair, makeup, and TV. Dyed, however, passes. She has had it done today; there is a burned tightness above her ears, the hair there stiff and pulled. All the curls are on the very top of her head. Underneath the fat hairdo, Louanne's grainy face is like an afterthought she could do without.

"Louanne," Daddy says. "Well, Louanne." And they hug. We hug. "Louanne." "Sue." She is wearing a pale-blue pantsuit. Her burnt neck smells like Spray Net. Mona watches.

"Come on in the den, ya'll," Louanne says, placing two fingers salute-style at the side of her mouth, shutting it off, as if telling a secret. "We're all in there," she confides, and smooths her upsweep.

Following Mona, we turn down the hall beyond the double doors, a long narrow passage flanked by closed doors. The hall is dark; at the end of it is a bright, noisy room. Cigarette smoke twists in the yellowish light. A reclining chair pushed back to a near lying-down position is next to the door, blocking it.

"Push up, Hugh," Louanne commands from behind us. "We can't get through, Hugh. Push *up.*"

Hugh Graustark obeys. The chair pops up. Hugh's head comes around the arm.

"I bet ya'll didn't know the house," Louanne says. "I bet anything ya'll didn't."

Daddy hits against a wall.

"Was this the living room, Louanne?"

"I knew it," Louanne says, hustling by us to get in the den first, in the process nearly knocking Mona to the floor. Following, we stand in a cluster behind Louanne as she makes her announcement.

"Listen, ya'll. Uncle Jimmy thought this was the *living room!* Isn't that something? The living room!"

She is Frank Sinatra, we are her chorus. I feel like we should make some background response. Some doowah Ink Spot noodling to finish out her song. But Uncle Jimmy? *Uncle?* I never heard one Stovall referred to as Aunt or Uncle. Walt Junior is Walt Junior; Lou, Lou. Louanne has picked up Uncle somewhere. Maybe from Hugh, who belongs to the nut-sect us-and-not-you church Louanne, from her hairdo, obviously has embraced.

We smile.

Everybody agrees it certainly is something that Uncle Jimmy thought the den was a living room.

Boyd Mullen, Mona's husband, gets up from his chair by the TV to come shake Big's hand and nod hello at me. Boyd has a red face. He is short, and totally bald. He then goes back to where he was, watching pictures; the sound is off. The show is a Sunday-night regular, about a black family in an all-white suburb. The black family has a multiracial set of children, adopted through the UN. In autumn, the show will be replaced. Boyd chain-smokes, watching his show.

Louanne's husband, Hugh Graustark, is more outgoing: he's been waiting for Big. As soon as introductions are done, Hugh offers to fix Daddy a drink which turns out to be jelly-glass size, using a juice glass for a jigger.

"Rum and Coke's all I got, Big Daddy," Hugh says and Big allows as how that will do.

The preacher is First Presbyterian.

"Reverend White," Louanne says and the preacher instantly corrects her. "Call Me Mike," he says, and turns to his wife, "My Wife Evelyn," who nods and smiles.

"Just got him." Mona whispers. "Africa."

"From there?"

Mona gives me a look. "Missionary duty. Teaching Bible to heathens."

"Oh."

Call Me Mike is a pretty young man, tall with dark curls. My Wife Evelyn is nervous. I believe she needs a cigarette. They have small children, she tells me in private, at home with a new sitter. She keeps getting up to make phone calls. "After Africa," she says, and rolls her eyes.

Call Me Mike nods and smiles, ignoring My Wife's signals.

Between den and connecting kitchen there is a bar, up to which six padded stools are pulled. On the bar is a feast: ham, turkey, several green-bean casseroles, potato salad, fruit salad, cookies, cakes, pies, homemade pickles, Parker House rolls, cobblers, coleslaw, and a jar of mayonnaise. Tupperware and Pyrex. Bake-'n-Take. Paper plates. A gallon jar of Russian Spice-y tea. Grieving Committee fare, no doubt.

The kitchen is Name-Brand City. Maytag, Frigidaire, KitchenAid, Tappan. No Sears in sight, not a trace of Monkey Ward in Lou Hart's house. Robby would approve. There is a microwave, a trash compactor, a double-door refrigerator-freezer with ice-water dispenser in the door, dishwasher, warming oven, a Jenn-Air, some stuff I don't even know about. An appliance salesman's dream. Pink Princess light-up phone. In the corner, a purple tape designed to kill flies and mosquitoes hangs from the ceiling, the letters GULF down one side.

"Mama liked up-to-date," Louanne reports. "She always bought the best. That wall-to-wall carpeting? Pure wool from

Burlington, you've seen it on TV, those circles they make to stamp it out? See that paneling? U.S. Plywood. That dining-room table? Ethan Allen bird's-eye maple. And that gold mirror with the eagle is real, genuine gold leaf."

Daddy asks about the hardwood floors, if they're still underneath. Louanne does not reply. Daddy sips rum and Coke and concentrates, looking about. Where are the built-in oak benches flanking the fireplace, the fireplace itself, the china cabinet and andirons, Big Walt's chair? The cut glass bowl on the Ethan Allen bird's-eye maple table is the only familiar thing. I recall its exact heft, lifting it.

To change the subject, Mona tells Daddy about a classmate of theirs who only last week had to have half his rectum removed and now has to relieve himself in a sack at his waist and how his wife said it was just killing his soul he was so embarrassed about it. My Wife Evelyn, looking dubious, gets up to make another call; Boyd watches a commercial; Daddy drifts.

"Louanne," he says in the middle of the conversation, "what happened to the dining-room suite?"

Conferring with Mona about the man who now shits from his waist, Louanne looks as shocked as if Daddy has interrupted church.

"Lord, Jimmy," she says, "that old thing?"

We will hear this refrain time and again as the evening goes on. Every time Big asks, same song, fourteenth verse, *Lord, Jimmy, that old thing?* And then Louanne goes on to describe how beat up the thing had gotten over the years and how while he remembered it as being the way it was when he was little, things just didn't stay the same and by the time her mother got there, those things were wore out, weren't they Mona? Mona segues in on cue. No market for old stuff, Mona says, people in Pine Bluff grew up with old, they are ready for new, aren't they, Louanne? and the thing goes on.

Big sits in a La-Z-Boy pushback, frowning, wondering by the time Mona and Louanne finish their song and dance just what it was he asked about to begin with and what their answer was.

Bird's-eye? What about Walt Junior's bed? Big Walt's desk?

In the dining-room buffet—third drawer from the top on the left-hand side—there used to be a rattlesnake tail, curled in a cotton-filled black box. Steve and I used to open the drawer and look; Steve would pick the rattles up and gently—they were dry —shake them. "If you ever hear that," he would say, "run." Trips home we'd ask the story and Daddy would tell how they got there, how one evening after supper Mother S. had gone to the home garden to get a melon for breakfast, how stepping across the rows she heard that unmistakable rattle, how she stood there screaming while Big Walt and Daddy sat on the Walnut side of the porch in the swing, watching the sun go down. How Big Walt, hearing Mother Stovall's yell, said "Your mother" and without a second's hesitation got up and ran. Took his cane and before Big knew it was gone. *I never saw Daddy move so fast,* Big says. How he, Big, wondered later if his daddy had known it was a snake from the way Mother Stovall had screamed *Daddy!* and how Big Walt picked up his cane and said Your mother, and was gone before the porch swing could make one full arc and was there beside the home garden already telling his wife what to do by the time Big got there. How Mother Stovall finally got quiet and Jimmy stood by the birdbath waiting, how Big Walt began to move across the rows toward her and when he got past the green beans and only the black eyes were between him and his wife told Mother Stovall to run and held his cane up high, handle end over his head. How Mother Stovall lifted her skirts and flew out of the garden like fireworks, and Big Walt brought the cane down on the ground time and again, grunting with each blow, *Unnh,* he said, *Unnh.* Afterward Big went over; the snake's head was blasted and buried, deeper than seeds. His body was still twisting. How Big Walt said to get him a hoe and when Big said the rattler was already dead, Big thought his daddy was going to turn on him, Big Walt's face was that red and sweaty. How Big Walt chopped off the snake's smashed head and rattles and said *Throw the body in a field.* "You can have the rattles," Big Walt said, "and the teeth." How Big

144

Walt would not touch the snake. "It's the one thing I'm scared of," he told his son. "Snakes." How Big Walt shuddered then. How surprising it had been that Big Walt was afraid.

How the rattles came to be in the buffet drawer, and now? No buffet, not to mention drawers. No dining room.

The glider? The piano-roll cabinet, the RCA phonograph? Mother Stovall's hand-painted china and Depression glass, her bedroom suite and the Philco and . . . and . . . *and?* . . .

Lord, Jimmy.

By the time Big has inventoried the lost green house of his past, he is all but dead-drunk. Hugh is fixing doubles. "Too much Coca-Cola's bad for your kidneys I hear," he says to Big, pouring extra rum, hee-heeing, and jabbing Big's ribs.

The brick on the outside of the house is not real, it turns out, but a new invention: thin sheets of bricklike substance, fitted over the green clapboard. "Better than brick," Louanne states. The green is still there, underneath. The sheets are only half an inch thick and will never ever crumble. *A lifetime guarantee,* boasts Louanne.

"Ya'll just don't know what Mama went through before Mother Stovall died," Louanne says, shaking her head. "No-body knows. I mean—"

"In her *bed,*" finishes Mona and Daddy starts to cry.

At that Call Me Mike says he thinks they should go and My Wife Evelyn says yes they do, and before they are out the door I could swear she has taken a red package of More from her purse.

Boyd sucks a cigarette. Watching weather, he has not said one word the entire evening.

Hugh offers Daddy a nightcap which Daddy heals from his tearful unhappiness long enough to accept.

"I've rolled you out a bed, Sue," Louanne says, ushering us back down the dark hall with all the doors, to what is called The Second Bedroom.

"Lord," Daddy says when we get to there. "Would you look at that, Sue. You see that rug?"

Beside the bed there is a small braided rug. It is old and tattered, obviously handmade.

"Know what it's made of?"

"Rags?"

"No."

"What?"

"Socks. Lou made them. Sat up listening to the radio knotting up socks to make rugs. We had them all over."

"Not just socks," Louanne, behind us, says. "All kinds of things. T-shirts, dresses. Not just socks."

"Socks," Big insists. "I'll never forget it." Ice tinkles in his glass. "Called them Knot Rugs."

"There's some in the old bathroom too."

"Knot Rugs. Lord, but Lou was mean."

I tell Louanne we'd better turn in. Placing two fingers over the side of her mouth, Louanne starts to say something confidential to Daddy, then, understanding his condition, thinks better.

"Good night, ya'll," is the last we hear of her.

Nighttime Loony

Linda described it as "like bones had come loose in his nose, rattling with the wind." Worse when he drinks, she always said which he always denied. *Stovalls snore,* Big says.

Sometimes Robby clothespins playing cards to the spokes of his bicycle tires: that. Sometimes the wind worries a loose venetian blind, making it persistently flapflap. That.

There's a digital clock radio on the table by his bed. In green numbers it shines the time. Bink. 2:11.

My lumpy roll-out is by some windows overlooking I can't tell what, the side yard maybe. There's a pecan tree I believe used to be in the back. Across the room, Big's in the double bed, sprawled across it in clothes and eye, bones loose in his nose. Rattle in. Rattle out.

Our beds have no headboards. They are simply mattresses on steel frames. The only other furniture in the room is Big's bedside table and, in the closet, a pink-flowered cardboard chest of drawers filled with unmatched socks. The beside table looks like something out of the Goodwill Last-Chance Room. Octagonal and dark, it has one chipped leg propped up with paper and a heart carved on the top. Inside the heart is somebody's initials + somebody else's, arrow and all. Next to the heart is the GE Snooz'n Wake clock radio. Bink. 2:13.

Lou's bedroom, which Louanne and Hugh are sleeping in, is no less bare. Their bed and chest of drawers match our octagonal table. There's a lamp, that's all. The house is empty, or nearly. Like a dollhouse you buy a child, promising to furnish it over birthdays and Christmas.

Walt Junior and Bootsey are due to arrive tomorrow. No one else seems expected. Services are to be graveside, a surprise. Big was shocked; he'd thought Pine Bluff First Presbyterian, what with all the people Lou must have known, after staying in Pine Bluff all her life. It seems however that in her fury Lou became a hermit, living here squint-eyed playing Sol by the window. The Grief Feast came from Louanne's nut-church friends, not Presbyterians. Call Me Mike is doing the honors only because Lou's membership is still with his church.

One room is the same: the main bathroom, down the hall, in which Lou died. Mona said it was a crying shame if poor Lou had to go she couldn't have gone in her own beautiful bathroom and Louanne agreed.

There used to be stone urns by the front steps, one on either side. Big says I ate dirt from the urns. Says he'd come on the porch and there I'd be, standing by the steps hand cupped to mouth. Hearing him, I'd jam in the dirt, swallow it, stand there mouth black as Oreos saying "I didn't eat dirt, Daddy, I didn't."

"There you'd be," Big says. "Sweet Miss Sally with a mouthful of dirt, saying 'Didn't, Daddy, didn't.' "

Now? No urns. No steps. No porch.

So? Robby would say. Why mourn what's over with and gone? I'm a city girl after all who likes her chicken in a plastic bag with a Holly Farms label on its wing.

Why weep? I'd like to take a look at those urns is all, sit on the L-shaped front porch, check out the bat grave and birdbath, move my ass back and forth on the glider, hear it squeak. Like to know something lasts. I forgot to ask about the cellar. Like to see if it's there. The stove. Those gray humps by the cellar steps.

"STAHHP." .

"Daddy. Hush."

"STAHH-P!"

He's sitting straight up, hair in horns, eyes wild.

"Big! You'll wake up the whole house. Are you all right?"

Bink: 2:22. By the green glow of the numbers, he searches for landmarks, trying to find out where he is. Then, as if motorized, he falls straight back onto his pillow again, sinking into snores that start easy and in time build up to bone-rattlers.

Once again the night has its pulse. Silence was an interruption. The beat moves us on. Outside my window, the branches of the pecan sway against the Pine Bluff sky. Always the last to green up, the pecan is as naked as if we were still in deep winter. In the night against the stars, its limbs look like arthritic old fingers, reaching for help.

Are there monkeys jumping in it? Daddy mumbles; blubbers. Blubber. A whale. What did he say he dreamed about on I-30? A new kind of animal, a combination whale/dog, with gills and spout, a wagging tail: a whog. The whog lived under water, he said. Crossbreeding. Oh, Daddy.

Sleep

Snoring fills the house, thumping out a count to breathe by. Jim Stovall's door is closed. The new house does not bounce sounds the way the old one did, but holds noise inside the pale-gold carpeting, the champagne draperies, the lowered ceiling. Still, he is loud enough to hear from any part of the house. The china does not rattle; the china is gone. The low rumbling underscores the bink of digital clocks moving time ahead, the switching gears of the refrigerator-freezer, the filling of the ice-making machine, the tinkle of chandeliers, the sounds of a nighttime new house.

Awake, Louanne lies in her dead mother's bed looking up at ceiling tiles, moving her tongue against the roof of her mouth, making a clicking noise, sucking her cheek and then releasing it, sucking and letting go. Hugh sleeps deep as a shoe. Turned toward the wall, his back greets her. Hugh's hair stinks; she can smell it. He'll have to wash it before the service tomorrow. Hugh is beginning to have that old-man smell. Louanne has an accordion style net tied over her hair to keep it set. A lady from the church opened up her shop special so that Louanne's hair would be fixed and ready for tomorrow. Another church lady had opened up her shop so Louanne could buy black clothes. Louanne wanted to be ready ahead of time. She had things to do. A deal will have to be made, but what? And with whom? She doesn't want to give up anything. Not one stick.

It's her house. Her mother fixed it up, she deserves it. None of the others would come to Pine Bluff to live in it anyway. And it is her mother dead at Little Buford's. Louanne shuts her eyes to ward off bad thoughts about Lou. So newly dead, ill thinking is not proper. Louanne must let a respectable grieving time pass. Then. Then. To calm herself, Louanne Graustark sucks her cheek and checks her hair, makes a mental note: tell Hugh to bathe. Something. She will figure out how to get it all. It has to

149

be. She is as smart as her mother. A deal must be made. She licks her teeth.

A pink heart beneath her head, half-sitting as if reading herself to sleep, the star of the show lies angled for viewing like a miracle-size diamond under glass in a museum. Her stone-gray hair is curled in ringlets, her face is golden tan, her lips and cheeks blue-pink, her eyebrows painted on. Her Mrs. Roosevelt jaw is clamped shut, a broken-jaw look done with wires. Cotton is inside her cheeks and eyelids to make them look not dead but sleeping. Wearing baby-blue chiffon supplied by Little Buford, she lies on pink satin sheets with lace at her wrists, clutching a frilly handkerchief. The hanky is a special touch from Little Buford, who likes to add small extras. The human touch, he calls it, designed to ease the stern look about Lou Hart which however he tried he could not tone down. Pink and blue were used to soften her looks and give her a sweetness in death which alive she had no portion of. Stockings cover her legs. She wears baby-blue dyed-to-match pumps on her feet, half-shoes with no backs where the feet don't show. Everything is cut out in back . . . like paper dolls, with tabs at the shoulders to hold the dresses on. Her hands are crossed at her waist, her nails painted an old-lady shade of dusty rose.

Like she was sleeping, Hugh Graustark said. *I swear. Like. Like she might get up out of here any minute and say she'd had a good nap.* Hugh shuddered. *Lord, Little Buford, but you done a good job.*

Louise Mildred Stovall Hart's eyes are fixed shut. Beneath the lids they stare at the ceiling, beneath Little Buford's careful work, wide open and awake. The clamped Mrs. Roosevelt jaw is ground permanently shut.

She had decided to take a bath and fell . . . of all things in the old bathroom, the one room in the house she had not remodeled, when she had a perfectly good stand-up shower stall in her own.

But she decided to take a bath, the more fool she, and the hot water made her dizzy and she fell, broke her already weak and shifting hip then lay there like a beached fish while her heart bubbled, flopped, broke. Split. Lying there in the altogether. Old white body, frame too big for feet and hands, bad combination, like a cur dog with too long a tail and too short a backbone. Ugly. Big Early bones, little Stovall feet. Did she have to have all the bad family traits plus being the oldest, plus being a girl? *Give me boys anyday,* Mother S. always said. Not enough feet to carry her size? Always about to trip? Did she have to decide to take a bath?

She had been thinking about Cure 81 hams on sale at Safeway, with their what they called—fat chance—Our Own Home-grown Tomatoes, when—

Flop. Fish-belly white flopping on the bathroom floor. She hated that bathroom. The architect had explained how much she would save by leaving it as it was, but she should have had it ripped out like the rest of the house. Now she'd gone and died there. Tits and hairless you-know for the world to see. Toenails needing clipping. All her pale stuff, wet and woozy.

Under the sink her eyes were open, fixed on the underside of Mother Stovall's old sink. The other bathroom had a vanity table and gold-plated faucets in shell shapes, American Standard, the best. Lou stared at ancient cracking enamel. Rusted legs. Peeling tile. No one knew how it had galled her all her life, living like renthouse trash.

At least Louanne covered her with a sheet before anyone got there so when others came she didn't look so fish-belly stupid. A bath!

Beneath sewn lids Lou Hart's eyes are wide, dead open.

Gravediggers work Sundays for double-time wages. The services are not until three o'clock Monday, so they will have plenty of time to get the plot ready tomorrow morning at a regular hourly fee. Sunday night, Lou's plot is yet a green space solidly grassed. Pines like ancient grandfathers sway in the night. Sometimes the wind coos inside them. The gravedigging order is on the custodian's desk. The custodian is at home, across the road from the cemetery, sleeping. At six, the gravediggers will arrive to do their work. By seven they will be done. They will then go on to whatever other job they hold down. Pine Bluff gravediggers work cemeteries part-time freelance, a moonlighting profession for ditchdiggers and street-builders and construction help. At noon, the funeral home people will come with Lou's tent and flowers. Then the others. The body. The preacher. The custodian sleeps unbothered.

When Bootsey Halstead Stovall found out the deal Walt Junior had made with Lou she hit the ceiling.

"Cash!" she shrieked. "CPA! I don't believe it, I just don't believe it. Me taking china-painting classes all those years and all that hand-painted china Mother Stovall had and now it's gone and I'll never see it. You take the cake, Walt Junior, you flat take the cake. Think of the parties we could have given with that player piano. Think about our children. You think Lou ever uses it? You think Lou gives parties? I'll tell you if Lou gives parties—no she does not. Last time we were there, remember, you said something was missing you couldn't say exactly what, turned out it was the china rattling in the night. Gone. Every last saucer. Where? I'll tell you where. Lou. Sold it. *Sold* it. She'll sell the floorboards before she's through. You watch."

Walt Junior sat in his chair watching baseball, waiting for Bootsey's rage to play out, wondering what made him think when he married her that her fits of temper were cute.

Let it go, Boots, he had told her through the years. *Let it go.*

"Let it go, let it go, all you ever say is 'Boots, let it go,' well I tell you one thing I am *not* letting it go, I am going to get something out of that woman if it's the last thing I do, you wait, you just wait I will throw rocks on her grave when she dies, she can burn in hell ashes to gall before *I* give up and let go."

Lord, Walt Junior thought, but women could say things. Worse than any man. Boots had such a mouth on her when she got mad. Not that she hadn't helped; she had. When they first got to Hot Springs and business hadn't come right away, she had gone out to the racetrack and the gambling casinos and told people over blackjack and between horse races how he could do their taxes and hide winnings so the IRS would not know. Then to the baths to see the old ladies in towels, explaining how much they were paying out of their retirement money that they didn't have to and how much they could save themselves with a good CPA. Boots was a fighter all right. But did she have a mouth on her.

"Talk about a mess of pottage. You watch. Lou will fix it so nobody wants that house. You just watch. She's got something up her sleeve you and that high-flying brother of yours never would have dreamed of—don't tell me, I know. I know Lou Hart like the back of my hand."

Bootsey had been right. And now that Lou was dead and the house, as the will stood, would go either to Jimmy or, if he didn't want it, to Louanne, Boots was riled up all over again.

"Now look," she said. "Your own children have to suffer. Halstead might have liked to have had his grandfather's house. Why, Walt Three has his grandaddy's name. They certainly deserve the house more than that whore Louanne Graustark and her no-good white-trash husband."

And what would Walt Three do with a corner house in Pine Bluff? Put up his boyfriends? For if Louanne was a whore their eldest son had to be called queer . . . no, *gay,* he was supposed to say. Walt Three clearly had, as they called it, come out last year but Boots, if she noticed, never let on, and he certainly wasn't going to bring it up. Their younger son, Halstead, was long gone to California, not much heard from. Walt Three lived by his wits in Memphis. Currently he seemed to be a travel agent but he had come home for Christmas last year in a Mercedes and Walt Junior doubted he could afford a peach-colored 450 SL on a travel agent's salary. But Walt Junior didn't say anything, he just rode in the car and said how nice it was.

No telling what Walt Three did to get by.

I don't want to think about it. He hoped Jimmy would come to the funeral. He hadn't seen Jimmy in years.

"If I just knew where that hand-painted china was. Or the

wicker daybed. Those matching vases on the mantel. That picture: 'Innocence at Bay.' "

Let it go, Boots, let it go. Don't stir it up let it go.

Let it go my foot, Bootsey Stovall swears, turning over to her side to try to get some sleep. She'll need it. They have to leave Hot Springs early the next morning to get to Pine Bluff in plenty of time for the funeral. A cold day in hell when Bootsey Stovall gives in.

Outside in the driveway an orange-and-silver U-Haul van is hitched up to the peach-colored Mercedes 450 SL Walt Three drove to Hot Springs from Memphis. Bootsey and Walt Junior had been surprised. When they told Walt Three about Lou's death, he immediately volunteered to drive them to the funeral. Said he wouldn't mind going to Pine Bluff anyway, to, as he said, "Eyeball who comes." Whatever that meant. Bootsey couldn't tell what Walt Three might do now . . . anything was possible. At least he didn't bring one of his boyfriends; that would have taken the cake.

It wasn't her fault. He didn't get it from the Halsteads, that was certain. Well, but maybe Walt Three would be more manly than his father, maybe he'd just go on in there and demand what his father should have taken for his rightful own, years ago.

Bootsey frowned. More manly wasn't what she meant. More something.

Walt Junior is sound-Stovall-asleep, snoring erratically, three minutes of noise to one of held breath. That was what drove you crazy. Waiting for him to breathe out. If you're going to snore, snore, Bootsey told him. I could get used to that.

Crack. Crack. Crack . . . zzzwipppp. . . .

Silence.

No breath.

She waits.

Walt.

Walt?

WALT! she slaps him across the chest with her arm. He lets

out his breath and starts crack-cracking again. Every night. Walt. . . . Walt? . . . WALT! It gets old. Oh Stovalls.

Hands folded together beneath her face in a nursery-book prayer pose, on her side, Bootsey Halstead Stovall closes her eyes and wills herself to sleep.

In his room Walt Three sips orange juice and reads wedding announcements in the Hot Springs Sunday *Sentinel.* Every now and then he tears one out, to take back to Memphis to share with a friend. His eyes are bright. He looks altogether content.

They will have to drive all night long to make it. The children are bedded down in the back part of the van in bunks built especially for them. They are coming from the northeast, across Tennessee, skirting the mountains on interstates to get there on time. The driver, sandy-haired and mild-looking, peers steadily out the windshield, singing songs with the radio to keep himself awake, driving like the wind. His looks are soft and placid, yet put him behind a wheel. As a boy, Steve Stovall was known as a hot-rodder, a hood, nearly a juvenile delinquent. Not that he got into trouble, just the crowd he ran with. He had wanted to be a race-car driver at one time. Now look. A van. His fuzz-buster shows a clear road, no highway patrol, no radar. He keeps the speedometer at a steady ninety. He has fixed up the engine to run smoothly at high speeds.

His wife—who swore to stay awake with him—has, thank God, conked out. Otherwise she would be leaning over this minute to check his speed and tell him yet again what the speed limit was and how much more gas he used going fast. Her head is against the window with only the flat of one hand to keep it from bumping. Her other arm is flung over her stomach, as if in protection. She is pregnant; five months' gone. She couldn't be comfortable. But if he wakes her, and suggests she move to the back part of the van and sleep awhile, she will insist she has not been asleep at all and in fact isn't sleepy now and where were they, what time was it, how much farther, how fast are you

driving, Steve? Let her sleep. Sleeping dogs. Her bark was fero-
cious. Not to mention her bite.

He hated the van. Seated high over the interstate, he feels like
a bus driver, delivering people Greyhound cross-country. He
would like a Corvette. A Porsche. When the kids grow up he
will have one. When he can.

This deep into night, stations from all over the country come
in clear. This alone, the voices from so far away seem like private messages whispered in his ear. The announcer is his announcer, they are driving west together across this endlessly
long state, from easternmost tip nearly to its western edge. The
van rides smooth, down the interstate without cracks or bumps
or stoplights. Across the grass island separating them, cars pass
going the other way, back toward home. The music is country,
a low-life taste he saves for when he is alone and doesn't have
to take gaff from Brook. "Making the Best of a Bad Situation"
is playing. The station is from El Paso, from all the way across
this state, then Arkansas and even Texas. Earlier he listened to
Chicago, then New Orleans. This time of night, bizarre pro-
ducts are advertised, plastic crosses, pictures of Jesus, thousand-
dollar Bibles, side by side with public-service announcements
about child abuse, Mormons, CP, polio, drinking. Salvation in
the night, driving west or east down boring interstates. Five-
record sets at an amazingly low price, R&B, country, rock and
roll, fifties, easy listening, choose your music then order your set.

At Brook's insistence, he had been to a weekend seminar in
Morgan, sponsored by an organization she liked, called U.R.U.
He needed to be more aggressive, she said, more in control of
his life, the Steve Stovall he chose to be, not some automatic
life-tape. He should be cause, not effect.

WHEN I WENT TO SEE *Star Wars*, the moderator said, I KNEW IT
WAS TRUE. THERE *is* A FORCE. THE FORCE IS INSIDE YOU. YOU HAVE
TO FIND IT. USE IT. MAKE YOUR OWN FORCE WORK FOR YOU. YOU ARE
YOUR FORCE.

LADIES AND GENTLEMEN: I AM HERE TO GIVE YOU A GIFT. YOUR OWN
LIFE.

156

The gun club was closing. Its founder, a Morgan, had died and his son was going to break up the property and sell it in half-acre tracts. In two months Steve would be out of a job. Then what? What could he do besides drive fast and shoot guns? He had to find the force within him, make it work. YOU CHOOSE, THIS IS IT, CHOOSE. The man made the karate chop gestures as he talked, pointing at people. YOU CHOOSE. He pointed at Steve. YOU. MAKE CLEAR GESTURES. SHOW THEM YOU KNOW.

"Lily of the Dawn" came on, one of Sue's early songs.

Never knew where she had gone,
Called her Lily, White Lily of the Dawn.

He was proud of his sister and scared of her. He couldn't see the purpose in going to this funeral, an aunt nobody liked. He had told his father they wouldn't come. But as Brook understood the will, the house was to go to Big Daddy next and if Big Daddy didn't want it maybe he would pass it on to them. Maybe we could move there, Brook said. Start a gun club in Pine Bluff.

Steve couldn't imagine what had come over her. Brook, leave Morgan?

Brook's father had said Steve could work for him. Sell.

I AM A SALESMAN: SAY THAT TO YOURSELF, SAY IT OUT LOUD: I AM A SALESMAN AND I LIKE MY WORK. I AM A SALESMAN AND I LIKE MY JOB.

Baloney. Big Daddy could sell broken light bulbs, Sue could sell songs. All Steve could do was shoot guns and drive and he needed all he had of himself just to get by. There was no margin, nothing to sell with.

He checks the speedometer and then his wife. Still curled up and sleeping. He eases the accelerator down a bit more, singing with the chorus of his sister's song.

Born in a song. Lily of the Dawn.

Brook is dreaming about Mick Jagger.
She had been to a Rolling Stones concert with a college friend

who had been a fan since she and Brook were roommates at Vanderbilt. Brook hated the Stones then. But times had changed and the Stones had outlasted everybody and seemed now more a cultural force than a band. Brook was curious about fame and trash and besides, there was nothing to do in Morgan. That was before Buddy Cape came home.

So Brook went and with a throng of stoned and screaming kids watched the thirty-year-old man strut and pose and fondle the microphone like a lover.

In the dream, Mick is on a platform. Strutting across it, he calls one of the audience up. They take turns, kneeling before his jeans, rubbing Mick's penis. Each hopes to be the next one called. Mick's knees are bent, his tight black pants unzipped. Feeling privileged, they do their work in shifts. Mick's lips are open and oh, Mick's lips. Near the shivering end, he pulls back and, finishing himself off, sprays them. They glory in being chosen. Laughing, he moves back and forth, like a gardener watering plants. *Brook!* Somebody's calling her. She wakens in a heat, slowly coming into her name, up and out of dreams into the real Brook. *Brook?* She sits up, focusing. Mick wore boots, a slinky yellow T-shirt. The road, the highway, lights in a red ribbon disappearing up ahead. Mick Jagger. Beneath her she feels the engine gear down as Steve takes his foot from the gas. The Stones.

"You're driving too fast, where are we?"

"Past Nashville. I'm not. Were you dreaming? You were making a noise."

"I guess."

Why Mick Jagger? Did she get her turn? She can't remember.

She is known as the rational one, Steve as the dreamer. But Steve sleeps deep as a tick silently sucking and she wakens in the night, again and again, stirred up and puzzled. Things come from the sky, dark ravenlike clouds turned to black moleish beasts that bite her face and chase her to the wall. The least serious domestic crisis becomes in her dreams a dark underground plot she can't control, some conspiracy, some siege from

other worlds. Spiders emerge from woodwork she has spent all
day cleaning. Raw meat changes into an erotic rubber thing.
Beneath every safe thing is something unknown.

She straightens her long legs.

"Change the station."

Sue's song is off. The everything-you-ever-wanted-five-
record-set is being hawked.

Steve reaches to turn the radio knob.

Brook's life is neatly divided in two. One half never sees the
other; she has it worked out. This dreaming, unnamed Brook is
the one she keeps for herself, inside the sureness of her step, the
authority of her voice. Her hair is short, brushed back like a
boy's. She smooths it. Her glossy eyebrows curve back against
her forehead as if brushed, the hair growing up, toward her
scalp. Her eye sockets are so shallow, they look nearly Oriental.

"Anything from the kids?"

"Solid sleep. How about this?" He has found a station from
Cincinnati, playing rock and roll.

"I don't care. None of it is decent. Put it back on the other if
you want. I just didn't like that commercial."

She turns onto her other side, drawing her legs back under
her, nestling in his direction. His profile against the window is
clear. Such a baby. Soft cheeks and freckles, Van Johnson on
"The Late Show." The All-Around Hi-Mom Kid. Beaver
Cleaver himself.

"Steve?"

"Yes."

"I want you to be firm. I want you to tell Big Daddy what we
want. I want you to tell the truth and not beat around the bush."

His profile nods. He pushes his glasses back up on his nose.

"Blue Eyes Crying in the Rain" comes on. Steve sings along.
She hates it when he sings along.

He suspects she has had an affair the past year, with a high-
school boyfriend who showed up in Morgan six months before.
Having lost his sizable inheritance first in a Superslide business

and then a diamond mine escapade, Buddy Cape had come home to see if he could beg some of his mother's oil and telephone stocks free. Buddy had a hole in his right earlobe . . . left over from the gypsy sixties, when Buddy left home. Brook denied Buddy had a pierced ear but the hole was there. She also said Buddy was gay, but Steve had his doubts. Brook and Buddy laughed together and played like children, telling old stories, spending hour after hour playing backgammon, shuffleboard, and Boggle . . . finding words within words. Buddy took Brook to the Country Club to swim, cooked her lunches of barely steamed vegetables and chicken breasts poached in wine. With Buddy, Brook was so lively. With Buddy, she was light as meringue. Steve got to be the heavy. Some choice.

Buddy drove an MG. With the top down, Buddy and Brook cruised Morgan. No one criticized. Hometown people thought they looked like the perfect couple. His hair was longer than hers. His flew back when they drove; Brook's was cut like a boy's. They looked like adolescents: you couldn't tell which was which.

Whose baby is she carrying? It doesn't matter. He will father the child, welcome it, be its daddy. The children are Brook's anyway, and so is he. Her town, her family. Toy people to move upstairs and down in a miniature house just their size.

He checks. Asleep again. Steve presses the accelerator to the floor.

Linda's mind whizzes. She cannot sleep. Joseph is curled around her spoon-fashion. She can feel his ribs at her back, his hipbones against her behind. They left at eleven, Caroline said. If anything had happened she would know. The highway haunts her; memories. No one had called to tell her about Lou until Caroline, in tears, telephoned to ask if she could spend the night at Nalandya. After Linda quickly agreed, Caroline had told her about Lou's death and Sue and Big driving to Pine Bluff for the funeral. In the end, Joseph drove to Houston to get

Caroline. He could, he said, drop off some film as well. She would call Sue in the morning in Pine Bluff and ask her to come by on her way home to pick up Caroline. That way she will know they are all right. Joseph flops onto his back, stretches, rolls to his other side. Linda follows, cupping his back. They sleep turning over together as if bound. Outside, crickets sing incessantly in a steady song that after a while seems like night itself. Her mouth against his spine, her midsection cradling his slim behind, she closes her eyes. She had been asleep. It is a question of going back.

Joseph? Nothing. Cartoon Z's. Some nights he doesn't sleep at all. His bones won't lie still. So near the surface they are too insistent. He may go a week getting only a few hours' sleep a night, then sleep two full days. After picking up Caroline, he left them, Linda and the girl, to talk. Smoked enough dope to ease his imagination, then turned into night itself; pure blackness; gone. No dreams. No Joseph. He is sleep itself.

From the sofa bed you can see the lake. Caroline sits up looking out. There is a moon, not full but nearly . . . lopped off on one side. Far across the lake, a light burns. One clear white dot in the deep blue-black. A boat or a house, something to get to, she can't tell. She was bleeding and bleeding. She hated it. Calling Linda seemed silly now, but she felt panicky: where would it all go? And Joseph. Did he know? She had heard the smell was different from regular blood. Joseph was weird. But no, she was careful, she had used Lady Bee, a powder her friend had recommended. Surely she was safe, but how could you know? When she moved, sometimes the napkin did not shift with her but stayed out of place to one side. It was disgusting, she hated it and the clasp of the belt in the back had rubbed her and it hurt. Joseph and Linda were in the bed, asleep? She couldn't tell. Could she hear them? Were they going to do it? With her in the next room still awake? She pushes the pad back in place, the fifth she has used today. At this rate the box will be empty by morning. Linda will have to buy more. But she can't stand to keep one on long enough to feel wetness, not wet like water but like something raw against you there, a slab of something bleeding. And it was yourself all the time. Every time the damp feeling came—sometimes in a noticeable gush—she changed, put on a clean napkin, dry and white and medicinal.

It's like being tied down. Like something has buckled her in straps. It isn't fair. The elastic against her stomach accentuates its softness, making her look fatter. Stuff is coming out. No one told her she'd be able to feel it. Sometimes when she got up from a chair or made a quick movement or turned, there it was. Flowing out. It was not her, it was something outside of her, some other life, nothing she had chosen. But this was it, wasn't it, from now on. Her tailbone felt raw and sore.

"Caroline?"

"Linda, you scared me."

"Are you all right?"

Caroline drops her head onto her hiked-up knees. Her grandmother, coming to console her, smells of Shalimar, Musk, and Joseph.

It is the moon, reflected in the water, making the white dot of light. There is no other light. Only the moon.

Robby and Ricky sleep in their clothes, stretched out on mattresses in the living room fully dressed, down to socks and shoes. The TV set flickers gray dots and blue haze, making a shushing sound they both sleep better to. They had fought over the couch then settled the argument by bringing in mattresses. Neither wanted to be in a bedroom. Whenever their mother left they liked to sleep somewhere different. It was fun. Like camping out. Their mother said it wasn't true they slept better with the TV on, something about rays and waves, but she doesn't know. The sound is a comfort. It lulls them to sleep. City children can't stand pure quiet. Whenever she comes in, in the night, and turns the TV off, they wake up. Then it takes them forever to get back to sleep again. She says it isn't true, but it is. They don't argue about it anymore, but it's true. On their own, with Buttface Caroline gone to Linda's, they have the house to themselves. The doors are locked and they are fine, nothing will hurt them in Post Oak Place, with the lowest crime rate in the city, a policeman for every seven citizens, its own police force not Cowtown's. Post-oh keeps them, rocks them gently.

Ricky's on his back. His stubby fingers are curled. Next to his face there is a brown apple core, a half-filled glass of 7-Up and melted ice, some cheese gone hard. By Robby's slim wrist there is a bowl of leftover wet sugar in a bowl and three soggy Cheerios. Neither boy is covered. His bony shoulders hunched, Robby, in a ball, looks chilled; Ricky, however, is spread-eagle and sweating. Ricky is never cold. In winter he refuses to wear jackets except his Yankee windbreaker and sometimes, a sleeveless down vest he got for Christmas. He wants to live in a cold climate someday, where winters are truly cold and summers aren't steaming like here. Ricky dreams about a girl named Kelly, riding a bike; Robby is caught in a submarine . . . a real one he remembers, dry-docked in Mobile, a tourist attraction along with a Navy battleship. His mother says it was such a long time ago he couldn't possibly remember, little as he was, but he does. It is a recurring dream. He is inside the submarine. The last tourist. They have forgotten him. No one knows he's there, not even his mother. They are shutting the door and he is closed up inside, alone. He curls tighter and tighter in his ball of cold, until his knees reach his chest. The TV buzzes. Ricky snores.

Call Me Mike has wakened, thinking of the funeral ahead. Poor white trash married to Mulberry Street was worse by far than African natives. White nut-church trash. A nut sect that allowed no lipstick or singing yet there was Hugh Graustark, a deacon, drunk as a lord. Three o'clock. The night is so long when you wake up.

My Wife Evelyn has just dropped off. From the missionary years they sleep in shifts. It was not something they talked about but in Africa they learned to take turns. He slept then she did.

One watched, the other dozed, like guards on shifts. It works
out. It is a way of being married. It works out.

On her back in a wide X, Mona snores. On his back in a wide
X, Boyd snores. Neither dreams.

Big dreams. *We have perfected it now,* the voice of the voice of
the authorities says, *we have combined the strains to cross over the
animals and make them one. I am the I, there is the he.* The animal
approaches. It has slippery skin and small eyes. A horn grows
out of its nose. It is fat. Blood oozes out its pores like fat coming
out slowly like greaselike glue. Fat the animal is I am, the animal
is another something altogether two put together to make one,
it comes.

A bird sits on its head, the animal has eyes so far down the
side of its head it cannot see straight ahead, the bird is its eyes.
Bird's eye . . . something. Eye-bird. I see what it sees, only to the
side nothing ahead. I am the I, he is himself, what is the inbe-
tween. When he moves drops of bloodfat come out. Drip down
his sides. And here comes the black girl. Her swift hands.

"Have they, have they—"

"Daddy."

He sits straight up, throws his legs around the side of the bed,
sits. Checks the clock. *Bink.*

His head is bowed. He could be praying.

The dream, the dream . . . water!

"You okay?"

"Yes. A dream."

"Listen." We're whispering, our voices like quick shadows.
"Louanne's going to want to talk about the house."

"I don't want it."

"It's your turn."

"I thought I might but—" he shudders. By the light of the
clock radio the dreamy, displaced look flashes across his eyes.
"Go to sleep, Sue," he says.

"I'm trying."

Down to bones, Mother Stovall is serene. Next to her, Big
Walt has crumbled to nothing. Her will, however, survives. It
rides the night sky, shaking broom and dust mop. Havoc like
fallout from fireworks sprinkles from the sky onto the heads of
whoever would rob a wife of her place. Havoc sifts onto their
pillows. Their sleep is uneasy. Mother Stovall is content.

Girl of My Dreams #4

June Day singing her song, standing in the spotlight in a tight
dress, a flower behind one ear, moving to a new beat.
HIT IT.
Stars shine, romance, can't live without you baby, don't go.
Love. A soulful June Day, on the offbeat. Sweet sliding; in the
background a sax. Romance, belief, romance. The sax wails.
In the night, in the smoky smoky night: vampire time. Rebop
syncopate do the dirty bop, request "Sixty-Minute Man," hear
the Shammies, sing the song. Sing the song, Aretha, sing the
song.
Oh, Questionnaires. Heart and *soul.*

Walt Three

"I hope ya'll like aigs."
Standing over the stove, Louanne splashes bacon grease onto
the yellows of two frying eggs. Her back is to us. She is talking
to the eggs.
"I heard ya'll up, so I went ahead and started you some."

"Eat eggs every morning," Big says brightly.

"Help yourself to coffee." The pot is a West Bend Electric Percolator. There is a magnetic sign on the dishwasher, shaped like a cloud, saying DIRTY. I turn it over. CLEAN.

"I like my aigs good done, don't you?" Louanne says and, giving us no chance to answer, flips them. "I heard you can get worms eating underdone aigs, same as pork. Raw birds nearly. Turns my stomach. Myself I cannot stand the sight of a runny yellow. Reminds me of I hate to say."

With her spatula, she presses down on one egg so hard the flat of the spatula bends. Then the other. Her shoulder heaves to one side with the effort.

"I don't eat nothing aigs is in that isn't cooked. Pudding? Can't fool me. Aigs go in after the milk is cooked. You are flatly eating raw aigs when you eat pudding. Ever think of that? Makes me sick, that moogy yellow stuff, that hard little snotty thing. Makes me sick. You ever had worms? Terrible. Worms is terrible."

Louanne spanks the yolks. I pour two cups of coffee. It's weak as water. Louanne is wearing a pink-flowered sleeveless shirt and matching darker pink slacks made of a knitted stretch material. Her behind looks like two flat dinner plates.

Daddy frowns. The minute Louanne said runny yellow and raw bird, he slipped away again, back in his glassy world.

I reach over and touch the back of his hand. He blinks and comes back.

"You take your eye out last night?"

"No. I slept in it."

"Daddy!"

"It's all right. It stayed. It's all right."

Louanne turns around for a quick look, checking out Daddy's eyes, then goes back to her cooking, poking a yolk with a knife.

"There," she says, satisfied. She slides an egg onto a plate.

"I'll just have toast," I say quickly as she turns to get mine. "Daddy can have my egg. I'm not much on breakfast."

"Baloney, Sue. You need you a good breakfast, you eat you an aig. Right after ya'll eat we are going to Buford's to see Mama. So you eat you a good meal to get started on. You'll be glad later on you did."

From the warmer oven she takes two pieces of bacon cooked so hard that when she lays a strip on my plate it breaks into chips.

"Ya'll put you down some toast," she says, gesturing toward the electric toaster. "There's oleo and jelly. I'm going to get ready. Ya'll take your time."

A yellow plastic bottle of Kraft Margi-Squeeze sits next to the toaster. Next to it are a giant-sized jar of Welch's grape jelly and a loaf of Wonder bread. The toaster is a Toastmaster. We work it. Daddy puts his bacon and egg on top of his toast—which he has thickly oleoed and jellied; the margarine comes out in a swirl, like the top of a Dairy Queen cone—and eats it open-faced.

"You want mine? You're used to two."

He rolls his eyes. "Big favor. Hard-boiled in grease."

"Well? Do you?"

He piles sugar into his coffee, stirring it so hard the coffee sloshes. The spoon makes a scraping sound against the bottom of the cup.

"Oh, fork it over."

I jab the yolk of the egg with my fork and lift it, impaled.

"Did Louanne say anything about the cellar last night?"

"The what?"

"The cellar. The basement." The egg hits his plate with a splat.

"No. Was she supposed to?"

"No, I just thought you might have asked."

"She probably sold it."

"That old thing?"

"Why?"

"It's the only basement I've ever been in. I'd like to see how it compares to the cellar I remember. What it smells like . . . if it's there."

The light-up Princess phone beside us rings twice then stops. Louanne yells it's for me.

"By the microwave," she says.

It's Linda. "Why didn't you tell me about Lou?"

"Is anything wrong?"

"No."

Daddy reaches for the Pine Bluff *Commercial,* pretending not to listen.

"Sue. Caroline is with me."

"What for? What happened?"

"Well, you know she got her period."

"Yes."

"She was upset and wanted to come up and I said she could."

"How'd she get there?"

"Joseph. He needed to go to Houston anyway."

"The boys okay?"

"I talked to Jane. They're fine. Everything's okay. I just wanted to know if you'd come by here on your way home and pick up Caroline."

"It'll be awfully late."

"I know."

"I mean, two in the morning."

"It's okay."

"I don't know."

"Nothing will happen."

"Well. Tell her to be ready. No telling what time we'll get there. I want to pick her up and go on."

"I wish you'd told me Lou died."

"What for?"

"I don't know. I just like to know what's going on."

When I was young I wanted to be small like her with size 5 feet and slim hips. I envied her her frailty, her pale skin, her thick blond hair. Of my group of friends, I always won Prettiest Mother and Best Personality. I wanted her prettiness. I picture her now, at the telephone, wrapped in some casual robe looking stylish and unplanned, her hair coming down in wisps, her thin lively fingers cupping the telephone. With the other hand she is either gesturing with a cigarette or tapping out a drum with her long fingernails.

"Well, all right." I don't know what else to say.

"Is Steve coming?"

"No. Pee has a virus; anyway, it's pretty far."

In the background I picture Joseph, slouched in some chair, bones in a heap like leftover ribs. The prince of the house, my mother and daughter his fluttering serfs.

"What's she doing?"

"Now?"

"Yes."

"Sleeping. She had a bad night. Not bad; restless."

"Where?"

"Where? On my bed. She was on the couch. She moved."

"Why?"

"Nervousness. Do you mean why did she have a bad night or why is she on my bed."

"The first."

"I thought so. She was nervous. And angry, alone there with the boys. Also scared."

"I had to come."

"Not angry at you. Just angry. You know."

"Yes . . ."

"Is Jimmy all right?"

"He's fine."

"Well . . ."

I say "I'd better let you go," as if I called her and we hang up. Big catches my eye.

"I have to go get ready."

"Who was that?"

"Linda. Everything's fine. Just Caroline. She went to Linda's house. That's all."

Big rattles the paper.

I hit it to The Second Bedroom, where, I don my ragtag weeds.

———

"Can we all go in one car."

This is not a question. Louanne is giving orders.

"No." But I'm too abrupt. "We might want to come home at different times?"

We are in the circular drive, and they are all looking at me. Mona says "Hump" in a snippy way as if to say *she* knew why I didn't want to ride in Louanne's car, she just wasn't saying.

Louanne pouts. "Well all right, Sue, if that's what you want." Her lip quivers.

Daddy is in the LTD.

Hugh allows as how he'd like to ride with Big and me and Louanne glares at him and Mona says "Hump" again in that same knowing way.

Mona punches in the button of Louanne's car-door handle.

Louanne says "Well, but—"

At that moment a peach-colored Mercedes pulling an orange-and-silver U-Haul turns down Walnut toward us.

As one, except for Big, we turn.

"Now who is *that?*" Mona says in her permanent huff as if knowing in advance who but not saying; at any rate, the wrong person. She consults her comrade Louanne, who has taken in car and trailer with a squinted eagle eye.

"I bet I know," Louanne says, smoothing the bib of her pale-green pantsuit. "I bet you anything I know."

"You do?"

"Yes, I do."

"Well, who?"

Tooting a hello, the car pulls up behind Louanne's. With the U-Haul in, there is barely enough room in the drive. The driver is tall, his head nearly touching the ceiling of the car. He waves.

"It's Bootsey I bet. With that U-Haul I bet anything it's Bootsey. I bet anything in the world it's, Hi Bootsey how are you, glad ya'll, see I told you it was Bootsey."

Three people get out of the car: a tall, angular woman with eyeglasses on a chain, a short plumpish man, struggling to free himself from the very tight backseat, and the young man driving, who is as tall as a basketball player and thin as a sapling.

I recognize the fat man. It's Walt Junior. He looks like a squeezed-down version of Daddy. The woman, all elbows and knees, must be Bootsey; the young man one of their sons, I haven't seen them in so long I have no idea which. He is dressed elegantly, in a dark three-piece suit, white shirt, and flowing striped tie. His hair is long and wavy. He looks like a slender plant.

Daddy gets out of the LTD.

The young man, my cousin, comes directly to me.

"I'm Walt Three," he says. "You must be Sue."

His hands bend and swoop like graceful fish. When we shake hands he takes my right one in both of his and holds it tight. His eyes are blue. He gives me a swift kiss and then a meaningful look. What? A signal of some kind. What?

We speak at once.

". . . been years. . . ."

". . . so long. . . ."

He dips his head in a certain way, with a studied flamboyance reminding me of Al Theater. His voice is as evenly modulated as a preacher's. Bootsey keeps darting quick looks in his direction.

Walt Three lifts his chin. Something. Smiles. Something? Yes. I know him. I've got it. The city has arrived. Yes, Walt Three, I feel better, in this Pine Bluff garden I feel not so alone. Walt Three, you devil.

The man toddling down the circular drive looks like a rolling frog, a rolling round dog. A birds'-eye, not rug . . . no. *Words.* A smile is on the round man's face, his hands are out, he goes side to side when he walks. Behind him is bones: two people. Bones are not us, Stovalls are round. Lou is not. A Not Rug. "Jimmy. It's good to see you, Jimmy."

"Walt Junior? Is that you, Walt?"

The voice is the same. It must be Walt. The baby gets the taters, Walt Junior gets the blame. Where is his daybed?

A rolling toad with Stovall eyes, Early nose, Daddy's forehead, Early short hands and feet. A chin of fat. Walt Junior never was fat. Now he is a round hog. A rolling ground going round round hog. Birds'-eye Maypo.

"I'm as fat as you, little brother. As fat as you." Walt Junior's eyes fill. Daddy's lower lip trembles. The two men embrace. Big is taller. His head bends down so that the bald top of it touches his brother's shoulder.

The clacking stops. Bones turn. Louanne turns; Mona, Hugh. The brothers are hugging. Their sister is dead and the brothers are hugging. Wives don't count, a wife is only My Wife after all, but these two are the same. Divided in two, the same.

The two brothers pound each other on the back and weep on one another's shoulder, saying *Walt Junior . . . Jimmy . . . Walt Junior,* to lift the weight of silence.

Louanne breaks it. "Did ya'll have a pleasant trip?" she asks Bootsey.

"Oh, yes we did," Bootsey says. "Walt Three is a fabulous driver just fabulous and of course his car rides smooth as glass. You cannot even tell you are moving in that car."

Everyone looks toward the car. Everyone pretends the U-Haul is not there.

"Where did Big Walt sit, I mean Walt Junior?" Louanne asks, pursing her lips in a fury at her mistake, having given Bootsey a point calling Walt Junior by his daddy's name. Louanne re-crimps a Church of God curl with her fingers.

"You haven't seen a Mercedes 450 SL before?"

"Well, I—"

"Oh, well. There's more room than you think. The backseat's plenty big and of course Walt Junior is short. You know that."

Bootsey says short as if being short is a crime, a Stovall curse.

"Well. And you and your son so tall."

Bootsey fiddles with her eyeglass chain.

"That Mercedes 450 SL, I swear, is a dream, a fabulous dream—"

"We are on our very way to view Lou," Mona interjects. Mona's hand has been on Louanne's car-door handle all this time. Pointedly she presses her thumb and sharply opens the passenger door of Louanne's car.

Mona gets in.

"I'm sure you all would like to freshen up first, then come down to Little Buford's," Louanne suggests.

Walt Junior and Daddy have come apart. They stand at arm's length wiping their eyes.

"Come with us, Walt Junior," Big says, his voice quivering. "I don't want to see Lou without you. You ride with us. She's at Buford's, you remember Buford? Buford is dead. Fell through the attic. Went blind, couldn't walk or talk. Buford's dead, Walt." Big's eyes mist up. "Little Buford runs the funeral home."

Walt Junior hesitates, his eyes darting in Bootsey's direction.

"I don't know, Jimmy. Bootsey—"

"You go on, Walt Junior," Bootsey says. "Go right ahead on with your brother. I think I'll take Louanne up on her offer and stay here and freshen up."

Only Walt Junior and Daddy are unaware of the politics of the moment. Louanne had suggested they freshen up before coming to Little Buford's thinking by the time they got there she could have established her center stage place. She meant for them all three to stay and freshen up, not Bootsey by herself, who was responsible for that U-Haul Walt Three's Mercedes 450 SL was dragging. Bootsey was the one to watch, not Walt Junior.

Hugh is no help. He looks drunk already, with a bulge in his back pocket the size and shape of a half-pint, and it will ruin the advantage by looking too arranged and last-minute if Louanne tries to pry Mona out of her car after she has already gone and got in, sitting there looking straight ahead. Like a dog, getting in first then waiting for the people. Mona was stupid.

"I'll tell you what, let's *all* go. Mama would like that." Louanne lights up. "Mama would like it if all of us came as one."

Bootsey works her jaw, right eye twitching. She lifts her glasses chain, lets it drop. "I feel tired," she insists. "I want to freshen up. It was a *long trip.*"

"We'll stay too."

Walt Three, all drama and style, looks down on the rest of his family with benign goodwill. Supple and fishlike, he bears no resemblance whatsoever to anyone else in the drive; he is purely his mother's son; pure bony Halstead. Beside him, his cousin, a true Stovall, is golden and fleshed.

"Who is that?" Big says to his brother.

"It's Walt Three, Jimmy. You remember."

"Your boy?"

"He grew up."

"But so far? Walt. . . ."

"What?"

"That boy's a beanstalk."

'I know." Walt chuckles. "You ought to see his—" The others turn.

"Walt Three," Daddy muses. "I can't believe it. A thin Stovall."

"Unless he's the milkman's," Walt Junior says, chucking Daddy in the ribs. "Ha ha. Unless . . ." Walt Junior does not know he has spoken loud enough to be heard until such a silence surrounds his feeble joke.

"HAH!" says Bootsey, shooting her husband a look.

"Walt Three. I'm your uncle. I'm Jimmy," Big says, holding out his hand and walking toward his nephew. "It's been a long time."

Walt Three meets him halfway.

"AHEM!" Bootsey protests.

"I hate," she says, "long good-byes. If ya'll are going, why don't you."

As if on command, they scurry in different directions. Daddy, Walt Junior, and Hugh have started to get in Daddy's car when Louanne, with one foot on the floorboard of her car and one on the circular drive, turns around and, seeing what is up, yells "Oh no you don't" to Hugh. But when Bootsey, who is already headed inside, turns from under the grape-cluster swag lamp to see what the matter is, Louanne's tone changes to pure Margis-queeze. "Whyn't ya'll come with us, Uncle Jimmy," she says. "There's plenty room." Hugh ducks his head back in Daddy's car, trying to convince Daddy and Walt Junior to stay where they are, but as Daddy is reluctant to drive, the three men get out of the LTD and head toward Louanne's station wagon. Mona has never budged.

"Ya'll be down in a little while," Louanne tells Bootsey.

"Soon as we freshen up," Bootsey, turning the front-door handle, replies.

Walt Three and I follow Bootsey. Under the swag lamp, Louanne's command stops me dead in my tracks.

"Sue!"

"What?" Louanne's voice is so shrill it makes your teeth hurt.

"If ya'll eat anything, help yourself to ham but save the roast beef, all right? Hugh can't touch ham." She two-fingers her mouth again and silently pokes the left side of her chest.

Once again, we wave good-bye.

By the time Walt Three and I get in the house, Bootsey is already at work, blood-hounding the house to sniff the trail of valuables left behind. She is furious. At every door she shakes her head. *Would you look at that, I knew it. Would you look at that. I told Walt Junior, I tried to tell him. Would you look at that.*

Nothing to claim, nothing to haul home, not one stick of anything. She has rented the U-Haul for nothing.

Walt Three and I go back outside, leaving Bootsey to her rampage.

"If the front porch was here, then over there's where the birdbath was."

Walt Three stands at the corner of the house, pointing in two directions.

"Porch swing . . ."

"Breakfast room . . ."

Walt Three takes a few steps. We are looking for the cellar door.

"The driveway was here."

"Turn here and . . ." We round a corner.

"The kitchen." (There was a banging back door.)

"Down there was the garage and the home garden, and over there the chicken pen."

"Chickens?"

Walt Three's amazed. "You don't remember chickens? Mother Stovall's chopping block? Her ax or was it hatchet? Stump-necked chickens running around the yard like—"

"—chickens with their heads cut off? I remember." But I hadn't. Chickens running headless through the yard while Mother Stovall chopped off more. A lot of chickens lost their lives when we came to visit. Chicken after chicken. She'd pile them in a tub. They'd lie on top of one another, flopping. The blood wasn't bad but oh the necks and gristle, those feathers, that flopping. *She?*

"Walt Three, did Mother Stovall do all the chopping?"

"You don't think Big Walt would bloody his hands? That has to be Louanne's room."

"Yes and . . . look. Walt Three, come look."

"What?"

"It's here."

"I don't—"

"The cellar door."

"Out here? Are you sure?"

"The house moved, but the door stayed. Look." Before, the door had been inside the house, within the back porch; now that Lou took off the porch, however, it's by the patio, next to the self-flaming gas grill.

Compared to the house, the cellar door looks ancient. Gray and scratched. The same door.

"Think it's locked?"

I want it to be and don't, want to go down, yet like a skydiver now that the hatch is open am dreading what I've spent all that time getting ready for, come all this way to do.

Walt Three tries the knob. It turns. "Shall we? Descend to the bowels of our grandfather's house? Investigate its nether parts?"

The stairs are gray, as I remember. Elephant gray: like my house. Beyond the first few steps there is only darkness. A switch is inside the door. Nothing. The switch seems disconnected.

"You go first."

"No, you."

"I found it; you."

"I turned the knob; you."

Here's the smell. Ashes, dampness, cobwebs, Mother Stovall's hair. Musty couches, mothballed closets, furniture oiled daily. Age and ruin. A cool drifting smell, the earth itself. Beside the steps are those humps I remember, a soft gray rise on either side, as if when the cellar was cut out, piles of earth were left and, later, cemented over, making humps. At the foot of the steps is a walkway so narrow I can barely get through it. I go Indian style, one June Day–shod foot in the track of the other. Past the narrow passageway I can see, now that my eyes have accustomed themselves to the near darkness, a wide lighted area.

The window: it's there, caked with webs and red dust. Through it, sunlight descends across the humps to the cellar floor, a sharp dust-filled slant. In the walkway a puddle of light flutters, birdlike.

"You remember?"

"Exactly. It's the same. I thought I'd mixed it up." Dust fills my mouth, cakes my tongue.

"Feel the walls." Walt Three is exhilarated. He palms a hump.

"I'm cold."

"Are you scared?" He sounds surprised.

"Yes."

"Why? Afraid of what?"

"I don't know."

"I like it. A bit of tension, to liven us up. Don't you think?

Edge City?" Walt Three turns his hand at a three-quarter angle and slices it through the air.

"Like when we burned the leaves with the cigarette lighter?"

Dust turns slowly in the sunlight. He smiles, remembering

"Buried the bat in blue ink?"

We're standing in the walkway, just at the end of it where the humps stop. Beyond us the path turns a little to the left. Walt Three towers over me; I have to crane my head against my spine to look at him. It's as if we have dreamed the same dream: children on their haunches around a bat grave humming tunes, saying mumbo jumbo, opening a pen. Sprinkles of Arkansas red dirt.

"And mayonnaise. Don't forget the mayonnaise."

"You know what Tina Turner says?"

"What?"

" 'Ain't nothin' you do can't stand a little greasin'.' "

It all happened. I feel cheered. Only the stove is left.

We take the jag to the left; stop. There is a wall; a barricade; stacks and piles going nearly to the ceiling. This was where the open place was, and the stove. Now there are boxes and chairs and sacks, fruit cartons, trunks, pots and pans, jars stacked on end tables, picture frames on their sides, pictures, paintings, stacks of thick 78's. A hat tree leans against a rolled-up rug crowned by an upside-down brass spittoon. There are books and maps and old drawers filled with boxes. Hatboxes, an umbrella stand, broken lamps, mounds of old clothes. The old things Louanne scoffed at.

Roaches scurry. There is a rustling sound.

Lou has made a wall, impossible to get through.

We bat cobwebs away; they tangle in our lashes, invade our throats.

"I wonder how long it's been since anyone was here?"

"All the old things Daddy kept asking about."

The whirling piano stool. Linens gone to ruin. A stove burner on its side. Big Walt's chair—splintered.

"Lou. Lou did it."

Walt Three is in shirtsleeves and vest, having taken his coat off upstairs. The starched whiteness of his shirt gleams, in startling contrast to the dust and the walls.

"Careful, Walt Three. You'll get filthy."

"I don't believe it. Look."

He points up high.

"Daddy's bed. The wicker daybed. Lou did it."

On top of a stack of boxes in a dark corner, resting at a downturned angle against a wall is Walt Junior's bed, its front legs poking high up in the air. The pillows are ripped. In places where the wicker is broken it looks like a stump-necked something. Some of the varnish is scraped off.

"Walt Junior's bed."

"She pitched it. Can you imagine. Every time we came here, Mama asked about that thing. 'Lord, Bootsey,' Lou would say, 'that old thing . . . ?' "

"You want it?"

Walt Three waits a beat. "Mama would give her eyeteeth for that daybed. Yes, I do. But if we let her know what's down here she won't leave till it thunders, so we have to do it in secret. Sneak it to the U-Haul, surprise them in Hot Springs. I'll think of something. That's what I want to do."

"I'll help."

Imagine Lou, at the cellar door, hurling. Some of these things she could have sold. Imagine her fury, rat-holing instead, as year by year she thought of more and more things she would give to the rats instead of sell or pass on.

"Here." On tiptoe Walt Three reaches a long thin arm past boxes and records and a mound of what seems to be only wool sweaters and topcoats, to grab hold of one of the daybed's feet. His shirttail pulls out; when his vest brushes against a box, it comes away white and webby.

"Got it." The only way he can get the daybed is to drag it across the boxes until it's close enough to get a better grip on.

"Watch out. I'm going to have to knock some things over." He rakes the bed across, turning his head as it comes to avoid falling debris. Two boxes tumble. Another. Some records. The hat tree hits a chair. Walt Three skips out of the way, keeping the daybed foot in his grasp. Turning, he tries to reach the other foot but it is still too far away and he is stretched out as far as he can go. Things spill. He pulls again.

"I'm getting it." He has the other foot, by the fingertips. From nowhere a vase rolls, bounces, spills dirt on his shoes, breaks.

"Fuck." His perfect shoe is a dirt pile.

But he's got it. The foot of the daybed is just above his head. Walt Three reaches to the center to lift it and brings it down, looking behind him for space. Sharing the weight, we take Walt Junior's bed to the cellar steps and prop it.

"I can't believe it. It's incredible." The crippled daybed, gnawed and scarred, is pathetic but restorable.

Walt Three dusts his hands.

We turn back to the open place.

At the foot of Lou's wall is the pile of overturned sacks and boxes the daybed dislodged. We squat to investigate.

There is a blue-striped hatbox with yarn twisted into a rope for a handle. Thinking it must be Mother Stovall's, I slip back the yarn, take off the lid. A silverworm darts out. A moth flies into my hair and when I shake my head, flutters across my lashes trying to get away. The hatbox is filled with carnival colors. There are ostrich feathers gnawed to nubs, fake pearls in long wrapped strings, black sequins nearly blue, blue ones iridescent as rainbows; rolls of grosgrain and taffeta ribbon in bright plaids and solid colors; patches of colored felt, swatches of bright-colored fabric, piles of gaudy theatrical decorations, meant to adorn a lady's head. Mother Stovall's, her Early Girl box, left-over from Cincinnati, remnants of Mabel, when Mother Stovall was not a wife. There are pieces of clunky costume jewelry scattered about with the feathers: a hand-painted enamel brooch, one pink earring, a painted ring with a huge green stone, an identical blue one. I try on the green one; a perfect fit. June Day will love it, flashing green in the spotlight while she sings. I bury it in some velvet. There are scraps of satin and bits of gnawed silk stained with watermarks. Underneath a velvet pincushion pricked solid with hatpins there's a bone-colored baby brush, its bristles soft as a powder puff.

"The piano rolls."

Walt Three is close, shoulder to my shoulder. I turn to him. His face is at mine; I can feel his breath. We are that close. He perspires in dots; the dots hang, as if unwilling to leave, outlining his lip.

In his hand is a chewed piano roll. "Oh Chicago," "Hot Socks," "Maple Leaf Rag" faster than fingers can go: whose fingers, going fast? Walt Three's hair is silky blond, his eyes pale blue with dark centers. He is nothing like a Stovall, this cousin. His ear is a perfect pink shell.

"It feels funny. Like burying the bat."

"I can't breathe." He sets his hand on my knee. "Sue . . ."

He moves his hand to the side of my face; I lean into it.

"What do you do, Walt Three?"

"You mean work?"

"Job, yes. Work."

His hand leaves my face, rests against my damp neck a moment, then retracts.

"Not much. I live with a man, Leon. He's well fixed. He owns a piece of the Memphis Horns, was on City Council awhile. Now he's opening a disco . . . dance emporium, he calls it. I do his legwork, cooking. Things. You?"

"You know I write songs."

"Yes."

"Then . . . it's a secret."

He rolls his eyes. "What isn't?"

"I sing them."

"You sing?"

"In joints on the edge of town under a different name: June Day. She's the singing me."

"Edge City?" He turns his hand in that three-quarter slice.

"Edge City."

"Well, here, June Day. Take this."

Walt Three hands me a piano roll. The song title on the label is indistinguishable but the credits are plain: COPYRIGHT, LONNIE STILES. ROLLOGRAPHY, MARTHA LEE. Big Mama Lee, beating out the tune. It was *her* fingers, flying fast.

"Sue. Leon's bought the block of Beale Street the old Daisy Theatre was on. He's redoing the Daisy, putting in new floors and neon and a blue dome. Imagine. A blue dome in Memphis; neon in cobalt and rose. In August he's having a grand opening: THE NEW BLUE HOT ROSE DAISY. Maybe you'll come? Meet Leon?"

"What kind of music?"

"Disco, what else? New Wave on Monday."

"You go for that one/two/three/four even beat?"

"I go for dancing. Like to move."

"Maybe I will."

"Do it. We'll let you sing a song.

"On Beale? No thanks." At the bottom of the hatbox is a large, floppy purple felt hat, flattened and on its side. I stick it on my head, strike a pose.

"Get this."

"Hot stuff. Wear it. Here, you can have this."

He passes me over a flat black box filled with cotton. Inside, is a long notched curl of hollow, teethlike things, thin as shrimp shells. The snake rattles.

Walt Three shivers. "I don't want any part of a snake."

"Robby and Ricky will love them." I start to put the tail into the hatbox when I see at the bottom, beneath where the hat was as if hidden there, as if put under the flattened hat so no one would find it, a black notebook, worn and warped, threads hanging from the cover, cardboard corners worn through. Black comes off on my hands as I lift it. Mother Stovall's diary? Hidden from Lou? I turn back the cover. Dust comes up in a puff.

LINDA SHANNON DAY STOVALL HER DIARY KEEP OUT.
1942–?????

Terrified, I close the book. It is as if Linda herself had spoken, was there. Walt Three's busy at his own discoveries. Slowly, I open it again.

There is a patch of watery brown at the bottom of the first page. The pages are brittle as dry leaves. Separating two, my heart knocking out a thump my eyes can feel, I smooth them.

Page one. The text is printed in capital letters.

> *THE QUEEN OF SHADES. SHE IS QUEEN OF THE IN-BETWEEN, OF LIGHT, SHADOWS, HEAT. SHE REIGNS OVER THE PLACE WHERE THERE IS NO THING LOVE IS NOTHING. WE ARE SHADOWS, SHADES AND HEAT. DARK/LIGHT. SMOKE. I LIVE IN COLORS AND HEAT, THE MOVEMENT OF LIGHT, RAINBOWS INSIDE GLASS. LIFE IS THE SPACE BETWEEN. I AM THE QUEEN, OF SHADES. L.*

New page.

> *REFLECTIONS. HOLD A BREAKFAST PLATE UP TO THE LIGHT, SEE ITS GREEN SHADOW. AS IN A BROKEN MIRROR. SHATTERED IS REAL, APART IS TOGETHER, TAKE A THING APART, IT COMES TOGETHER . . . L.*

Memories cross over. Merge. She and I were talking recently about mirrors. *Playgirl* had an article recommending mirrors when things got dull. Mama said no.

"I wouldn't like," she said, "to see myself in such one-on-one flat representational terms. It would be too depressing. And it would not be real."

Not real?

"If you took a mirror and shattered it, then put the pieces over or beside or over *and* beside the bed and watched yourself having sex in all those mirrors at once, a thousand yous, a thousand hims, a thousand angles of light back and forth, that would be the truth. The truth is in bits and pieces. You connect them up in your mind."

I asked her if that was conceptual art. She laughed.

MOTHER STOVALL HAD US WASH WINDOWS . . . something something . . . LIGHT, GLASS . . . MAHOGANY, THE HEAT OF . . . something.
TURNED STONE COLD, A ROCK.

On one page she makes shapes with her name.

LINDA

LINDA DAY

LINDA SHANNON DAY

LINDA SHANNON DAY STOVALL

SHANNON DAY

STOVALL

L

I

N

D

A

The coolness of the cellar has a double-whammy effect, hot and cold at once. Closing the notebook, hands wet and shaky, I put it carefully back in the hatbox, cover it with fabric.

"Look. Look." Walt Three has found a box of dishes that have miraculously escaped shattering. He holds a plate to the dusty slant of light. The plate is pale pink; shining through it, light turns rosy. *Light is real. Heat, glass.* A green cup makes the light lime.

"Depression glass, Sue. Look." *Hold it to the light.* He lifts an amber saucer.

"We ate breakfast off it. I liked the gold ones."

"Cheap stuff then, but Lord. Leon will have a fit." *Shades.* Enough.

"Walt Three, it's getting creepy down here."

"Not to mention late."

"Let's take up the daybed."

My feet are asleep from squatting. Standing, I shake them to

get some feeling back, and rub my stiff knees. Walt Three takes
the lower end of the daybed and we lift it up the cellar stairs to
the U-Haul. I agree to take the Depression glass to Houston to
keep for Walt Three. If Bootsey gets her hands on it, Walt Three
says, Leon will never see those dishes.

Where were the fairy tales then? In her real life or the notebooks? Which was actual Linda? Mama or Queen of Shades?

On the way down to get my hatbox, I stumble on the cellar
steps, catching the heel of one shoe. Prying the heel loose, I pull
the wrong way. The nails give, the heel pulls loose . . . not off
but undone on one side. I hammer it against the floor which
helps a little, but not much. I'll have to crip through the funeral,
arch hunched to keep the heel in place. Certainly I can't wear
Etonics.

After gathering up the hatbox, I try once more to peer between the chinks of Lou's wall to see if the stove is there. We
never went beyond this area; beyond it, there was only damp
darkness; rats, a dirt floor. Positioning myself so the sunlight's
behind me and I'm not casting shadows, I try to make out what's
there. A shape. Is it? *Who's stoking?* No way to tell; it's too dark.
There are more boxes and things. I can see a picture, impossible
to get to, of a girl in a bonnet with ribbons by her face.

Foot in a hunch I take up the hatbox. Walt Three is standing
by the Mercedes, unhooking the U-Haul so we can ride to Little
Buford's in the 450 SL. He points to his head.

"What?"

He points again, making a face.

The purple hat.

Lifting it, I toss the hat in the trunk of the LTD and shake
loose my hair.

"Let's get a drink of something and go to Little Buford's."

After washing up, Walt Three and I find Bootsey in the
kitchen, eating a roast beef sandwich so thick she has to stretch
her mouth yawn-wide to get it in.

"Nothing," she is mumbling. "Not a cotton-picking thing."

Oh Mother Stovall.

———

Little Buford's is an old house made over into a funeral home. Crossing the railroad tracks to go though downtown, Walt Three, driving the Mercedes, says, "Just like Memphis. Dead as a doornail." Sacks are tied over the parking meter heads up and down the main street of town; no cars parked in front of them. Across the street is a banner: SHOP DOWNTOWN FREE PARKING FREE. Store windows painted over are hung with signs saying FINAL REDUCTIONS/GOING OUT OF BUSINESS/LAST DAYS. Like the house, the town has made a quarter turn. The big old Victorian houses near downtown now look like low-rent poor-white city, while out on the other edge, which used to be where black people lived, there are town houses and ranch-style condominiums and shopping malls and all that.

Little Buford wears a black suit; a white carnation in his lapel. The carnation has seen better days. He hands us a pen saying BUFORD'S FUNERAL HOME 50 YRS. WE KNOW YOUR NEEDS. Would we please sign the register? At the top of the page is Lou's name and address, the date, underneath the signatures of Big and Walt Junior. No one else. "Miz Hart is in the Blue Room," Little Buford whispers. Next to the front desk is a door with an ornate bronze plate engraved BLUE ROOM. There is a high whining sound coming from the Blue Room door, wound up dog-pitch range, like radar.

"What's that?"

"Beats me."

We turn to Little Buford, who shrugs. We sign in. The door bursts open. Big comes out, followed by Walt Junior, both in a rush. "Crazy," Big is saying, Walt Junior hot on his heels. While the Blue Room door is open the sound increases in volume; goes down when the door is shut. Daddy sees me.

"Sue, thank goodness. Shall we dance?"

"Daddy, we just got here."

"Crazy. She's crazy."

Daddy has that wild look

"Who?"

"Lou."

"Lou's dead."

"I don't mean Lou. Louanne." Big rushes out and as soon as Walt Junior can get free from Bootsey, who is telling him there is not a stick of anything to take back to Hot Springs in the U-Haul, he follows Big.

Like Call Me Mike, Little Buford keeps smiling and nodding, nodding, smiling. With a sweep of his arm he urges us in.

Walt Three pushes open the Blue Room door.

These days funeral homes are like movie theaters: chopped up and puny. No grandeur, no size, no sense of occasion. Dead, so what, why should dead mean fancy? The Blue Room is simply that, a room painted blue. There are folding metal chairs, no rug. Our feet tip-tip on the linoleum as we traipse down a blue floor single file to view the remains of Lou. Mine tip-*top*. The room is dark except for Lou, and she is lit up like a museum display, a vision of bubble-gum pink and satiny baby blue. She reminds me of children in dance recitals I used to play for.

Louanne's in a chair by Lou's head, head back, hands up over her hair, turning. Her hands are going back and forth and back and forth, like somebody screwing, unscrewing light bulbs. The bulbs go in, come out, go in. Louanne's eyes are closed: the radar comes from here. Louanne, mourning the death of her mother nut-church fashion, is sitting at Lou's head making a noise that sounds like a nail going across a blackboard as she turns her hands back and forth over her dyed Church-of-God hairdo. When does she breathe? The sound goes on and on, through her nose and out, through her nose and out. We stand at Lou's feet. And Lou lies there like fierce Mrs. Roosevelt, looking ashamed if you ask me to be in pink and blue bubble-gum colors with a hanky in her hand and a daughter doing this nut-church act. After all, Lou was Presbyterian.

In the background, music plays . . . something soft and tinky, I can't make out the tune. Muzak has replaced SSS. Think: Muff never would have had his chance to sneak up on her.

Bootsey groans. "This takes the cake," she says without opening her teeth.

Mona comes up, bends over Louanne, and, as if shutting a window, draws down her screwing hands. They whisper together, and Mona takes a Kleenex from a box decorated with cattle brands, swaps it for a soiled one Louanne hands her. Louanne mops her brow. Mona motions us over. The Kleenex box says MAN-SIZED TISSUE. When Louanne hands Mona back the tissue she's just given her, Mona rakes out another.

Louanne upsweeps her hair in back, smooths down her bibbed stomach then comes over, hands out. "I'm so happy to see ya'll," she says, taking our hands one by one. Like we hadn't all just been in the circular driveway that morning squabbling like turkeys about tall and short and who would drive and eat roast beef.

Bootsey growls.

From the darkness of the folding chairs, Hugh Graustark ahems.

"Don't Mama look peaceful?" Louanne whines.

I'd forgotten how big Lou was.

We agree she looks peaceful and Louanne asks us to pray. Before we can answer, Louanne is on her knees, and so we get down on the blue linoleum too and Louanne says the Lord's Prayer for—we found out later—the fifth time that day. Muzak plays on: during ". . . for Thine is . . ." I figure out the tune: "Raindrops Keep Falling on My Head." I ask you. B. J. Thomas at Little Buford's Funeral Home.

When the prayer is over Walt Three takes Bootsey's hand, helps her up. "Lord," Bootsey mumbles with a grunt. "Lord God in Heaven, have you ever. And Lou a Presbyterian!"

Bootsey is an expert at talking without opening her teeth.

Mona, lurking in the shadows, tiptoes up offering Kleenex. But Louanne gives Mona a withering look and Mona retreats. In minutes, so do we. By the time we open the Blue Room door Louanne is back at her us-and-not-you sect whining, hands over her hair screwing, unscrewing. Little Buford wrings his hands, nods, smiles, thanks us for coming.

Big and Walt Junior are waiting by the Mercedes, silent as fat stones.

"Mama, you'll have to ride in the back with Daddy," Walt Three says flippantly. Bootsey growls, grits her teeth, gets in. Walt Junior follows. They are jammed up against one another in the rear, each grabbing a window roller to keep as much to the other side as possible. Big gets in the front, I sit on his lap On the way home, everyone is glum but Walt Three, who happily suggests we take a ride by the Martha Mitchell House, saying it's not far out of the way and it's painted this fabulous and perfect shade of sky-blue and we ought to see it. But nobody's enthusiastic so Walt Three takes us on home.

Five minutes after we get to the house, Louanne, Mona, and Hugh arrive. Louanne is over her grief. Methodically, she takes out the Tupperware and Bake-'n-Take, the Pyrex and aluminum throwaway containers. There are paper plates, and plastic utensils in a large grocery sack marked GRAUSTARK. Louanne says everything is ready. She does not bring out the roast beef.

"We'll eat on our laps."

"Where else?" Bootsey waves her hand signaling the lack of furniture. Louanne scowls, Bootsey gloats, Mona knits her brow. Bootsey and Louanne exchange looks. Big and Walt Junior dig in. Hugh sneaks off to the kitchen, to a nook behind the microwave. Boyd arrives.

We eat.

Graveside

"We are gathered . . ."

Not many. The Green House Nine plus a neighbor, a Mr. Bird, from down Walnut, who must be ninety. Mr. Bird is wearing khaki workclothes, a straw hat, and heavy leather shoes, doubtless so he can get on back to his gardening once this is done.

My Wife Evelyn, elbows crooked to serve her handbag, looks up into her husband's eyes with studied devotion. So does Walt Three.

". . . this pious woman of the church, this mother, this war widow, this wife, this Louanne Mildred . . ."

My Wife ahems, whispering Lou*ise* through smiling teeth.

". . . Lou*ise* Mildred Stovall shall we pray."

We are standing around Lou's rectangular hole, and there aren't any chairs. Call Me Mike's been gone too long, it seems. Standing over a hole in America is simply not done, not in Presbyterian or even nut-church graveside ceremonies.

Lou's behind us in her box, under Little Buford's canopy, laid out beneath a shower of vibrant glads.

Louanne has changed into head-to-toe black: shoes, stockings, dress, purse. Atop her yellow curls sits a black velvet clip-on circle hanging down from which is the merest suggestion of a veil. Her nose is in a Kleenex, her clothes are new: a tag remains, dangling from her armpit.

Red-faced Hugh Graustark is just behind Louanne; at her side, ever-present tissue-bearing Mona, eyes on Louanne.

". . . our sister, our mother, our aunt, our *friend* . . ."

Mother Stovall lies beyond where Lou will go. Beside her is Big Walt. Buck Hart's on down the line, out from under the trees. The graves are on a hillside overlooking Pine Bluff; beyond the road at the foot of the cemetery the land goes flat: nice view.

Beside Mona, silent Boyd Mullen turns his hat, his bald head reflecting the sun. His fingernails are edged in black. It was his car with the engine inside.

Bootsey's stiff as a lamppost. Walt Junior's a puddle. Walt Three is all sparkle, eyes on Call Me Mike.

Big's shaky. I feel him teetering. Since the scene at Little Buford's he's been hazier than ever. If I call his name, he might respond in wonderment, utterly confused, eyes rimmed and bleary and he will not know who I am. Another time, I'll say "Big . . . ?" and he'll look over sharply, and say "What?" and he'll be all right.

"Ah-*men.*"

There's a coughy rustle: the blessing is done. Big and I are uphill from the others, at the place where Lou's head will go.

Louanne hands Mona a damp tissue. As Mona pulls out a fresh one, she drops Louanne's. The tissue floats, Mona snatching as if at a mosquito. The soiled tissue lands at the grave's edge. Just in time, Mona grabs it up. Louanne looks mad enough to spit and Mona, glancing back over her shoulder at Boyd, says "Shew."

My own prayer is simply to make it through this service so Big and I can go home.

Leaving Mother Stovall's house, there was another big to-do about cars. Louanne seems determined to keep us all together, under her eagle eye, to contain conspiracies. This time, however, I put my foot—arched in its hunch—down: I insisted we take Big's car. We were, after all, leaving for home from the graveyard.

"But, Sue," Louanne protested, "won't ya'll come back afterward to eat?"

I said no.

"Then at least come get you something to take. We've got all this food." With her hand Louanne indicated the Tupperware and Pyrex, in her eyes a faint glimmer, inspired by the hope that if we were leaving postservice we would not be planning to stake a claim on the house. I said no thank you to the food.

Hugh rode to the cemetery with us, having managed somehow to escape his wife's grasp. Louanne rode with Boyd and Mona in Little Buford's hearse. Then us. Then the Mercedes.

"I hate it when people do that," Daddy said in the car.

"Do what?" said Hugh, pulling a flask from his pocket.

"Go on at funerals. Nothing against Louanne, you understand, Hugh?"

"Go ahead, Big Daddy," said Hugh. "Go against her. I ain't been against her in years." Hugh hee-heed at his joke. "Get it?" He slapped Big's shoulder. "I ain't been against her in years."

"I hope she's better at the cemetery."

"Hmmh," said Hugh and he took a slug of roogle. "Don't hold your breath."

So far she's been tame. We are all however getting a bit woozy standing in one position while Call Me Mike preaches over the edge of the open grave. To our right, Call Me Mike is at Lou's waist, Louanne and Hugh, her shoulder. We're the head. The Walt Stovall Juniors face Call Me Mike from the other side of the grave's waist. My Wife Evelyn's beside her husband at the stomach; our guest, Mr. Bird is in My Wife's position across the hole. Boyd and Mona are stuck like glue to Louanne's backside.

". . . the Easter season is upon us, the time for gratitude and meditation, a time when we should look into our hearts to see what filth is there, to be cast out. The stone has been rolled away. The miracle is upon us: spring, salvation, resurrection, the life."

And Lou?

". . . ROLLED AWAY!"

Walt Three's eyes widen. He gives Call Me Mike a sparkling look. Call Me Mike frowns; in the middle of a sentence, he hesitates.

From my position at the head of the grave I can look down the cemetery hillside and see the entire Arkansas landscape, nearly to the horizon. Out there is a body of water somewhere; in the sunlight it sparkles. To the south of us there are thunderheads, a deepening color. We may catch a rainstorm on the way home. To the north, on the road below us, a van approaches, a putty-color breadtruck-type van, whizzing toward the cemetery gates faster than bullets. The thunderheads hang low, near the horizon caught in trees.

"Shall we pray."

I swear Walt Three answers a flirtatious "Mmmm-*hmmm.*"

The van turns into the cemetery drive, comes through the iron gate, races down the gravel road, parks by the LTD.

". . . in our loneliness and time of need, oh Lord *help* us . . ."

Heads down, our eyes are all up, as we watch to see who is coming. Louanne, facing away from the gravel road, hearing the crunch, seeing our eyes, surreptitiously edges her head back over her shoulder, like a right-handed pitcher checking a runner on first.

Big rocks.

". . . give us some consolation oh Lord, a sign . . ."

Big rocks faster. One hand is reaching down, toward his belt, then below it.

"Daddy?"

"Rhinos, hippos, it's coming out."

A sandy-faced man steps down from the driver's seat of the van. A tall woman in loose clothes gets out the other door. The man goes to the side of the van to open a sliding door. Two small children pop out; a girl in plaid pinafore and long socks, a boy in short pants. The children run toward us, screaming.

"BIG DADDY BIG DADDY BIG DADDY."

"Amen."

Daddy is fooling with his fly, knees bent.

"The fat is squeezing out," he says.

It's Brook and Steve. They join hands and come toward us, like an insurance-calendar couple Brook takes long loping steps.

"BIG DADDY BIG DADDY BIG DADDY." The children's arms are out. Their bright blond heads bounce up the hill toward us.

"Ashes to ashes, dust to dust, may the Lord bless you and keep you . . ."

He's opened it. Big's fly is down. I reach for his hand, digging into the zipper.

My hand slips. I touch not fingers, but hair.

"Sue!"

I draw back. He zips up.

Brook and Steve are nearly running. The children still scream for Big Daddy.

". . . make his face to shine upon you . . ."

"And give you a piece." Did I imagine Walt Three said that? Yes. I imagined it. Walt Three is gone from his place. Where is Walt Three? Everything is cuckoo.

Ess and Pee run up to Daddy, grabbing him at the knees, squeezing.

Big looks down in a panic, thinking whogs and rhinotamuses have got him. Recognizing his grandchildren, he comes to.

"Ess and Pee," he says. "You old rascals." He picks them up one by one and loves them up. They hug his big neck and wait for jokes and fun.

The worry, however, does not leave Big's eyes.

Steve comes. We hug.

"I thought you weren't coming," I whisper, as Call Me Mike's benediction continues.

"Brook . . . *we* decided at the last minute."

Nervous and indecisive, pale as milk, Steve is here one second, gone the next. He's wearing glasses now but his pudgy freckled face is as childlike as ever.

He looks to see where Brook is.

The women have gathered; Brook, Louanne, and Bootsey, Mona close behind.

". . . and give you peace. Amen."

Louanne, in the hot middle, resorts to theatrics. She tunes up. Her hands shoot in the air. It starts. Screw, unscrew. The radar, nonstop.

"Ma-MAH!" she screams. "Ma-MAAHHHH!"

"Now now, Louanne," Mona says patting Louanne's shoulder. "Now now."

Brook stands back and in profile I notice her rounded waistline.

"She's pregnant," Steve explains.

"I thought you weren't—"

Steve shrugs. Brook stares at Louanne. Bootsey's teeth clack but her lips don't move. Hugh, seeing his chance, ducks behind an oak tree fat enough to hide him. Boyd stares at the grave, still turning his hat. Mr. Bird disappears down the hill. Call Me Mike and My Wife Evelyn smile and nod, like brides at the reception, waiting for congratulations. My Wife Evelyn's knuckles are clenched, gripping her purse. She needs a More.

But Louanne's nut-church act is not working. Bootsey and Brook are in hard conversation over to the side, paying no attention to the light-bulb routine.

". . . will clearly provides," Bootsey is saying when Louanne butts in.

Taking a step toward the casket, Louanne throws her hands over her face. "Mama!" She screams, and runs beneath Little Buford's canopy to throw herself upon the gladioli. A pink head snaps, falls. Mona gathers it up, drops it in her purse, snaps the bag closed.

"Not even in the ground, Mama," Louanne says. *"Not even in the ground!"*

"I'm not listening to this." Bootsey sets her shoulders, "Not that caterwauling again."

"There is no 'Mama' now, Louanne," Brook explains to Louanne's shuddering black back. "Dead is dead and now is the time to choose."

Ess and Pee run up to Steve, to ask if they can go look at Alucard's house, pointing to a mosquelike mausoleum. Steve hesitates, looks toward Brook, who is a grave's width away, takes a breath and, as if deciding to declare war, says yes.

Call Me Mike and My Wife Evelyn are headed down the hill toward their car, My Wife Evelyn nearly in a jog. In the peach-colored 450 SL, sitting tall behind the wheel, Walt Three waits.

"Daddy!"

The sound of Steve's voice stops us all. It is not a voice accustomed to screaming and it is screaming now and, not used to being pushed so, sounds more like a bubbled croak than words.

We turn toward Steve. And then there is a sound. A rushing,

watery sound, a gushing. A waterfall rushing. It comes from Big.

The long yellow stream is perfectly aimed. A rainbow arc, from the top of the grave it shoots straight down into where Lou's face will lie . . . her Early nose and Mrs. Roosevelt jaw, her eyelids sewn shut. Discreetly, Big holds himself with a careful hand so that his penis cannot be seen. But the stream coming from him is as thick and pungent as horse piss. In Lou's grave it makes a steamy well; on Big's face is a satisfied look, head atilt, eyes rolled heavenward.

". . . Lou's chest," he says. "Not socks, not birds. Eye. Me."

No one moves.

We wait. There is nothing else to do. We listen. We are statues of listening.

Big pisses and pisses. We wait.

More piss. An avalanche of piss, a monsoon, more piss than a normal bladder can hold.

Piss on piss. Puddle on puddle. Bubbles, froth. The grave gets deeper. Piss digs a hole. Big pisses on. A Niagara of piss.

Finally, there is a lessening. The stream turns to a mere pour, a running trickle, a trickle, and then drops . . . drops . . . drop. Drip. He wrings it. Drip. Bends his knees, tucks it in, zips up, hands crossed over himself.

Standing at his sister's grave, Big looks beatific.

"Good God," says Steve at my shoulder. And we all stand there. No one has moved.

"Oh my, Jimmy," says Walt Junior. Bootsey punches him.

Llavots's breaths are held. For once, no one knows what to say. I run to my brother.

"We're leaving, Steve. Right now."

"We just got here."

And Steve and I have a conversation as if piss weren't in the grave, as if nothing had gone wrong. He tells me about the gun club closing and being out of work and I'm amazed we're doing it but sometimes things go that way. Meantime Brook comes over and like a sturdy nurse, practiced in trauma, leads Big down the hill.

Ess and Pee cavort about the mausoleum. From behind the oak, Hugh takes a healthy swig.

"We're coming to Houston."

"We?"

"Us, Brook and me. The kids. We thought we'd visit Mama, then you. Is it all right?"

Brook opens the door of the LTD, sees Big safely inside. Louanne is standing at grave's edge, mouth in a steady hang. Speechless, she is staring at her uncle's piss.

"We don't want the house, Steve."

"We?"

"Big. Me. Him. You do what you want. He doesn't want the house."

Steve's eyes jump. Something. Certainly he would never leave Brook's precious Morgan? But something. I turn to go.

"Steve?"

"Yes."

"Call Mama first."

On the way down the hill to the LTD my heel snaps off completely. Taking both shoes off, I finish the trip barefoot. At the wheel of the Mercedes, Walt Three is in a state, gripping the steering wheel to steady his hands.

"I'd forgotten," he says, "how much I hate funerals. I was okay until the benediction, ashes to ashes and all that."

I reach my head and arms through the car window. Walt Three and I kiss like lovers.

"Come to the opening, Sue. August. Don't forget. On Leon's birthday. The ninth. I'll send an invitation."

I promise to try.

"Don't forget the DG." He points to the trunk of the LTD. The Depression glass. I promise.

By the time I get behind the wheel, Big is snoozing quietly, his regular nap.

Grateful, I crank the car.

Up the hill, graveside hags and harridans are emerging. Brook's long arms flail the air, Bootsey's elbows fly, Louanne's hands are up, begging attention. Her hair is starting to come loose. Curls hang limp. Ess and Pee play tag among the gravestones. Uncles, husbands, fathers—the men—stand still, turning their hats and waiting. Another truck has pulled up beside Steve's van. Inside, cemetery workers patiently wait out this family squabble, patient because, having already punched in on grave-digging clocktime, their meters are clicking. *Bink.* They shuffle a deck of cards, deal out a hand of gin.

Call Me Mike and My Wife Evelyn are long gone.

High in the swaying pines against a perfect sky I imagine I see Mother Stovall in the needles, head back, laughing and shaking her mop. The dust flies, sprinkles down. Havoc ensues.

Her will be done, amen.

We back out.

Girl of My on the Road Dreams

Under a blue light on Beale Street, dancing: The Hot Blue Rose in August.

Memphis: home of the blues and the Peabody, of Elvis and white rock and roll; of the girl shaking and moving her feet, doing fancy twists and dips. Me. Heart high because feet move. The dream is to dance. My dream. Fangs appear: I am the other me. Deep into night on the road, the darktime strutting one comes out. Alucard.

Elvis sings "That's All Right, Mama," Tina does "Proud Mary," The Questionnaires slide and swoon and she/I is/am dancing to a New Blue Day hot August beat.

Doing a snaky step Walt Three flings his long arms. His ear is pink sweet as a baby's. His hand makes swooping fishlike arcs. My face still carries his scent, where he laid his hand in the cellar.

Emphasis on every beat. One-two-three-four. Once you have the beat the song falls in line. No beat stronger than another, it moves into your head, determines the pace of your heart, pumping your blood in its tempo, three-four.

I/me. June Day. Rock-steady.
Disco blue. Under a cobalt dome.

Across on I-30 down through Texarkana, we turn onto 59 again. The nightmare stretch. A New Orleans station tunes in, playing country. Sad songs about married love and the end of it. "Mama."

Listening to Willie Nelson sing "My Heroes Have Always Been Cowboys" to the rhythm of Big's snores, I fight to stay awake.

Steady. Get the beat; the song will come.

A commercial comes on, selling thousand-dollar Bibles made of once in a lifetime leather, the proceeds of which go to an organization called Hallelujah, Inc.

Tammy's up next, singing "Two-Story House" with George.

Listening to country, I head south. Low clouds cover the stars and the wafer of a moon I saw last night. On my way, I sing along with Tammy, watching out as I go for hungry east Texas police.

The Queen of Shades

The LTD lights sweep across the small frame house. Lights are on in the living room and kitchen; otherwise the house is dark.

Linda opens the front door, motioning me in. She is dressed in jeans and a loose cotton shirt. Her feet are bare.

"Let's go in the kitchen. Caroline fell asleep waiting. She's on the couch with her suitcase."

"I told you it would be late. Actually we made good time. It's only two."

In the kitchen she draws me close. "I was so worried."

"I told you we'd be late. I don't want to stay long. Daddy's asleep but he might wake up. And Caroline has school."

"He'll sleep," Linda says firmly. "You want a glass of juice? Some coffee?"

"Coffee."

She gets out a glass jar filled with coffee beans. "How was it?"

I give her a quick rundown, leaving out the cellar and piss. "And are you ready? Brook is pregnant. They're coming."

Linda turns on her grinder to pulverize the beans. "Coming?"

"Tomorrow, with the kids. To visit you. Then me."

Linda runs hot water in a pot, folds a paper cone, fills it with the ground coffee. But her hand trembles and some of the coffee spills.

"How far gone is Brook?"

"I don't know. She barely shows. But she's tall."

She lights a cigarette, watching the kettle of water. "I thought they were finished with babies."

"So did I. Something's going on. Something funny. I couldn't tell what and . . . Linda."

Like a startled child she turns from the stove. "What?"

"Walt Three and I found the cellar. Everybody was gone and we went down, just the two of us. There were things down there. I found something of yours. In a hatbox. Hidden."

She checks the water. "What?"

"A notebook. A black notebook. I brought it. I didn't mean to pry but I read some of it. What I could. It's a wreck; the pages tear."

Linda looks blank. "I don't remember."

"You don't remember writing it?"

"No"

"That year we lived there?"

"No. I forgot a lot of things. Deliberately put them out of my mind."

When the coffee is finished, Linda lifts the wet filter from the pot, dumps the grounds into a can marked COMPOST, throws the filter away. She pours a cup, then sits at the table across from me.

Close up, her age shows. There are deep lines around her eyes and her lids are crepey. Her pale skin weeps in folds. Behind the glassy sparkle in her eyes—way back—is a leveled-out plane of utter weariness.

"Where is it?" Her hand is trembling.

"In the trunk of the car. I wasn't sure you wanted it. I just didn't want anybody else to have it."

"I want it. Oh yes."

"Well. I didn't know."

Cigarette smoke sifts up through her piled-up hair into a kind of halo.

"Great coffee."

"Yes. Joseph brought it. The beans are from—"

"Yes?"

"Oh—Jamaica. Blue Mountain, I think."

"You know Mother Stovall's house is gone?"

"I heard Lou remodeled it."

"Remodeled? It's gone. Fake brick is over the clapboard. She turned it into phony Colonial Whispering Mesquite. Faces Walnut instead of Pecan."

"I can't imagine."

"No. You can't."

"What else did you take from the cellar"

"Some things of Big Walt's. Ledgers, piano rolls, a watch fob for Big. Some hatmaking supplies from Mother Stovall. An old leather coin purse."

"You twist it to the side and it opens?"

"Yes."

"I remember Big Walt used to offer me coins from it. He'd lift my skirt with his cane and say—" She laughs. "Big Walt was awful."

"Also, a cream-colored baby brush, hand-painted with flowers. I thought it might be mine."

"No. I'd have taken it if it was yours. Probably Louanne's."

"Well. It's mine now. Oh, and you won't believe it. For the boys. Wrapped in tissue good as new."

She shakes her head.

"The rattles."

"The snake rattles?"

"Yes."

A door slams.

Daddy. He stumbles in, hair in horns, eyes puffed and traveling. He has no idea where he is.

The Jack of Diamonds scored. They have a new kind of, you know, on the water, a riff? No. Rough. No, not rough. Something. First one to get to the end is king. Jack of Diamonds did it. Zip. Fast as this.

He holds up his left hand and makes his thumb-to-finger tracing sign, up and down the angle there. He watches his finger go up, down. We watch.

"Is he awake?" Linda whispers.

"I don't know. Don't say anything. Daddy, let's go back to the car."

I take his arm. Meek as seaweed he goes with me to the car. His door is open. He slides willingly in. As I turn to close the door, he takes my hand. *The pediatrician said to miter the flashing where the green bird's eye is,* he says. And then, clear as anything, "Did you tell her? You didn't tell her what I did, did you? Don't tell her, Sue."

His hand drops. He closes his eyes, collapsing.

"Here." I hand Linda the notebook. "I think he's safe for a while but I don't want to chance it for long."

She stares at the book, clearly recognizing it, but does not take it. "I wonder who found it. I wonder if they read it. It must have been Mother Stovall. Mother Stovall put it where Lou wouldn't find it."

She takes the notebook, runs her hand over the cover, pressing down, as if to feel what's inside. "You were the main thing, Sue. When I remember that house and time, mostly I see you. You were the prettiest baby. Fat face and and dimples, that high Stovall forehead. Mother Stovall said it meant smart. Lou said it might be water on the brain. Oh, Lou was shameless. All in all, the only happy times were with you."

"From the book you were pretty miserable."

"What does it say?" She lights another cigarette. In the ashtray, the other one's still smoking.

"Here."

A page cracks when I turn it, rips down one side.

" 'I live in the in-between. In spaces between acts and table and words. Life is in shadows and shades, in light trapped inside glass. Rainbows in windowpanes, the reflection of a lampshade in Mother S.'s glasses. A green cup held to light makes birds on the tablecloth. The Queen of Shades, I am queen. The Queen rules the in-between long live.' " There is a silence between us, thick enough to cut.

Her blue eyes jump. She stands; sits back down, looks beyond me as she talks. "I nursed you the entire time we were at Mother Stovall's. After lunch I'd take you off to ourselves in the bedroom and we'd be alone awhile. That was the best time of the day. I'd nurse you then put you down for a nap. Logy with milk you'd sink straight down to sleep. You were so fat. But it was a sign of health for a baby to be fat then. Louanne was thin and we were constantly trying to fatten her up. Your little thighs were pure rolls. And we'd go to the bedroom the two of us and afternoon light would be streaming through those windows Mother Stovall rubbed so hard with ammonia to keep clean. And . . . that was the good time of day." Her eyes close, then open, and she looks toward the ceiling. There is a picture of her posed like that, blue eyes lifted to the light. A door-to-door photographer took it; draped her shoulders in velvet, asked her to lift her chin. Daddy never liked that picture. He said she looked whorish. "So fat. I'd rub oil in the creases. Then sprinkle baby powder on top. You'd drop off sweet and milky. It was during that first deep sleep of your nap that I wrote in the notebook. I remember now. I hid it under your crib mattress. When you'd fallen asleep I'd slide it out. Like a dirty book."

She laughs.

"After a while I'd go back into the kitchen to help with the dish-drying or whatever there was to do. There was always something. Mother Stovall was a maniac about housekeeping and after Big Walt died she was even worse. Lou would give me a look when I came in and I would have to look away, feeling guilty for my secret because, in truth, I *had* been up to something. This." She points to the notebook. "Lou couldn't nurse Louanne. She had no milk. It killed her soul that I ran with it, milk in my lap. Jimmy had to pump it off.

"Then when we moved to Memphis—" she stops abruptly.

"Tell, Linda, go on. What?"

But there's a leap in the story. Something she's keeping for herself.

"I had to change my routine. In Pine Bluff you were just learning to walk by the time we moved out, but Memphis? Lord."

"What?"

"Oh, I've told you. About running away."

"But the notebook."

"That's the point. Once you started running away, our afternoons changed. In fact, I don't think I wrote in it again for years. Not until—"

"Ophelia."

"Yes. Not until then." She changes the subject quickly and I get it: there are other notebooks: Ophelia notebooks. None from Memphis. She has been writing the whole time. She always had a secret self, a June Day, Shannon Day, hidden behind motherhood and names. I don't believe for a minute she didn't remember the black notebook.

"I'd put you to sleep, think you were down for the afternoon, go about my business, maybe take a little nap myself, and zip you'd be gone. Quiet? A perfect criminal. I never heard a thing. You'd sneak up from your nap and take off. Going, no-telling. Going actually nowhere. Just going. Up and out and down the street. We had to call the police several times. And every time you did it you'd come home with your pants full. You'd go off by yourself, to mess in your pants in secret, you understand? That and eating dirt were your two private things. But I always knew. The look in your eyes always gave you away. You never were good at hiding your thoughts."

She laughs softly.

"I caught you at it once—running away—and took your picture from behind. You're on a sidewalk, trucking down, heading out, on the road . . . to somewhere, anywhere, just going for the sake of the trip. Not going to get someplace. The sun is on your hair. It's pulled back with a barrette, thin and wispy and feathery gold. You're in overalls and your foot's up, moving you on. The sidewalk's cracked; tilted. You're slanted the other way to counterbalance, fat arms up. So fat.

"I remember those overalls. They were red. And the blouse you have on is one Dolly made. The collar had embroidered bears on it."

She looks at me.

"Were the stone urns there, Sue? By the front steps?"

"The front steps weren't even there."

"That's where you'd get your dirt. 'Diddent eat dirt, Mama,' you'd say. 'Diddent.' "

"Then what?"

"What what?"

"Happened next. When did I stop running away?"

"When Steve was born. I had a hard time with Steve, one thing and another. I was sick a lot. Jimmy had to work odd hours, long hours. You were my little nurse, caring for him and me both. You gave up your precious *bavvah* when Steve came —bottle, you sucked it all the time—and stopped running away. I don't know about the dirt. Maybe that went too. I needed your help and you gave it."

"Well. You were a good mother, Linda. You know it?"

She looks up. I have never said that before. It frightens us both. The weariness in her eyes comes to the surface.

"No. I should have stuck to what I believed. Been this Queen of Shades notebook me, not Miss Bridgeplaying what I thought I was supposed to. But I didn't know. There were things you didn't question then. I have never been daring, or brave. The things in the notebook seemed then like so much craziness. Plain crazy. And until the wreck I was terrified all the time of what people would think of every single thing I did or said. Dolly did some of that. Some I don't know just *was*."

She stops, opens her mouth to continue, then presses her lips together as if to keep herself quiet. She will never give it all away. Some things she will save for herself, keep secret to use in her work. Behind her blue eyes, she's left me.

To rouse her, I reach across the table, to touch her hand lightly. Brushing a cigarette stub, I dislodge it from its perch. It collapses into the well of the ashtray.

"I have to go, Linda. I still have a drive ahead."

She comes to.

"Stay. Spend the night?"

"Me and Big and Joseph? No thanks. And the boys are there. I can't. Let's gather up Caroline."

In the living room, Caroline is wedged into a corner of the couch, head dropped forward, hair wild and loose about her face. She wakens instantly, wide-awake the minute her eyes open, like Big. Her pink satin overnight Neiman-Marcus bag shaped like a tennis shoe is over her shoulder. In sleep, she cradles it.

" 'Bye, Linda. And thank you." Caroline gives Linda a brief kiss and goes out.

Linda and I follow. At the front door we stop a minute. She's still holding the notebook. There's more, something she's not saying having to do with the notebooks, having to do with her whole life and maybe, maybe, things being the way they are, with mine. But there's no time now and we say our good-byes.

When we back out of the drive, Linda is in the doorway, waving. Light from overhead shines through her hair, making it silver. Behind the house is the blue-black lake. The moon is high now, out from under the clouds. It hangs dead straight over her. Stars out here are astonishing. They dot the black sky like so much silver glitter, tossed onto a swatch of black. From here you can't see the lake. She waves. On the gravel road in front of her house, I stop where the mailboxes are, at an intersecting Y. There are no cars this time of night, but I stop, and when I look in the rearview mirror, she is still standing under the porch light, in her hand the worn black book.

The LTD takes off heavily in the gravel. Big's radial tires spin a minute, throwing rocks, and then we are gone, headed south down 59 toward the Loop and home.

Joseph is asleep, one of his dead unshakable times. Linda curves against his back, pressing her breasts into him, rubbing her hand down his chest. His penis is tucked between his thighs like a child's. He does not stir. Linda turns away.

Mother Stovall's house hangs like a crystal in her mind. She never forgot a second of it, she had wondered time and again what happened to the notebook, who found it, read it; why she had left it, if it was some kind of troublemaking gesture not to have remembered to take it.

It was her secret self, the rest of her. Until the wreck she'd confined that part to paper. In Ophelia, unknown to Jimmy, his friends had propositioned her: the banker he had such trust in, the one-armed handsome lawyer, numerous drunks, and golfers led on by the glassy blue sparkle of her eyes . . . like mirrors to see their own reflection in. She turned every one of them down. She had her notebooks and that, for a very long time, had been enough. In Oxford, Mississippi, when she was a secret wife hidden from coaches and Ole Miss, it was all she had. She wrote and wrote. Secret wife, secretly missing a period. Holed up secretly in an apartment, she'd lie in bed and feel her stomach, wondering. She wrote everything she felt. She had tried to read the notebooks from time to time but there was so much pain there; she couldn't bear it. In memory, those times had become washed out, paled, smoothed over. In the notebook, her days were sharp as blades. Then, years later, the siege of accidents began. The trip to Hawaii; the knife, the broken rib. The notebooks from that time are fat; they go on and on. She can barely stand to read them now. The notebooks are scarier than dying. When she came to from dying she asked Dr. Creekmore to bring paper, pens: she wrote that too.

Even as a girl. All her feelings, the things that got stirred up. *Made for sex,* Dolly told her, and Linda knew it was true. She was safe from it, as long as it was only words.

Reaching up, she pulls out the pins in her hair, to let it fall past her shoulders. When she smooths it from her face, it makes a fan behind her. She curls on her side, away from Joseph. The tips of her hair graze his ear. Turning in her direction, he cups her to him.

Tomorrow. Brook is coming . . . she checks the clock. Not tomorrow; today. Brook, Steve, her grandbabies. Ess and Pee. Brook, Queen of the Instant, Mistress of the Real. Linda trembles with dread, imagining Brook's uncomplicated eyes.

Joseph pulls her close. Not that he's waking; by habit. Her pretty boy, wait until he hears. Tomorrow she'll be a grandmother, to babies he's never met.

Something will happen. It will.

Nearly three. If she could glue the numbers still, stop Brook in her tracks! Breathe. Breath is all. She turns on her back out of Joseph's hold and begins to relax, starting at toes, moving up. Soon she is heavy, sinking into the mattress, breathing deep. Relaxation moves through her thighs and up, to her mouth, eyes, and . . . concentrating, she is nearly there, when something —a quick wisp of light; something too soon to name—stops her. And then gets back into it, folding back into the space Joseph has in sleep saved for her. She will wake him early. Wake him up with her skin. *Complete the circle before the wheel makes its revolution.*

———

As the car slows for the Houston off ramp, Caroline rouses.
"We home?"

"Close."

"Mama?"

"What."

"Do you like Joseph?"

"I like him fine," I answer, dodging. "Do you?"

"He's weird."

"Weird how?"

"I don't know. He says weird things in that funny accent and
he's supposed to be funny and he never is. How come he talks
that way?"

"He's from Connecticut."

"A girl in my class is from Newark. She doesn't talk like that."

"I think Newark's not the same. But it was nice of him to
come get you, wasn't it?"

"Mmmmm," she murmurs. Agreeing?

Caroline flops against the backseat. We are quiet the rest of the
way home. I've lied to her about Joseph, once again confining
the June Day heart of my hidden self to dark streets and back
alleys. June Day is awash in lust for Joseph, I could tell my
daughter. She'd like to suck his bones, that's the truth, dear
bleeding daughter. But I can't bring it off. *You know.*

I wheel off the freeway down Kirby, past a CITY OF HOMES sign,
through our sleeping town within a city, down the better streets
of POP, over to our section, POP's lesser edge.

Our house looks like Astroworld: every light in the house
seems to be on. From the living room, the steady late-night glow
of the TV makes a blue square on the window.

"Caroline. We're home. Caroline?"

She has fallen back asleep. Her head is tilted, exposing her
neck. Her mouth is open in a tender childlike O, her hands are
flat against the seat as if holding her up. She wears blue jeans
and a soft print blouse with tiny pink buttons and a Peter Pan

collar. Her legs are slightly spread. A dark stain runs down the seam of her crotch.

Oh Princess.

I cup her knee with my hand. Waking, she draws back. "We're home."

Reaching for her pink satin bag, Caroline gets out and disappears in the house, without a word.

"Daddy."

"HUH." He shivers.

"Time. We're home."

He sits straight up, looking deep at me, as if I were something he was studying.

"Your mother needs help."

"Daddy—"

"The police. If they put her in jail. . . ."

I don't know whether to play along or correct him. "What?"

"She'll be in jail." He pauses to check his vision, making sure he has it right.

"She's at the commune, Sue. They're having an orgy. She didn't want to go at first, but her ears have holes. The hippies and the niggers are there, dagos and Jews. They have ventilated Linda. I mean. No. Crenulated her hypotenuse. Aerated the diatribe. . . . Laminated . . ."

He knows what he wants to say but the words are coming out wrong.

He holds up his big left hand, palm toward me.

"Daddy."

He makes his sign. "What?"

"We're home. It's four-thirty."

"Oh, home? I didn't help drive. Shall we dance?" That quickly, he's back.

"Jive and mambo."

Heavy as wet clothes, we unfold from our long-distance positions; stretch; lumber up the drive into the house.

Daddy zeroes straight for the bathroom. I hear the familiar

sounds, aspirin bottle popped open, the childproof *ping*, pills shaken, bottle set down, water runs. He sighs, in advance of the relief ahead, then barrels out the bathroom door, aimed straight for Robby's bed without good night or undressing. He did not replace the aspirin bottle top.

The house is a mess. Clothes all over, newspapers, food, skateboards, and baseball gear. The boys are asleep on homemade mats in the living room in front of a buzzing TV.

Reaching to snap it off, I step into a bowl of sour milk, tipping it. A clot of white stuff slops out. A limp Cheerio hops onto my toe. I lean across Robby, push the ON/OFF button, remove the Cheerio. Robby stirs. Ricky sits up a second then falls back to his pillow. Sometimes—even with his dark Italian hair and skin—Ricky looks just like Big.

On my way to bed, I turn off the rest of the lights.

Big starts to snore.

Chessboard

"Did it rain?"

"Big duh, Mom."

Robby's reading the Cheerios box, eating cereal. It's morning, too early.

"Well?"

"Look out the window. The backyard is solid water."

The box offers Cheersbees: a Frisbee with a hole in the center for $1.50 and boxtops.

"When?"

"Only as soon as you left, that's all. It was great, Mom, just great."

"But it was pure blue sunshine when we left."

Robby shrugs. "So?"

I can't get a hold on this conversation. All I'm getting is chips and dust, nothing solid to hold on to. Ricky left early to play Horse behind the school. Big took Caroline. Robby and I are alone.

"Did everything go all right?"

"Oh it was great, Mom, just great. Asshole Caroline left, then buggerbrain Ricky invited about twenty-five guys over and they started puking around." Robby does a hunchback pantomime, chin out, mouth down, neck stretched, poke poke with his head.

If I hadn't brought it up he wouldn't have thought of it but now that he has it's making him angry all over again just remembering.

"What kind of puking around?"

He drops his spoon. It slides into his bowl, disappearing among the floating O's.

"Oh, nothing much. Just crapping up all my things. Just eating the stuff you left. The cookies, the Pop-Tarts, the Nacho-flavored Doritos. Oh, just all the bananas and my Hi-C."

His tongue drips junior high sarcasm.

"I had to go, Robby. I couldn't help it."

"Let's see. Number one, Shawn cratered my X-15 and left the top off the glue. Number two, he said he'd pay me back but he won't. Number three, Kevin got into my baseball cards and number four, stole George Brett. Only my favorite player. That's all."

He looks down. Finding his spoon vanished, he pushes the bowl away. He'd rather do without than get caught looking.

"Next time you go someplace I'm going to invite about thirty kids over. Little kids. Tell them they can play with Ricky's skateboard and glove. Watch them rack up his Super-Go and his Kryptonics. See how he likes it."

He won't. This is Robby's revenge. It has to be somebody's fault, somebody safe, namely me. Ricky's too tough. The world has done Robby wrong; I represent the world. He is out to get me. Easy mark.

"Did Ricky do Field Day?"

"Mom, I'm trying to tell you. It was black night in the afternoon. The electricity went off."

"They postponed Field Day?"

"Big duh. I have to go."

He gathers up his stuff, starts out.

"Robby?" He turns. "I'm sorry your stuff got racked up."

For a moment he sheds his protective crustiness and is there in his skin where he stands, my reedy middle baby in his Superlite Adidas. His thin fingers remind me of Walt Three.

" 'Bye." He closes the door.

It opens.

"I forgot."

"What?"

"I need money. I'm joining the band. $32.54 made out to Keyboard City."

"The band? The . . . well, here. I'll write a check. The band? What instrument? That's great. When did it happen?"

"Not today, I'm late. Saxophone. Yesterday."

"Saxophone?"

"They tested my mouth. Said it fit." He shrugs: so? If it doesn't work out he won't have lost much.

"Robby—"

" 'Bye, Mom." He's gone.

The band. Robby?

A saxman. Honk and blow. Romantic noodles, soulful swoons, wind instead of fingers, who'd have thought it. A wind man. A Questionnaire.

And Field Day's been postponed: I can still do my Team Father chores. Rats.

The house is dark and damp and quiet and I'm going back to bed. Cowtown Crud has returned. Mildew. The dishes from last night are piled up all over the kitchen. Never mind: back to bed. It's Tuesday, time to move. Get the funeral out of my mind. Time to go sing. Make a Friday singing date, introduce "Mama." Sitting alone in dark dampness June Day comes alive. Like vampires at midnight, or Namflow with the moon. The snake rattles will go to Robby. The watch fob to Rick.

On his way to the Zodiac, after letting Princess Grace off at school, something like fireflies dance in front of Big's eyes. Sparkles. Like waterflies.

Everything seemed possible once, every dream. Now look. Door-to-door like Bob Hope, sample case in hand: HAVE I GOT A DEAL FOR YOU. Crap. Of all the bright possibilities not one paid off. Down the drain every one, fast as shit from a pig. Drag him down. Somebody always got in his way.

Hot Socks was a good time. The Shine. Those were good times.

He pulls into the parking garage with the Pisces sign over the doors. The garage is cool and dark: the driveway angles down. As the LTD moves down, water rises. It starts to fill the car, to his chin and higher, over his head. He is under. Whales swim about; a seahorse looking prim, a turtle the size of a bed. A lazy creature lumbers by, slow and moody, an underwater cow, a baby is in the sea grass, a monkey. Watch out. The cow might eat them. A black man swims to the LTD, demanding rent. Big must protect his family, fight the black men, he must daddy his family. When he opens his car door to defend himself, water pours in.

When Sue was born he said to himself, Jim Stovall it is time you did something with your life. Time to stop fooling around, time to be a man, to father that button-faced baby, to daddy that forehead so high it wrinkles, the fat rolls in her thighs,

Stovall eyes. Llavots nose. Went to medical school. Stayed awhile. Didn't take long to get an MD those days but not long was too long. Things happened. Linda had no black lace and there was his baby girl, needing to be daddied. Anyway, he reasoned: Why serve when you can sell? He found Ophelia, took wife and baby girl, hit the road. From then on the world was divided into territories and routes; time was making calls. Town to town he went, sample case in hand. *What'd you bring me,*

Daddy? Sue would say when he came in from the road. *All my love, sugar. All my love.* But it wasn't enough. She wanted presents. Things. The right kind of skirts. Lipstick, stockings, black lace . . . no, the black lace was for Linda. Linda. My wife, what wife, I have no . . . everybody all over the northern part of Mississippi remembers him still. How he would roll in the door, dark eyes shining making jokes bringing light with him when he came, saying HOWZ IT GOING, WHOZ IN CHARGE, WHATZ THE NAME OF THE TUNE? Saying LET IT ROLL, FOLKS, LET IT ROLL and his trademark HOW ARE YOU GETTING ALONG WITH YOUR WORK. Life rolled in with Jim Stovall. No wonder he could sell tadpoles to frogs. Happy was having it going. Feeling that zing when you got hooked in. Pow! One hop. A hot hand.

The streets are slanted. Big is atilt and so the world is. Watch him.

The black man knocks on his window, Big having locked the car door against his threat. The black man will drown. Black people can't swim. Remembering the swift black girl, Big takes out his wallet, slides it under the seat.

Never had been a divorce in the Stovall family. Still had not. He and Linda were still married, he had but had no wife. Sometimes he sent money. She cashed the checks. No one knew. Big never told. Were they married? Far as he knew. When is a wife not a wife? When she's a hoer. Get it? Hoe/er?

Someone is holding his elbow to guide him, a two-toned man, black in the face but there are white spots here and there and the rest of him is white except for his hands, which also are spotted. Like the rhinotamus. The whog. Half-and-half. New things all over.

"I've got to hand it to you, buddy," Big tells the half-and-half man. "I never thought they'd do it."

"Do what, Mr. Stovall?"

"Make one like you."

"Careful here, Mr. Stovall. Do what?"

"Half-and-half."

"Three steps. There's one. What you mean? Two."

"I mean, I know about mixed marriages, misrepresentation, and quatrains but I never saw one black some places, white some others. You an albino?"

"Three. Down this hall and you're home."

"Pigmentation, that's it. I saw a nigger one time had white eyebrows. Skin black as coal, hair nappy, everything nigger but those eyebrows. You got freckles?"

"Nossir. Nearly there."

"Most albino-nigger skin has freckles."

The man takes out a key and opens the apartment door.

"In here, Mr. Stovall, easy now."

"In medical school we had cadavers. One after the other every one of them a nigger. How was I supposed to know how a dead white man looked, I said, when all the cadavers were black as the A of spades? That's what my grandson used to call it, you know my grandson Robby?"

"Nossir. I don't."

"Used to say A of spades. His favorite card in the deck. Not niggers like you, you understand. Trashy types. Family let us cut them up like dogs."

"Lie down here, Mr. Stovall."

The man puts two pillows under Big's head.

"One of them had the biggest dick I ever saw. Purple. Partly from pre—no, post—metastatic, no. Livid. Blood something. You know. Blood gathers, I can't think what it's called. Partly that and partly because it was just naturally a purple dick. You got a purple dick? Or a white one?"

"I'm going to call your family." The man lifts the phone, dials the Zodiac office.

"Biggest I ever saw. Down to here. Stovalls have short dicks. Did you know that? All of us. Short Stovall dicks. I told my son when he was little, 'Son,' I said. 'You are going to have a short dick; there is nothing you can do. But a short dick can get the same work done and women don't mind if you do it right.' That's what I told him. Not true, though. Some women just don't like a short one. Know what I mean? But that's what I told

him and sure enough he does have a short dick. My daddy did.
I saw it in the bathtub. A Llavots dick.

"Just a minute— Mr. Stovall, do you have your wallet?"

Big's eyes widen. His hands clap quickly over his back pockets.

Gone!

"I don't think he wants to—all right. Let me, *Sue Stovall Muffaletta* . . . " the black man is writing.

"My daughter? No. She doesn't have a short dick."

The black man turns.

"What did I just say, Chessboard? Can I call you Chessboard?"

Chessboard holds his hand over the receiver. "You mentioned
your daughter. Your daughter's dick, a matter of fact."

"Don't get smart with me, Chessboard. You know as well as
I do girls don't have dicks. And don't talk about my daughter.
Next thing you know she'll be—" He starts to whimper.
"Crooked," he says. "Cattywompus. What's the tune?" Big takes
his hands from his back pockets and weeps into them.

The black man dials Sue's number.

Suddenly Big's crying jag stops. "All niggers have big dicks,"
he says. "It's a known fact. Down to here."

"Mrs. Muffaletta, this is James Burnside from the Zodiac
Apartments . . ."

"Chessboard? You ever seen a crooked dick?"

". . . sitting in his car threatening to hit me and talking about
being underwater. . . ."

"Muff had one. It's a funny thing to see a dick and know
where it's going. I mean when you've got a daughter."

"Something is wrong, Mrs. Muffaletta. I think you should
come over. The man's not right."

"You should have seen her, Chessboard, she was a doll. I
would have done anything for that girl. Anything."

". . . for a while but I have work to do. Ten minutes. You get
over here fast as you can."

"One nut and a short dick. Other one never dropped. One nut
and a short dick."

". . . all right, Mrs. Muffaletta. Good-bye."

"Was a time she didn't do it all. Sweet Sue. Like a princess. Don't get me wrong, I'm crazy about my son. But oh that Sue." He stops; looks around. "Chessboard. Did you hear about my wife?"

Chessboard hangs up the phone.

"No. I didn't."

"We have to do something. *Sue!* Queers and hippies. The police broke it up and there was Linda. I need to talk to *Sue.*"

Chessboard, from a distance, nods.

"She didn't want to but they talked her into it. Promised her black lace and White Shoulders. And you know what?"

Chessboard shakes his head no.

"I asked you a question, Chessboard. I said, *Do you know what?*"

"*No,*" Chessboard says, "What?"

"I forgot."

"That's okay, Mr. Stovall. It'll keep."

"She is with a Jew photographer. Did you know that?"

"No. I didn't."

"I never heard of a Jew photographer. You?"

"I couldn't really say."

"Man in Rosedale took pictures was Syrian. I knew a dago did it. But not a Jew. That's a new one on me."

They are both silent. Chessboard hopes the man is drifting to sleep.

"How about yourself?"

"What?"

"You ever see a Jew photographer?"

"I don't think so. Now that you mention it, Mr. Stovall, I don't believe I ever have."

Jim Stovall turns his big head over to one side, away from James Burnside. His arms are down by his side. He looks very vulnerable. Suddenly he raises up on his elbows, looking straight out in front of him, at the wall across the room from his bed.

"Goddamn her soul," he roars. "I knew she'd pull something like this. I should have left her where she was, barefoot in Arkansas, little blond thing. Sugar-baby tits, cute and sassy. Should have left her there, not put that black lace next to her ass. Once they get it, Chessboard, you know what I mean. You get my drift."

He waits for an answer.

"Yessir."

"I know you do. Once they get used to it they are never the same. Take my advice. Watch out what rubs up against their ass. Look at Linda. That commune. The orgy, with niggers, excuse me, Chessboard, and Jews. Even hippies."

He turns over on his side and instantly falls asleep. Snoring. The loudest snores James Burnside has ever heard. The black man tiptoes out; locks the apartment door. It is a shame what happens to people sometimes, he is thinking. A shame.

As he makes his way down the Pisces hall, James Burnside is hoping two things: one that the man stays asleep until the time his daughter gets there and two that Sue Stovall Muffaletta has a key. In any event, James Burnside has done his part. He walks fast, toward Cancer. An apartment there has been vacated and needs painting. I am going to shag it on out of here, James Burnside is thinking, before they haul my ass further into that white man's mess. Chessboard, indeed. He walks fast, looking out as he goes for Jim Stovall's daughter.

For his daughter he would be a doctor. Buy a home, ruffled dresses, white shoes, short white socks with scalloped edges and little pictures embroidered in the ribbing. Wallpaper with roses. A bed with a white canopy. Gold bracelets. A locket with pictures inside. A music box, playing "Here Comes the Bride."

For his girl his daughter his loving baby firstborn girl child, who made his life feel lit up and new, he would become a real *daddy.* He would be a daddy who knows, prescribes. Listens to your heart, interprets its beat. Doctor Daddy. No banjo. Big

Walt would be proud. Everybody would say, Baby Snowball was the baby but look at him now.

Music was not respectable. From football, the banjo, The Chunk, he moved on.

Medical school was no more difficult than playing the banjo. Others studied long hours. Jimmy skimmed, crammed for exams, passed easy. Others barely got by. His memory was for things seen. Once the formulas had been written on the blackboard he never forgot them. He still remembers. He can recite chemical formulas and enumerate the elements and their symbols as if he learned them yesterday. He can tell you how the body's cardiovascular system works, in detail. He went for day light. All of it was the same.

Then Linda got pregnant again. Sue was three. The second time around, Linda had a hard time. Sick all the time, she spent half her pregnancy in bed. Sue kept running away. Linda's angel face was turning into folds of worry. Veins popped out in her hands.

He couldn't stand to see them hurt or wanting. He would get them whatever they wanted: that was what a daddy was. *Don't worry,* he said to Linda: *I'll take care of it.*

And Big hit the road.

Before he quit medical school he had seen an experiment done on a guinea pig. A synthetic female hormone was fed to a daddy pig. The daddy pig's tits swelled; filled with milk. The babies came to suckle. The daddy pig daddied them with breast milk.

It was terrible. He had never been able to forget it. That was twenty-five years ago and it still gave him bad dreams. The look in the daddy pig's eyes.

"Sue?" He is alone. Chessboard has left. *"SUE!"*

IV.
Four-Oh-Two

The Monkey Ward

"What can I tell you? He's atilt."

"A what?"

"Atilt. Awry. Confused. Seeing things wrong. Maybe seeing them right, calling them wrong."

"Hallucinations. Sounds like hallucinations." Brook is our medical textbook.

"His moon is entering Uranus. I looked it up. A time of chaos and uncertainty." Linda, our *Houston Post* Astrocast.

We are all here, in the fourth-floor waiting room, gathered to offer maps by which to chart Big's very mind.

I turn to Steve. "It's like he's inside a dream. In his mind, between thinking and saying everything gets screwy. He knows what he wants to say but it comes out wrong. It's a matter of language. He looks in a tree, sees a leaf; somewhere in there before it gets out, leaf turns to fish. He says fish. Monkeys are everywhere. He was parking in Pisces when he thought he was underwater. You see?"

"Like I said," Brook says flatly. "Hallucinations. That's what a hallucination *is.* Tripping. You can't baby him, Sue. It's not just words. You could say everything is words. You could say this room is a room because we don't call it baby. It is what is *is,* that's all there is to it. A room is a room. Period. It's not okay to call a leaf a fish."

I have been over all this on my own. Yesterday after the man at the Zodiac, James Burnside, called, I took Big to the emergency room of this hospital; spent six hours in the waiting room listening to him rant and rave about fish and dicks and Linda, trying not to imagine what might have happened.

Steve and Brook came last night, then, this morning—a surprise—Linda. And so the Llavots are all gathered, sitting side by side in Fiberglas contour chairs joined at the shoulder; we have to swivel our heads all the way to the side to talk. Brook's in a blue chair with Pee on her lap sucking her fingers. Brook grabs the child's wrist, slides the fingers out. Pee jams them back in deeper and Brook looks the other way. Slumped against her mother's chest, Pee stares at Linda. Linda's in a red chair, Steve's in yellow, I'm in orange. Shannon is running from one bank of chairs to another, sliding down the Fiberglas. Steve, who hates hospitals, has not said a word.

A Mexican woman sat by me yesterday, the entire time. She held a baby, who slept most of the day and jiggled against the woman's large chest as she rocked it. Muzak played and we waited. "Raindrops Keep Falling on My Head." "Michelle." "Rocky Mountain High." I was in a blue chair. She was in yellow.

Finally, well after dark, they called me in. Big was on an examining table, strapped down.

"Shall we dance?" he said. Doctors were all around, a fleet of earnest young men with clipboards and charts. Eyebrows shot up.

"It's not crazy," I explained. "*Shall we dance* means let's go. It's his way of talking. Like a code. If I answer, 'Jive and mambo,' that means I'm ready too and we'd hit it. All right?"

Blank doctor faces: one Arab, two blond pretty ones, a bearded rugged type. They all stared. A specialist came in, a fast and tense, black neurosurgeon from this floor. There was a flurry when the black doctor arrived. Daddy greeted him warmly.

"CHESSBOARD!" he said. "LONG TIME NO SEE."

The neurosurgeon was not amused. The other doctors fluttered.

"IT'S ME, CHESSBOARD. YOU REMEMBER. ONE-NUT SHORT-DICK STOVALL?"

The Arab asked me to step out please, and he and I and the other young ones went out into the hall. In an official semicircle, they grilled me.

"He is not crazy." I said. "He is seeing the world wrong or at least it comes out that way. He knows what he wants to say but it won't come out right. It's a matter of words. Language."

"Can you give us an example?"

"On the way over here he said if you cliff this hypotenuse and veerio pool you will accelerate the lesion. That's talk he knows, technical terms plus family lingo. He was telling me to cross the highway, pool is loop spelled backwards, *the* Loop, Loop 610 and—" They weren't buying it. "Veerios is the cereal Robby eats. My son. Cheerios?"

From the closed cubicle, Daddy sang.

"HOW'S IT GOING, WHOZ ON FIRST, WHERE'S ROBBY-MA-HOBBY WITH MY BAMA GLASS TODAY? IT MUST BE FIVE O'CLOCK SOMEWHERE IN THE WORLD. BOTTOMS UP! DOCTOR'S ORDERS TWO GLASSES A NIGHT."

Fast-and-tense, the black neurosurgeon came out; asked me the same questions.

Remembering the elephant dose of Pentothal during the cataract operation, I told the black man. He said "Mmmm" and didn't write it down.

I went back to my blue chair next to the Mexican woman. She jiggled the baby. We waited.

Sedation had no effect, even a double dose. They tapped Big's spine; he hardly noticed. He only protested when they stuck fingers up his behind.

"HOW COME YOU GUYS ALWAYS FIND A WAY TO RAM YOUR FINGERS UP A GUY'S ASS? IF A MAN'S GOT A HEADACHE YOU RAM HIS ASS!"

Shifts changed. A new fleet of nurses arrived; more doctors.
I told the story again: his dreams and confusions, the progress
of the disorder, the renovated house, his sister's death, the Pentothal. I stared at the wall at the picture of a red covered bridge.
At six, I called home. Steve and Brook were there. They went
to the Zodiac to sleep.

Daddy's heart man's partner came by. The heart man himself
is at a convention in Hawaii sponsored by an organization called
"Private Practice."

I told the partner the story. The partner, like the other doctors, paid the Pentothal information no mind but went on to ask
about aspirin and booze and bananas. Bananas!

"Does he take aspirin?" the partner inquired, looking down
half-glasses at his clipboard, flipping by graphs and charts.

"Yes. For his thigh which has a steel pin in it, and his knee
and his back. His arthritis."

"How many?"

"What?"

"Aspirin."

"I've seen him shake out a handful."

Doctors nodded. DT's and aspirin, they clucked. Blood. Potassium. Bananas. Electrolytes.

"Is your father a drinking man?" the Arab asked.

"He takes a drink."

"How many?"

"Two glasses of sherry a night." Oh Daddy. Not saying Bama.
Or Econo-King size. "Doctor's orders."

One doctor came out sweating. "That guy's strong as an ox,"
he said.

Past nine, they wheeled him up here, locked him in Neurolog-
ical IC: the Nut Ward, Room Four-Oh-Two.

We can see the door from the waiting room; it's green and it's
locked. Big's inside. There are outsized numbers on the door:
Four-Oh-Two. You wouldn't want to confuse it with any other
room. We can visit him one at a time, four times a day for twenty

minutes at seven o'clock, eleven, three, and seven. A maximum of two people can visit, each session, one person at a time. The others have not been in. I went in at seven this morning. It's a quarter to eleven now. We're awaiting the call.

At seven, most of the patients were quiet, still sleeping. One struggled to waken, another babbled and drooled. One particularly red-faced man spit furiously toward the woman who came to visit him, trying to put into words information trapped in his mind. The others looked altogether gone. Wired and taped, bottle-fed, bottle-drained, they lay there. Like fenceposts.

Their families came, to pat the patient's hands and brush their hair, to lean down close and speak to them, telling the news from home. Mostly the patients did not respond. Small dots and lines appeared and reappeared on the electronic monitors. Tubes and wires hung from their beds. The tiny green light came and went, making that sound.

At the nurse's station by the door there are eight TV screens identical to the ones by the patients' beds. A nurse is at the desk beneath the screens. At seven, the nurse was reading a novel, *Sweet Bliss*.

A young boy with a shaved head is across from Daddy; round disks attached to wires dot his whiskery head.

While I stood by Big, the boy's mother talked to him.

"David?" she said. "Can you hear me, David?"

Big was tied to the bed.

He was still in his undershirt, smelling sour and foul. His hair was fluffed up in horns, his beard growing out. I realized how careful he was to keep himself shaven. I had not known his beard was so gray. There was a yellow bruise on his shoulder and his sleep was abnormal. In drugged vacancy, he was gone. His cheeks sank deep as caves, then blew out. Sucked in, blew out, shuddered. His diaphragm collapsed, ballooned, collapsed. His breath was shallow. Crazy sleep.

"Daddy?" I didn't know what to do. We had twenty minutes. I called his name, understanding that the other visitors jabbered on and on, even when it was clear the patients could hear nothing because there was nothing else to do. And you had twenty minutes.

"It's me, Daddy. Sue." How could he change so, in so little time? Only hours before he'd been yelling about fingers up his rear. Now?

The nurse at the front station looked up from *Sweet Bliss* long enough to throw me a look. I lowered my voice. "Can you wake up a minute, Daddy?" Nothing. That rasping. Breath seemed to come from his throat, no deeper. Suddenly I wanted him to waken. What were they doing? Why tie him down? Big? I wanted to see his black eyes. I stood there.

"Big?"

The nurse licked her fingers, turning a page.

At the wrist, his hands were tied to the bed frame with what looked like pieces of ripped sheets. The knot was secure, the rags short. Suddenly, in his sleep, he pulled against them. Fists doubled, his huge arms pulled, his face reddening with the effort, shoulders pressed to the bed. Once. Again. Again. No more. His face melted back into its original pie. As if it might break apart, like overcooked meringue. The Chunk was tied. The Kid could not break loose. Weep for Baby Snowball.

I watched David's mother awhile then left, before the twenty minutes were up. There was no reason to stay. I didn't see any doctors from the emergency room. No one said anything except, on the way out, the reading nurse.

"You're his daughter?"

"Yes."

"Your father's a strong man."

"Yes."

"Lord, he gave us a time."

"Why is he tied?"

"He'll be better at eleven."

She went back to *Sweet Bliss.*

He looked so gray. And his breathing . . I can hear it still. His chest; it rose, then fell, in great thunking heaves. Nightmare breaths. Deep drugged rasping. How did she know with such certainly that in four hours he would be better?

"Who's going in?" Brook says now, smoothing back her hair and once again removing Pee's fingers from her mouth. "The sign says two."

No one answers. Steve clears his throat.

"Me, I guess. I think I should," he volunteers without enthusiasm. I have not told them about the restraints, hoping in the four hours since I was here Daddy will have improved as the nurse promised, at least enough not to be tied down.

"I shouldn't go." Linda looks frail, her eyes like old china ready to break. She appeals to me.

"I think not, too. After Steve goes, I will. I think seeing Linda will only confuse him more."

"What's it like in there?" Steve is nervous. Ess has crawled into his lap to pull his hair and try his glasses on. Steve says "Don't, Shannon," in a voice Shannon knows he does not have to heed. Steve rears his head back away from Ess.

"Don't ask."

Steve frowns and with one fingers presses his glasses back onto the bridge of his nose. Shannon pats his face.

"If I tell you you won't want to go and if you don't go you'll always wonder."

Just beyond our waiting room, a thick green plastic rope bars entrance to that end of the hall. The rope is low, strung between short silver poles. There is a silver hasp at the end of the plastic rope connecting it to a hook on the wall. A woman in a red-and-white candy-striped pinafore approaches the plastic rope. We all stiffen. She unhooks the hasp from the wall and chains it to a pedestal. There is a small desk. The candy-striper sits, takes a stack of cards, cracks them on the desk. She arranges them in twos, looks at us, and nods.

We walk to the desk in a group.

"One at a time," the candy-striper warns, "total of two. Name?"

"Stovall," Steve says and, as if volunteering for the firing squad, steps forward.

The candy-striper scans her cards, comes up with Daddy's, gives it to Steve. There is one card for each patient.

"Well, this is it." Steve turns to me for support. "Let's go." All I can do is nod. Steve trudges down the hall. Halfway there, David's mother passes him, her purse hugged to her waist, heels click-clicking, head pushed forward as if to get her there faster.

The door to Four-Oh-Two opens. Steve and the woman go in.

The numbers stare us in the face.

The door opens. Other visitors go in. The door thunks shut.

"One at a time, total of two. Name?" Smiling efficiently, the crisp candy-striper says the same thing every time. Only three people go into the women's ward.

"Well . . ." Linda sighs, and as if on command we turn from the door.

Shannon and Priscilla are on their knees on the vinyl couch, stomachs against the pillows. They are looking out a window and whispering together.

"When's the baby due?"

Brook blushes. It's the first time her pregnancy has been mentioned to her. I've never seen her blush. She avoids looking at Linda. Linda, on the other hand, is pinning Brook to the wall with sharp stares.

"Not until August. Maybe late July."

"Lord," Linda says. "Another Leo."

And then, for the first time Brook boldly turns to Linda and meets her gaze head-on. Brook is a full head taller and together, they make quite a picture, each the opposite extreme of the other . . . Linda small and dramatic, her hair piled and wispy, that spiritual hopeful look. And Brook. Tall and lanquid, her long stride and close-cropped hair, her belly long and lean and lightly protruding. Yet they are dressed similarly, in imported cottons hand-dyed in soft colors, drawstring pants and loose tops. Sandals. Authentic ethnic: the kind of thing I walk right through, seams that tear, straps break.

Something crosses between them. A flash, quick and electric, like the beeping light on the screen above Daddy's bed. It's there and then it's gone.

"I don't believe in astrology," Brook says, lifting her eyebrows as if to clear her mind.

"I know." Linda will not let her go.

Brook moves away, to check on the children who, in deep conversation, have turned their backs to us

I turn to Linda. "You don't have to stay. You have your appointment with Sasha Moon; go on. I know you don't like the city."

"I'd like to help but I don't know how."

"There's nothing to do. He'll come out of it. I don't think it would help you—or him either—for you to see him."

"You have to convince him there's a reason to get well."

Everything is splintered; haywire; yet look. This is still my part to play. Big sister, top mama, SSS. Big and me to figure it out. I will be in charge because it's easier.

"Did Joseph come?"

"Joseph—"

"I told you—" Brook admonishes Ess and Pee.

Four-Oh-Two opens and Steve comes out, looking as pale as thinnest skimmed milk: Blue John, Big calls it. Steve looks like Blue John. He's coming fast.

"—is gone."

Steve replaces his card. The tap-tap of Brook's sandals approaches. Linda's eyes shine. She said *gone*. But there isn't time. Only ten minutes.

I go to the desk and show my card. The candy-striper nods me past. Joseph is gone?

Big is awake, staring at an upside-down bottle high over his left arm. The bottle drips a golden-yellow fluid into his vein. He looks better. He is wearing a white hospital gown stamped METH HOSP and someone has shaved him and combed down his horns. His wrists are free and he is awake.

"Hi." I touch his right shoulder to get his attention.

His head turns my way slowly, in underwater speed.

"Heh-oh, *Sue*," he says. "Steve was here." He seems delighted, and essentially all right. A bit thick-tongued but evened out; in the world, at least.

"I know. You look better."

"Sue." His face begins to crease. "Chessboard tied me down."

I take his wrist, hold it up.

"Not now. You look better, Big. This morning I couldn't rouse you. You were out."

"Tied me down. Half-nigger. Said he wasn't but I know. Tied me to the bed."

His attention drifts to the yellow fluid. His expression changes, becomes milder, a kind of studious rapture. Dazed again. Where is he?

"Daddy." I touch his face to bring it back. "I only have ten minutes." His face comes willingly. "I have a message from Robby. He said to ask you if they had any SLAW up here."

Big doesn't smile. Nothing is funny. Nothing connects. What will I do if nothing is funny. Who will Big be without jokes?

"Sue," he whispers, turning to check for listeners, as if anyone in Four-Oh-Two had room enough in heart or mind to eavesdrop.

"You see that bottle?" His big face is on its side, cheek against the pillow. Without looking, he points over his shoulder to the bottle of yellow fluid.

"Yes."

"There's a little boy fishing in it. He's sitting on the bubbles around the edge. See him? Now I have to do this quick or he'll hear, but watch the bottle."

I can't help it: I look. *When kids sat on his lap, adults believed he was Santa Claus.* Big jiggles the IV tube. The yellow fluid sloshes.

"You see him?" Big says, "You see? That kid belly busted on in, didn't he."

He is all glee, that sly wherz-the-muzic look in his eyes.

"He fell in," he says like a giggling schoolboy. "Fishing pole and all. He fell in." He makes a "V" with his fingers, then points at his eye. "Get it?" he says winking. "Bird's eye." He makes a vaudeville joke-face. "Vee. You. I. IV!"

I look at him. At the yellow fluid. At him. Shall I agree? Do his dance? Swing out when he twirls me?

"Sue."

What, Daddy, what, who, what, I don't know what to say or how to act.

"Get me out."

Time to go. *Click,* thunk. Four-Oh-Two is locked behind us. Door shuts like a vault. Behind it, pain. The words won't come. I turn in my card. The candy-striper says, "Thank *you,* " and cracks my card against her desk.

"Crazy," Steve says between sobs. "Dead crazy. You all just don't know." Brook and Linda are huddled about him, their hands on his back, rubbing in circles. Ess and Pee sit on the couch, fingers in their mouths as they watch their daddy cry, their feet straight out in front of them, legs too short to bend at the pillow's edge. Brook's fingers are long. She has bitten her nails so close her fingertips are fat pads. Linda's hand stops from time to time, to press expertly in at a certain place, to relax him. Steve's face is in his hands. His contour chair is red.

"Ready? Time's up."

"Sue. What did he say? Did he tell you about the horses in the IV bottle having a race? The floating emergency dock?"

"Horses? No. A boy fishing. He tipped the IV bottle and knocked him in the lake."

"Hallucinations," explains Brook. "He's tripping. You all do not understand. Those of us who—"

"Fuck off, Brook. Nobody cares."

She shuts up, midsentence. Everyone stiffens. Brook's hazel eyes turn to flint.

"Sue!" she says. "The children."

"We should go home to talk this out," Linda says.

"There is nothing to say. You all should go home."

"Sue. You have no right."

"I've been here. I got him here. I'll see this out. There is nothing to talk about."

"You think you know everything, Miss Know-it-all, know every smart thing straight A's and muckety-shit. Always have."

"Steve!" Brook is aghast.

The candy-striper, reattaching the green plastic theater rope, shushes us. "This is a hospital," she hisses across the hall. "Take your family arguments elsewhere."

"Fuck off, Brook," Ess says giggling, mocking me.

"Ah-ummmm," Pee puts her hand across her mouth like a no-speak monkey. "Not supposed to say fu-uhh-ck."

"Shannon! Priscilla!" Brook seems reduced to shouting out the names of her family.

Steve stands. We are face-to-face. He is taller but not much.

"This is not the time nor the place for this, but I tell you, Sue, I have had it." With his finger he replaces his glasses on his nose. "Now I tell you what. I am going home. I am going to take my wife and my children and I am going to go home but—" He's lost it. He turns to Brook, who places her hand over her belly. Steve melts. It's over. Whatever it was he started to say he is not sure enough of to face waking up tomorrow to live with.

"Let's go." Virtuously, he gathers up his family. Ess and Pee skitter ahead, having never witnessed this version of their daddy before. But Brook rises slowly, in her own time. She comes to me.

"Join the real world, Sue," she says. "Your father has gone crazy. He drinks too much and now he's gone crazy."

"*Your* real world, Brook?" Linda says quietly. Brook's head jerks around as if Linda had hit her, and once again the look passes between them, steady and unflickering, nearly erotic. What? Brook turns on her heel and, gathering her family to her, goes to the elevator doors. They wait.

Linda and I retire to the contour chairs.

The elevator arrives.

As the doors close, Brook says, "It moved, Steve. The baby. It moved." Holding hands, they move to the back of the elevator and stand against it, in a row, Steve in the last gasp of his momentary huff. No doubt his anger will disappear altogether before they get from four to one. By the time they get to the parking lot he will feel regretful. The last we see of them, they are looking up at the floor numbers waiting for the doors to close.

Girl of Big's Four-Oh-Two Dream: Always Linda

I gave her a watch. It had a cat on it, in a tree. Its tail pointed the time. Finest watch money could buy. Such a thin wrist, so white. Last night on TV they announced a new kind of emergency room. I AM IN THE HOSPITAL. It was on the water but it could go on land too. The boatdock is down the hall. Then when people get sick at sea the hospital can. Floats right up to where they. Bisect the hypotenuse. By sexual in the. Fluid drip-dripping. THE NUT WARD. LOONY BIN CITY. Stole everything. Came and took it all. When the fish leaps it halves a loop and crinkles in a whisper. Chunk was a who. A chunk, irrigate the femur, cast it on waters bread. Get out. The Pack, pack it in. I HAVE TO. A nigger whore from Memphis came, a friend of Linda? No. Not friend; nigger. "Marry me," she said and cut a heart from her panty hose. Stuck it on my chest. Nothing you can do about it, Big Daddy. We are married now. Whore skirt slit to here. Whore hair. Linda. Sue. Sweet Sue. Chessboard tied my arms. Shit in the bed I said. Shit in the bed if you . . . Mother Stovall. Girls. Whores. Whore. Wheels. The radius of a circle is. Hypotenus is. Pie. Daddy me big, Daddy. Don't tie down The Chunk. *Where is his wife?*

The Frog Prince

They came midmorning, Brook in Mexican cotton, a long purple tunic top and drawstring pants, espadrilles so as not to be taller than Steve. Her short brisk hair was brushed back in ducktails and she looked lovely, in her tall, boyish way. The kids popped out of the van like puffed oats, Shannon the pistol first, then Priscilla: damp shy Priscilla, in pink dress and scandalous white tights. The weather was steaming, the first hot day of spring. Thunderstorms predicted to blow in that morning had moved on, leaving the weather still and uncertain. The day felt shut down, closed off.

Steve hugged Linda warmly. He looked pudgy and frayed; more indecisive than ever. He was wearing glasses.

Linda had been reading the Queen of Shades notebook when they came. Joseph had gone to town, saying he'd be back when her family was gone. They had made love that morning. She woke up first and gave him a back rub to stir him.

The children wanted to go swimming. Steve said yes, no, maybe, looking at Brook. Brook said, "In thirty minutes." And Shannon and Priscilla raced off to check the time. Steve and Linda went to the kitchen to make snacks, leaving Brook on the couch with her espadrilles off and feet up.

When they came back with trays and glasses, Joseph was there. Joseph who said, Joseph who didn't want to meet. What brought him back? But there he sat, listening to Brook, as Brook's toes stretched and flexed, stretched, flexed. She had long bony feet, wiry tendons. Aristocratic feet. Anklebones like knobs. Her pants' legs were rolled.

Linda introduced Joseph to Steve. Joseph stood. They shook hands, lover and son. Joseph is younger than Steve. She offered orange juice and cheese. They ate. Brook ran her hand through her short hair and flexed her toes.

When the thirty minutes were exactly up, the children were exactly there, bathing suits in hand. It was time, they shouted, time time to swim, time time, you promised. You promised. And Brook asked Steve to take them down, saying she would come as soon as her feet were rested and Steve said yes and asked Linda to come too.

And Linda agreed. And wanted to go.

Single file they marched down the hill to the pier. And Brook and Joseph stayed behind.

Halfway down Priscilla started to cry. "Up me, Daddy, up. Hot stickers!" Steve lifted her. Sucking her fingers, Priscilla looked back over his shoulder at Linda, her blue eyes level and serene and steady, four fingers settled deep in her mouth.

Dark clouds, leftover from the threatened storm, hung scattered about the blue sky, occasionally blowing over the sun. Uncovered, the sun was hot, the sky bright and clear.

"We better not stay long," Linda said, shading her eyes. "This early in the year, the children will burn."

"Not me," Shannon yelled back over his shoulder. "Not me, I never burn, do I, Daddy? I never burn. Pee burns but I never do."

"Don't call her Pee," Steve said in a Brook-like voice.

At the pier, Shannon dove off immediately. Brook had taught him, Steve explained. Brook believed every child was born knowing how to swim, that you had to trust that the natural ability existed and urge it up. If you didn't smother it, it would flourish.

Priscilla seemed certain about natural abilities. In her two-piece print bathing suit with ruffles across her rear, she sat primly on the edge of the pier and complained to Steve how hot it was. Her belly was soft. She smelled like indoors, dolls, and closets. There were Indians on her bathing suit, joined at the hands.

Steve did a near belly-bust dive.

"You're getting fat," Linda teased.

"Living fat," he said. Out of Brook's reach, he seemed easier, more relaxed.

"What'll you do about your job?"

"It'll work out. I've got some ideas." Steve swam away.

Linda sat by Priscilla, who paddled her feet back and forth. The lake was warm, as usual.

"You like water?"

Priscilla stared straight ahead at her father.

Linda tried again. "Shannon's a good swimmer, isn't he?"

The boy went happily back and forth, back and forth. When he got to the pier he'd grab hold of the ladder, come up for breath, take a quick gulp and say, "Watch this," and set back off again.

"Water is not my water." Pee's hair was reddish-blond like Steve's. A strand by her ear lay pasted on her face in a perfect C.

"What?"

"Shannon's water is his water. Mine is inside."

Linda understood perfectly.

"Maybe you'd like to come look at the lake at night. Just look at it in the moonlight. That's when I like the water. Then it's mine."

Priscilla looked suspiciously at Linda frowning. She shook her head *no.*

Steve swam out farther. His stroke was short, choppy, his rhythm irregular. Sue was the swimmer, not Steve. A swift cloud ran over to cover the sun, then moved away and they felt scorched again.

Steve kept swimming. There was a slight growl of thunder from the distance.

"I want to go up," Priscilla said suddenly, and she stood. Cupping her pink hands around her mouth, she yelled across the water. *"Daddy!"* But Steve was too far and his head was underwater too much of the time to hear.

"Daddy!"

Linda stood and bent to the child.

"Baby, he can't hear you. I'll take you up."

"No," she said adamantly and began to cry. She turned on her heel and started to climb the bank, crying furiously as she went.

Joseph had set railroad ties into the side of the bank for steps, too far apart for a baby's stride. Her fat feet were burning and the steps were too high. She stood on the second railroad tie on one foot and then the other, fists turning against her eyes as if to rub them into her head.

Linda lifted her.

She looked out at the lake. When Steve's head poked up and he looked in their direction, she pointed to the baby and then up the bank toward the house. She thought she saw him shake his head to indicate he understood, but she wasn't sure. Shannon made it to the pier again and said "Watch this" and was off again.

At the edge of the patio, she put the baby down and took her hand. Priscilla jammed the fingers of her other hand in her mouth. They circled the edge of concrete, keeping on the cooler brick that outlined the cement. At the glass double doors, they stopped. Were stopped. Something told them. Holding hands, Linda and Priscilla looked in.

On the couch, Brook was stretched long, toes pointed, her untied drawstring cotton pants below her hips. Pale as a fish belly her taut belly rose . . . tight as a shell, filled up with baby. Joseph was on his knees beside her, his long skillful hand rubbing her belly and between her breasts. His hands: sometimes Linda lay on top of him and came from the way he rubbed her back. But that took time. Could they risk it? With the others so near? No. There. Joseph's other hand worked more seriously. Not enough time for patient stroking; he had to move her along. Joseph watched her face. Brook's head was back, the top of her head against the couch pillows, her eyes closed.

"Women get more out of themselves," he said once and Linda hadn't known if he meant more outside themselves than men, or get more from themselves than from men. Brook's eyebrows were up, her chin lifted: up to get it, hips lifted. Up. Against the striped couch, her full belly was white, like the moon.

Linda waited. Priscilla sucked her fingers. What did the baby see? Where would this information go? Far back? Until the woman on the couch turned to somebody else and the real Brook was the Brook she knew. The mama she needed her to be?

Linda had never seen a woman come. She watched Brook. Up to get it. High as the moon. Shuddering she moved up. It was so clear, when it happened. Her white belly like a shell, navel inside out with the baby, hips lifted. Head went back, neck arched, mouth moving. Joseph watched, his dark eyes mysterious as night; Priscilla watched. And then . . . Joseph turned.

Turned? Yes. She had gone back over it in her mind to make sure of it, and he did. Saw them. Grandmother; baby; voyeurs.

His dark eyes focused quickly. He was expert at this, at finding quick pictures and snapping quickly and then quickly moving on. He shielded Brook's face, so she could not see them.

Brook dropped her hand to the floor. Joseph smiled, licked her belly. Brook drew back. Linda knew that flesh gasp. Too soon, too much. Joseph looked pleased.

Brook reached for her pants. Joseph stood.

"Daddy's back."

Turned toward the lake, Priscilla pointed a wet finger. Steve had swum back to the pier and was up on his elbows there, looking toward the house.

Loosening herself from Linda, Priscilla headed off down toward him, paying no heed to stickers or hot steps. Linda followed.

"Is she all right?" On the pier, Steve squatted to the baby's size. Priscilla's head was on his shoulder, altogether fagged out. "I heard her yelling."

"She didn't want me to help. But I think she's used to me now. Aren't you, Priscilla?"

They sat, looking out over the water. The baby patted her father's leg. A dark cloud came over and turned the lake sour. When it left, the water sparkled once again. But in fact brown was its true color. The sun make it look silvery and blue but in truth the lake was murky.

A long shadow moved across them.

"Where is Shannon? It's time for him to get out."

Behind them, Brook—pants tied up once again—was giving commands. Steve called to Shannon, relaying Brook's command, and Shannon got out.

"I swam it forty-three times, Mama."

"That's nice."

Brook stood tall over the others, who sat awhile, swinging their feet. Looking out at the lake, she frowned, and smoothed her hair back behind her ears.

"Looks dirty," she said.

From up at the house, Linda heard Joseph's gray Toyota back up and drive off.

So.

Midafternoon Steve and his family left. And Linda sat on the patio watching the water, doing yoga to a jazz record she liked, a mellow mourning flute. The phone had started to ring. She ignored it. There was no one she wanted to talk to. It would stop ringing long enough for the caller to redial the number, then ring again.

She would write her version of The Frog Prince. In hers, the frog won't win his kiss, the princess having become enamored of tricks he performs with his sticky tongue. She would call it "Someday My Prince." The princess keeps promising, putting the frog off, biding time. "Just once more," the princess says, "with the tongue." Hrunert. The frog's name would be Hrunert. With a Jewish growl.

She concentrated on yoga and work, to keep other pictures from her mind: Joseph and Brook; Joseph seeing her; Joseph turning back. Sometimes the time came for change so fast.

He did not come back.

She called Houston, made an appointment with Sasha.

Late that night the phone rang and she answered it.

Mama One-Two

The cafeteria is not a cafeteria but a series of food stations. There is no single line to go down. For salad, you go to Salad Bar. For a sandwich, to Sandwich Bar. For a plate lunch you travel to Hot Meal City. Desserts are at Sweet Things.

Linda chooses a funny salad. I get soup, iced tea, oatmeal cookies.

We sit at a table in the corner where the vending machines are. This section is called SNAK-TYME. All around us are machines dispensing a variety of foods . . . grapefruit juice, milk, corn-nuts, dry-roast peanuts, Mi-T-Goods, Campbell's soup, candy bars, Eskimo Pies, Coke, and Dr. Pepper.

The residents and interns seem to prefer the machines. They are in our section drinking juice and eating peanut butter crackers. Hands in cellophane bags, they eat without noticing, hand-to-mouth while their intense conversation continues.

"So what happened?"

"With what? Where?"

"With Joseph. When Steve and Brook came."

"I told you. Joseph is gone. And if he isn't, I am."

"*Something* happened."

Linda looks up from her salad. Her eyes are filled. When she cries, tears collect; hold; don't drop. The blue is pale and glassy; they have a silver cast. My eyes are brown like Daddy's, yet I see myself in hers. In Daddy's, I fall in, go soft, feel lost. These glinty blue ones cast me back to myself.

"Sometime's the time, that's all." And once again, as at her kitchen table, Linda closes the conversation. She is behind her eyes again, and will not say.

She dabbles in her salad, arranging apple bits in pictures. I eat soup and wait.

"There's something else, Sue."

"I knew there was. What?"

"I got a telephone call last night. Did I tell you about Grace McDonald?"

"At *Skin?*"

"Yes. Well you know she's been high on my stuff for a long time and thinks it ought to have a shot at a wider audience. One thing led to another and well, they've sent the stories to an agent who's interested and she's found a publisher."

"You had a busy day."

She shakes her head. "I'm in a spin. All these things at once. I knew there was a reason for Brook and Steve to have come. . . ."

"You're not going to tell me what happened?"

"No. No I'm not. Maybe later."

"Okay. Then what?"

"Well. Grace wants me to come up. To New York, can you imagine? I told her about the Queen of Shades notebook plus other ones I have and she's interested. She thinks the stories ought to be done with woodcuts for illustrations, fairy tales for grown-ups from a woman's point of view. She says they'll be a smash. A combination of what did she say, Jung, Jong, Roth, Grimm, and Nin? I don't know about any of that, but—"

"But you're going."

"What do you think?"

"Go. Yes, go. Of course. What's to lose?"

She sighs.

"I'll have to find out."

"What name will you use?"

"I figure if I'm going to do it I'm going to. My own. Linda Day."

"This calls for a celebration."

At SNAK-TYME, I consult the machines. Something sweet is in order. The M&M's slot is empty. Lifesavers take too long. Here. A Zero bar. I put in two quarters, bring back two bars.

"Ever had a Zero?"

The wrapper is ice-colored, decorated with a polar bear holding up a paw.

"You know I don't eat sugar."

"It's a one-time occasion. Come on. Bottom's up."

"It's white."

"So it's a Zero. The snow? The bear?"

The Zero is disgusting. The worst candy I've ever eaten. The icing tastes like sweetened glue. Still . . . I down mine. Linda eats a little, then puts the candy down, covering her teeth marks with the wrapper.

"You'll be famous."

"We'll see."

"Who's *we?*"

She shrugs.

"Sue." She wipes her mouth with a cafeteria napkin. "I'm going by to see your kids, then to Sasha's for my appointment, then home. You want to go? I mean to Post-oh? I'll bring you back in time for the three-o'clock visit."

"No. I'll wait around. See if a doctor shows. I'll be home between now and the three-o'clock visitation, but I don't know when."

"Will you call? About Jimmy?"

I want her to go home too. "Go to New York, Mama. Do it. Be a combination of all those people, Ring, Rung, Joth, Nim and Grin."

We kiss, a brief touch.

As she reaches to push open the cafeteria's glass doors, the doors abruptly pop open. Startled, she hesitates a moment, then goes on. Her Mexican sandals make a kind of squeaking noise when she walks.

By the time I stop staring at the glass door where she disappeared, my coffee is lukewarm and the line at HOT DRINKS is long. I go to SNAK-TYME. No change. Slide a dollar in the change machine, get back three quarters, spend two on a cup of muddy stuff that comes out with cream, though I'm sure I pushed BLACK.

When I get back to my table it's taken.

Back to the Four-Oh-Two waiting room. I'll stay. No sense

rushing home and fight finding another parking place at three. It's quiet here. I'll buy some slick magazines and sit in a blue chair. Maybe see a Nut Doctor. Maybe Fast-and-Tense. Something may come to me, some explanation.

Four-Oh-Two. Four-Oh-Two.

Have mercy on the Nut Ward.

Four-Oh-Two.

Brook

The house smells like Linda. Essential oil, essence of some herb, supposed to turn some magic. Soon as this is over, I think I'll paint the house. Post Oak Plain: a white house with dark green trim. Like in pictures.

"Anybody home?"

The kitchen is a picture. When I left this morning the mess was staggering. Dishes in the sink, table sticky with jelly, a lidless jar of peanut butter, Robby's Cheerios. Now it is immaculate. Floor mopped, pots and pans put away. Cabinet tops wiped, floor shining, garbage taken out, stove wiped, grease spots gone. Mr. Clean City. Big Wally and Glow.

"In here," Caroline calls from her room.

She is doing homework and lying in her bed against her ruffled pillows. Beyond her feet, the TV is on, "Love, American Style," one of her favorites. When Robby and Ricky are here they make such fun she won't watch it.

"Hi. How's Big?" When she looks up from her schoolwork, it's to look at the TV, not me.

"Better. Not well but better. I have to go back at seven."

They put me in a straitjacket, Sue. I believe him.

They tied me down. Yes.

Stole my things. Yes.

Put me in a store window, so everyone could see Yes.

Is it daytime or night? Isn't it Halloween? Is Linda still at the orgy? It was awful, Sue, what was going on.

She is still at the orgy, Big, yes. Bodies are all around her, filling her mind; shades and gaps. She is their queen, Nin, Goth, and Rim. What can I say? I understand him. I can see what he sees.

"Have they said what caused it?" Caroline asks.

"So far, aspirins."

"Aspirins?"

"That's what they're saying."

"You believe it?"

"He was taking twenty to thirty a day, for his back and legs and arthritis. And yes, I think they had an effect. But that's not the cause. I don't know what did but it wasn't aspirins. I suspect an overdose of Pentothal, from his cataract operation. He's having flashbacks. But they'll never say so."

Fast-and-Tense admitted using a straitjacket. "The man was belligerent," he said. "We could not control him. And you know . . ." he cocked his head, ". . . your father is strong as a bull, Mrs. Muffaletta. Four of us could not hold him down. We do not like to use the jacket and he was not in it long, trust me, not more than half an hour."

Caroline, looking doubtful, studies the TV.

"Remember that friend of Jane's? They gave her Pentothal when she had her baby. After she got home they found her one day hunched naked in a corner saying her sister was after her. Nobody would believe it then either."

Fallen into dreams. Nobody listening.

Imagine Big, cramped into an X. Imagine a world unable to turn.

"Mrs. Muffaletta, we are going to bring Mr. Stovall out of this, I assure you. It's a matter of time. What we are working on is cause."

"I thought you said aspirin."

"Well, that is our belief at this time. But we are doing other tests as well. His brain scan is normal. But there is an imbalance somewhere. Something out of whack."

Big duh.

Fast-and-Tense wore a starched white medical jacket and white pants. The chief resident in neurosurgery, he is a West African and very black. He, I take it, is Chessboard. Half-and-half, a new phenomenon, Daddy says, and no wonder: black men in his pill-pushing days wore green orderly suits and cleaned slop, never were in a position to tie white men down. Black men were cadavers to cut on. This man looks black, acts white. Half-and-half: black-and-white. I am beginning to understand Big's dream world. The green house turned on its side haunts him; Bird's-eye maple; Mother Stovall's revenge; Lou's.

"Where is everybody?" I ask Caroline.

"I don't know. I'm the only one home. Robby stayed for band practice. Did you know he joined?"

"He told me today."

"He'll be late every day. It's queer."

"Caroline. What do you mean?"

"It's queer, that's all. Queer. Weirdos are in the band. Especially ones who blow. I'll be glad when this year's over and I'm in high school."

"You'll only have one year, you know. Then Robby will be in high school too."

"It's bigger. It won't be as bad."

She is looking down now, writing furiously.

"Caroline, you're a snob."

She doesn't reply.

"Did you see Linda?"

"No," she says, "but I smelled her. And Steve and Brook were here too."

"How do you know?"

"There's a note. You didn't see it? In the kitchen."

"I didn't see it, no." A commercial comes on. Bill Cosby touting beans.

Propped up on the kitchen table against the sugar bowl is a sealed envelope saying SUE.

Sue,

We are waiting at your house until it's safe to leave. When we started out of town, Steve turned the radio on, and there had been an accident . . . on Loop 610, just where we were headed. A truck filled with ammonia veered off the spaghetti bowl overpass there and fell down on Highway 59 below and exploded. Ammonia gas is all over. People are in hospitals out there. The driver of course is dead, and the highway and the Loop are closed off. We can't get past the Loop for a while until it is clear. So we came here to wait, not knowing where else to go. We gave back our key to Big Daddy's apartment to the Zodiac office and I convinced Steve you wouldn't mind, though he didn't want to come here at first, after your tirade in the hospital.

Anyway I cleaned up your kitchen for you, for something to do and to help out. I understand where you are, Sue. This is a bad time for you and you are allowing the situation to control you instead of the other way around. I don't want to tell you what to do, but I did think a clean house would be a help. To my mind, it's easier to make decisions when you start fresh.

We are not angry. Steve was, but he understands. It has been a difficult few days, what with the funeral and the hoo-hah about the Pine Bluff house and then Big Daddy. Please call us and let us know how he is. We are as concerned as you are, you know. Big Daddy is welcome at our house. We will be happy to have him come there if he needs to or would like to, to stay as long as he likes. We have room and of course Shannon and Priscilla would love it. We have decided to stay in Morgan. Steve is going to try working for my father, though I don't think he wants to sell. We'll work something out.

Please come to Virginia. Possibly when the baby is born? Lucky we didn't leave sooner. Imagine what the ammonia fumes might have done to the new baby. It just goes to show you. You make your own luck. We chose not to be there.

249

You can only do what you can, Sue. Big Daddy will either come out of this, if he decides to, or he will stay. It's his choice. You cannot make anybody else do anything. They must do it for themselves. He is playing old tapes, using you the way he did Linda, and other women. His mother, the teachers he talks about. You are the principal of his school, slapping his hand. But I don't want to interfere.

Steve now tells me he's talked to Triple-A and we're going home a different way. East on Interstate 10 to Mobile, up to Atlanta then north, home. We've gone that way before and it's awfully boring. All that flat country straight across from here on, until past Mobile. But the highway is clear in that direction, and it will get us there. It is two o'clock now. We will drive all night and try to get home by tomorrow night.

Please let us know how things go. And come to see us if you can. My best to the children.

Brook

Big's News

The pool is dangerous. You must stay inside it. Trucks fly. The way is free but you must keep a bird's eye on it, it will loop you if you don't hold it down. Otherwise, the gas will run out and take over. The green will turn colors, change to brown; it will never live again, it will never reach back green again so you must hold on to it while it is still snakes in the cantaloupe rows.

Gas is running out, crossing over.

There is no gas.

Go underwater where it can't get you. Escape the Loop of the pool. Or black people will come. Whores. Wives will eat gas and turn into nigger whores.

Veerio the pool, stay outside it.

The hypotenuse of the pie will tell you where Loop is buried, piss in her face, knots in hot socks, play the tune, dance out your eyes bird's-eye, I am. Maple.

Crossed over. The daddy pig suckles. Tits like rubber sacks. Hairy milk tits. It all runs out. The floating emergency dock is necessary to cure all the swimming people.

Blues in the Nut Ward

The TV news that night told of nothing else. How the tanker truck was speeding on the overpass and could not make a curve and plunged over the guardrail to the highway below where it exploded. All the vegetation surrounding the area was killed, and people trying to escape the deadly ammonia cloud swallowed the gas in spite of themselves. Only two people were reported dead so far, the truck driver and the driver of another car who swerved to miss hitting the truck and slammed into a freeway support bunker. Hospital emergency rooms in the area reported hundreds of people coming, their eyes and lungs damaged. "I've seen them tanker trucks before," one eyewitness said. "They come barreling over the Loop like a house afire. Ought to do something. Ought not let them fellows tool around the city fast as they like when they're carrying gas. It's not right." Investigations were ordered.

At the seven-o'clock evening visit, Daddy was sitting straight up in bed, his back up off the pillows at a perfect right angle.
"Daddy?"
His eyes were alert and open, but did not seem, exactly, to see.
"Daddy?"
Other visitors whispered in patients' ears, telling them the news. With his hands cupped one on top of the other in his lap, Big looked like a choirboy about to sing. And in fact, he did.

His eyes on the bottle of yellow liquid above his bed, he opened his mouth and music came out.

"*Georgia . . . Georgia . . .*" I looked around, checked the nurse. The room was still . . . no time, no clock; night, day, all the same.

Big's voice is high and sweet, a sexless bluesy Bessie Smith kind of voice, higher than his own throat can imagine. When he sings you can see him reaching up inside, pushing for higher notes, like Nightingale Norris. Eyes closed, his eyebrows lift toward one another, and his face looks sad enough to melt. The room was filled up with Big's song.

The whole day through.
Just an old sweet song keeps . . .
Georgia on my mind . . . Oh yes. . . .

Shaking his head, in rhythm, with the slow sad beat, a thin stream of sound, a high sweet woozy wailing, it moved to the beat of electronic beeps.

The room grew quieter. Visitors stopped telling the news to patients blanked out as ever. The angry man with the red face and popping eyes glared in Daddy's direction, redder than ever.

I say Georgia, Georgia. . . .

Hands in his lap, he was angel innocent, like a round-faced boy. Like a sweet soul *daddy*. Tears rolled down his cheeks. His eyes were shut and the tears squeezed out; ran together in a stream.

Other arms reach out to me . . .
Other eyes smile tenderly. . . .

Unashamed, he sang the whole song. On the last verse, he took it up an octave. His eyebrows reached high up on his big high forehead, up to his hairline, and he strained for the highest note he could reach. He got there. He couldn't hold it but he got there. ". . . on . . . my . . . mi-ind." His eyes opened. The monitor beeped. The mother of the boy across from Big clapped her hands together once, then, embarrassed, stopped, looking

around. Daddy's dark eyes came around to mine, and when he
looked at me, everything was there. Aunt Lou. The funeral. The
dreams we share. Linda and Brook, Joseph, everything. He
knew. He knows. Everything. Even pissing in his sister's grave.
Bird's-eye maple replacing the dining-room suite; no urns, no
steps, no porch.

The moment passed.

By the time I left, he was underwater again. Cows swam past.
Oh, Daddy.

ANNOUNCING:

A NEW TALKING BLUES SONG IN THREE-QUARTER TIME BY M. S. SUE,
BASED ON A TRUE STORY SHE READ IN A MAGAZINE WHILE SITTING
IN A RED CONTOUR CHAIR IN THE METH HOSP FOURTH-FLOOR WAIT-
ING ROOM. (THE TALKING PART IS IN PARENTHESES.)

BLANCHE AND RALPH

(This is a true story about the misuse of the Golden Rule and
the consequences therein. About how people instead of doing
what they would have done unto them end up giving back to
somebody else whatever bad treatment it was they got dished
out early on and how hard that cycle is to break.)

When Ralph was born, his poor mother died,
Leaving his daddy four children, no wife.
His daddy blamed Ralph for the hard times they had,
Unemployment, cooking supper, no wife in his bed.

He hit Ralph with his fists and the back of his hand.
Burned him and bruised him till he could not stand.
Ralph just took it, what else could he do?
When a man is your daddy it's like he owns you.

(But some time afterward the child Ralph—trying to figure out what was what in the world—would bury his head in his hands and cry.) He'd say:

"I didn't do it, I didn't do it, it's not my fault,
Dad, please.
Don't hit me, don't hurt me, I'm down on my knees.
I don't know what you want, I don't know what I did.
Don't beat me up, Daddy, I'm only a kid."

(But nobody stays a kid forever and one day Ralph discovered himself grown up and at sixteen, bigger than his dad. He was known as a tough kid around town, handy with his fists. Only his daddy never noticed. His daddy thought Ralph was the same kid he'd always been. A mistake on his part.)

One night Ralph's father came home roaring drunk.
Ready to fight, he said, "Where is that punk?"
Ralph jumped from his bed to stand up to his dad,
When he drew back his fist, to his daddy Ralph said:

(Chorus)

"You better make it good the first time.
Miss, and you draw back a nub.
I been pushed around the last time,
Punched out in the name of love."

(Ralph's daddy was so stunned by this unusual act of defiance he didn't know what to do, so he prepared to swing. Ralph, seeing what was about to happen and not wanting actually to hit his father, held up his hand and warned him again.) I said:

(Repeat *Chorus*)

(At that the point was made. Ralph's daddy finally got the message and turned around and left. But Ralph knew it wouldn't last and that someday they would undoubtedly come to blows. Ralph left home that night. Went to a new town, got a job as a mechanic fixing cars. One day a young girl came driving up to the station. Why, she said, was her Pontiac's red HOT light on? Ralph took a look inside her engine and said, Why little lady you're boiling hot and flat out of water. And proceeded to fill her up, to cool her radiator off. Blanche.)

Blanche was her name, she was sixteen and shy.
Never been out on dates, never kissed or told lies.
Her mother was strict, she made Blanche stay at home.
The minute Ralph teased her, her poor heart was gone.

They ran off and got married, two kids barely met.
Swore true love forever, their future was set.
Had babies, had troubles, money was tight.
Blanche worshipped her children, they filled up her life.

(But Ralph changed. In fact, as soon as they got married he seemed different. Turned from a regular charming guy into a pure raving maniac where Blanche was concerned. Accused her of all manner of wanton activities, hitting her in the face to get her to admit to a promiscuous past that never was, slapping her until her cheeks turned blue.) And Blanche would say:

"I didn't do it, I didn't do it, it's not my fault, Ralph, please.
Don't hit me, don't hurt me, I'm down on my knees.
I don't know what you want, I'm your wife, Ralph, to keep.
Do it quiet, please, Ralph, the baby's asleep."

(Fists became the rule of the day in Blanche's life. Bruises and aches, a broken heart, and silence. If she told, Ralph said, he'd hit her harder.)

Ralph kept Blanche in fear for her life.
She had nowhere to turn for a wife is a wife.
Till one day he threatened to turn on their son.
Blanche picked up a bread knife, told the boy, quick, to run.

(Ralph just laughed. Blanche stood thẻre with the bread knife in her hand not knowing what to do and Ralph pointed a finger at her.) He said:

(Chorus)

"Girl,
You better make it good the first time.
Miss and you draw back a nub.
No wife's got a right to hit back.
Obey in the name of love."

(Blanche hesitated. Ralph explained it to her again. He said, Did you hear me, girl? What do I have to do to get your attention?) He said:

"You better make it good the first time.
Miss and you draw back a nub.
You do what I say or make tracks.
Straighten up girl, for this is love."

(Blanche dropped the bread knife and Ralph lit into her. Blanche didn't scream. She had got to where she didn't any-more. So nobody knew. Nobody heard her yelling anymore so they figured it wasn't happening. Blanche's life seemed set. She never thought out how it would turn out, just went at it, day by day. Keeping on. One night, however, Ralph made a mistake and went too far. That was the night Ralph stopped beating his wife.)

Some neighbors were over. Ralph started to boast,
About a barmaid he'd dated, the best and the most.
She had blue eyes and blond hair and a body that wouldn't
    quit.
Ralph said when she moved it, he flat had a fit.

Well, Blanche had had it, he'd just gone too far,
Marriage is marriage, a bar a bar.

When the neighbors had left, Blanche took down their small
    gun.
Some time is time for the time to be done.

(It was a small-caliber pistol they kept for protection. Still, at
close range, it was vicious. Ralph had gone to bed. He wasn't
asleep. Just lying there.)

"Ralph," Blanche said, "you better open your eyes.
One last fond time, Ralph, to say your good-byes.
You've done it, my husband, this time gone too far.
I won't share my bed with a girl who tends bar.

"I didn't do it, I didn't do it, the things that you said.
You hit me, you hurt me, you slapped my poor head.
I didn't know what you wanted or why I got hit.
But last time's the last time you son of a bitch."

(Well, Ralph opened his eyes at that. Looked up to see Blanche.
At the foot of their bed with the pistol, aimed dead straight at
his eyes. He started to get up and she cocked it. He lay back
down, deciding.) Then, from flat on his back, he said:

(Chorus)

"Blanche,
You better make it good the first time.
Miss and you draw back a nub.
No wife's got a right to talk back.
Come here in the name of love."

(Blanche was ominously quiet. So Ralph, from his pillow,
started to explain it to her again.) He said:

"I said"—
Which was as far as he got.

(When the police got there Blanche was still standing at the foot
of the bed Ralph was lying dead in, still pointing the gun at his
body. Like he might get up. With all those holes in him.)

She shot him once in the cheekbone and once in the chest.
The one in his stomach put poor Ralph to rest.
Another she pumped out went straight to his heart.
The last one she saved for Ralph's private parts.

"I didn't mean to, I didn't want to," Blanche started to cry.
"He was my one true love, my husband for life.
He hit me, he hurt me, I went down on my knees.
But never again will I say oh Ralph please."

(Blanche got off eventually, after telling her story once to a jury
that deadlocked, then again to a more sympathetic group, who
set her free. She's at home now with her children. Blanche
doesn't feel like a hero, Blanche believes in the Golden Rule. But
at least she doesn't get beat up anymore and she prays every
night her children won't pass the tendency on. A time comes for
times to change. And even now, though she's shy, Blanche
draws the line a little differently.) Cross her now and you'll hear
her say:

(Chorus)

You better make it good the first time.
Miss and you draw back a nub.
I been pushed around the last time.
Punched out in the . .
Black eyes in the . .
Cracked ribs in the . . .
Broken heart in the name of
                    love.

V.
Turn Up the Music and Dance

Me

I have:

done all the things I have said I would not, ncluding with married men when I swore. (Nice, getting to an age where you have done enough things you swore you wouldn't that you don't have to apologize every time.)

I:

sang at Zoe's again, Friday night in the parking lot, to a big crowd. Sam Moore announced me. There was a four-piece band, a portable keyboard, an electric bass, a guitar, and a fiddler who could play like a fool. It's beginning to stay light longer now, coming on to the solstice . . . one of Linda's high holy days. We started at five, the sun hot and high as early day. Another singer went first, a Zoe regular. I was the star, saved for last. Wore my best swingy dress, a Brazos Belle gardenia whore-hair style behind my ear. By the time the first act was done I was already soaked; by the time I took the mike, streams of sweat had run down between my breasts and tracked my spine from neck to base. The gardenia's lemony Old South smell got stronger as the flower caught my heat.

I:

wore Mother Stovall's green ring;

sang "Blanche and Ralph." Not a dry eye in the house: I love it. Stood there singing, the great I me, with the foot-stompers, ultimate Stovall, the beat not syncopated but on the nose; solid weighted, a waltz-2-3. Leaning against Zoe's doorframe, Sam Moore sucked a beer. The gardenia smell got headier. The hot-fingered fiddler played like a madman, hitting the high notes bagpipe style. Like Caruso, Lanza, a Pagliacci in the parking lot, Nightingale Norris. The girl of my dreams. In my shoes.

I have also:

returned to the back room in Zoe's. I know what I said, but there he was sucking that beer from that brown long-necked bottle and looking at me and there I was after the week I had had enough with loony nut ward fishing poles in IV bottles and Shall We Dance? straitjackets. Electrolytes and bananas. I cried real tears in the real world as I sang. After I finished my set I was drenched with sweat, my Dolly/Crystal dress looking like something the cat dragged in, my gardenia limp, feet sliding like fish in strappy patent shoes. Finished but high. Flying. Sam Moore came up behind me while I was talking to the fiddler and ran one finger down the sweat on my nearly bare back. My back arched; ribs lifted; stomach drew in. Hot from heat, cold from sweat. And Sam Moore knew. Yes, I told him, yes, and when he rounded the icehouse toward the alley still drinking his beer, with an extra bottle for me, I waited a minute or so then followed. He was standing in the door between the garbage cans waiting, grinning, making sure I got down the alley safe. I walked past him into the back room without a word. Took off my swingy little dress and, Lord. Our bellies slid against one another in sweat. The end of the rainbow for sure. Everything happened. Up to get it, again and again. Yes.

I came:

home to find I had a small blue bruise on my lip and a gardenia I had by then forgotten about still pinned behind my ear. It was completely brown, a knot like a fist holding back my hair. My cheeks were flushed, my hair ratted and wild, my mascara smeared. I smelled of salt, and Sam Moore. I went to sleep relishing his smell, my salt, the peacefulness inside my head. Such a night does clear your head. If nothing else, it allows a person to start fresh.

I have:

waked up, thank the Lord, feeling no regret. Only greed. More only leads to more, excess wants glut, inches need miles. Enough is never enough. Some only makes you want more. Sing it;

taken a chance; checked Big out of the hospital, like it was a hotel. They still don't know. They took him out of Four-Oh-Two; put him in a room. They went over it and over it and analyzed everything from shit to brain waves and they don't know. Aspirin thins the blood, makes it flow too fast, gives a person funny symptoms. Light-headedness, craziness. Lack of bananas, potassium, an imbalance. Electrolytes. Some acid thing. DT's? Daddy had a fit. TELL ME THE BLOOD COUNT, GIVE ME THE LIVER ANALYSIS, he demanded. The Arab M.D. turned white. Said he wasn't allowed. I'VE *HAD* THE DT'S, Daddy shouted after him. THIS ISN'T THE DT's! The Arab flew. One day, I walked in and said SHALL WE DANCE? The nurse taking his b.p. looked at me like I was the one crazy. Daddy's face lit up. JIVE AND MAMBO, he said. MAKE IT CITY. DOOWAH DITTY. And we up and left. Sometimes the time is the time. Whether or not Daddy will ever be straight again, I can't tell. The monkey in the tree will always be in his mind, I know that. The fog will come back, chase him down to surround his face in a cloud, and he will be back there again, in the nut ward, off his beam; syncopated; in the gap. "It happened," he told me point-blank. "The monkey in the tree. The boy fishing in the IV bottle. The Jack of Diamonds in that race. It's real. It happened. I won't talk about it anymore. People think I'm crazy. But I'm telling you, to me it's as real as breakfast. It happened." He has quit his job with Simply Good. Told them he'd like to take a leave of absence, which frozen yogurt companies never heard of. *Okay,* he said, *I quit.* From now on he will get a disability allowance, Social Security checks, food stamps. "Didn't they check where you live? I'm sure the Zodiac would not qualify." Big said, "You have to know the answers to the questions, that's all."

I have:

seen what he saw up there in Four-Oh-Two. Moved inside his skull. Brought him back. One day we were sitting in the hall when a black nurse came toward us pushing a grocery-store style cart containing a huge roll of white gauze. Daddy was talking to me. Suddenly he was gone, that moony soft look. I watched as his eyes went over to the black nurse, her cart, the gauze. At that moment he was lost in cuckooland again, in some gap inside his mind. I went with him. That was a half-and-half black/white nurse he saw, pushing a baby carriage. Inside it was her very white baby, its heritage unapparent. They had done it. Crossed over. Chessboard. A new kind of people. It lasted no more than seconds. Then the switch happened and he came back; we continued our conversation without a hitch, although I knew in time I would hear the story about the half-and-half black/white nurse with the secret white baby. Another time some loud something we couldn't see was rolled down a hall behind us. It sounded like a metal barrel on its side. Again the conversation stopped. Daddy cocked his head, listening. The rumbling sound moved past us and then stopped. Had the boat docked? Were the animals stampeding? Had the helicopter landed at the floating emergency dock? I couldn't tell exactly. But I knew where he was.

I have:

decided to move Robby into the Zodiac with Big for the summer. Robby can take his sax over, to practice. Turns out, Robby adores his sax. He is a new man, Robby; beside himself with excitement over the move. Ricky, however, is not doing so well. He has not hit one out all season. No cakes. Rick did better with a sterner coach. Sam Moore is too kind. Caroline has surprised us. She had to fill out a computer card, listing all the courses she intended to take throughout high school. To me, it seemed ludicrous for someone so young to map out her next three years. But Caroline took to the task with grace. In the space marked FUTURE PLANS: OCCUPATION, Caroline wrote "Veterinarian." Veterinarian? "Yes," she said blithely, as if this were something we had known all these years and how could I possibly have missed it. Stitches and ticks? Fleas and dog gynecology? She says yes. She has already written the state's leading agricultural college, a place known for its reverse countrified snobbishness and crewcut down-home boys. Caroline? At A&M? It'll pass, I keep thinking; it will pass. Jane says don't bank on it, she's a stubborn-headed girl and of course Jane is right, she is. So I don't know. Jane meantime has broken her vow. A lawyer this time. A thin one, no wife.

I have:

taken no more pledges;

written to Steve apologizing;

felt, nonetheless, no guilt or regret for what I did. I just think I was rude;

received one postcard from Linda from New York saying, "All is well. The energy field here is bizarre but invigorating. Home soon. The solstice approaches," and another saying "Met somebody. Am I ready for an older man? A grown-up? The stars say yes. We'll see. I MAY STAY!" She will be famous I suppose. Rin, Noth, Sin. I hope she will. Or at least hope I hope so;

started to take more singing engagements, some inside the Loop;

raised my asking price. No one has complained;

begun using the name June Day more and more. All my writing from now on will be registered under that name and I am seeing a lawyer to find out about changing the old ones over ... consolidating my activities, trying to stand in my shoes in the real world where I am, myself myself, I me the same, by name in fact and dream;

realized if Linda publishes as Linda Day and I as June Day, well—;

not seen Sam Moore since that night. Decided to rethink Jack Auhl. Make lists. Unmarried is a start;

received more mail, including a note from Walt Three invit-

ing me to Memphis August 8–9 to the opening of the New Blue
Hot Rose Daisy. "Bring the Depression glass," he said. "We'll
dance all night";

bought my ticket and a new pair of shoes. Decided to do it.
Up and go;

received also another letter, this one from Linda:

Yesterday Camille *was on at a movie theater not too far from where
I'm staying. (You have to come here. They play all the old movies on TV
and in the theaters, too.) I went to an afternoon matinee. Oh her. That
face. Like pale china and such a smile. Loss is the worst.*

*Plans are afoot to, as Grace says, "make Linda Day a star." If this
thing gets published you'll have to come up. We'll have something better
than a Zero bar for a celebration.*

*Tell Caroline I think her plans to go to A&M are terrific. Tell Robby
to honk on. Tell Ricky to stay in there. One last thing: I have finally
made my peace with your father and my marriage. Did you know we
were never officially divorced? I am going to file. Not so much to free
myself as to indicate to Jimmy that the thing legally is as over as
spiritually it has been for a long time. To let him loose of the idea. Can
you imagine taking this long? Send me your new song. Love, Linda;*

heard from Pine Bluff about the house. Lou, it seems, was
heavily in debt when she died, what with all the renovations,
turning the house from Mother Stovall green to up-to-date
Whispering Baloney. The reason she didn't get the old bathroom redone was, she was down to the bottom of the barrel and
got scared. Which also explains the lack of furniture. A lawyer
representing a number of creditors has slapped a lien on the
house . . . we all got notices . . . and now it's completely tied up:
nobody's. Louanne must be fit to be tied. Big says they could
keep it locked up in litigation for years and it may not end up
belonging to any of us. Lord, Mother Stovall. How the story
turns out. How long-lasting an effect a thumbed nose can have;

written Linda back, telling her about Zoe's (the singing part)
and June Day. I ask you. All these confessions. No more, I
swear;

decided when I get home from Memphis and the weather

cools to repaint the house. Get rid of elephant-cellar. Try blue. A New Sky-Blue I found, with white trim, like Martha Mitchell. I went to the Bayou Bend Hardware Store and got a Sherwin Williams card the color I'm looking for. Brand-Name City this time, not Sears. Hope it works.

packed my bags, sent the Depression glass to Walt Three via UPS. On to Memphis, the New Blue Hot Rose Daisy, and Beale. Elvis and me and the blues. My new shoes are red, with ankle straps and blocky Spanish heels, the throat cut down past toe cracks. Big says it's whore shoes when the toe cracks show. My dress is cobalt blue, to match the Daisy's neon. I promised Big to check out the Peabody site, to see exactly what the roof was razed for. I plan to dance my red whore shoes altogether *off*.

Down here, a hurricane is in the works. Stalled in the Caribbean but on its way. They're naming them now for men. A daddy hurricane?

Never mind weather, I'm going. Turn up the music. I plan to dance.